THE NINE RED GODS DECIDE: THE COMPLETE ADVENTURES OF CORDIE, SOLDIER OF FORTUNE, VOLUME 2

OTHER BOOKS IN THE ARGOSY LIBRARY:

Eric of the Strong Heart

BY VICTOR ROUSSEAU

Murder on the High Seas and The Diamond Bullet: The Complete Cases of Gillian Hazeltine

BY GEORGE F. WORTS

The Woman of the Pyramid and Other Tales: The Perley Poore Sheehan Omnibus, Volume 1

BY PERLEY POORE SHEEHAN

A Columbus of Space and The Moon Metal: The Garrett P. Serviss Omnibus, Volume 1

BY GARRETT P. SERVISS

The Black Tide: The Complete Adventures of Bellow Bill Williams, Volume 1

BY RALPH R. PERRY

A Grave Must Be Deep!

BY THEODORE ROSCOE

The American

BY MAX BRAND

The Complete Adventures of Koyala, Volume 1

BY JOHN CHARLES BEECHAM

The Cult Murders

BY ALAN FORSYTH

THE NINE RED GODS DECIDE

THE COMPLETE ADVENTURES OF CORDIE, SOLDIER OF FORTUNE, VOLUME 2

W. WIRT

ILLUSTRATED BY

ROGER B. MORRISON
& JOHN R. NEILL

COVER BY

PAUL STAHR

STEEGER BOOKS • 2019

PUBLISHING HISTORY

"I'm Shootin' Vely Good" originally appeared in the July 13, 1929 issue of *Argosy All-Story Weekly* magazine (Vol. 205, No. 1). Copyright © 1929 by The Frank A. Munsey Company. Copyright renewed © 1956 and assigned to Steeger Properties, LLC. All rights reserved.

"The River Lies in Front" originally appeared in the August 17, 1929 issue of *Argosy All-Story Weekly* magazine (Vol. 205, No. 6). Copyright © 1929 by The Frank A. Munsey Company. Copyright renewed © 1956 and assigned to Steeger Properties, LLC. All rights reserved.

"What Kept You?" originally appeared in the September 28, 1929 issue of *Argosy All-Story Weekly* magazine (Vol. 206, No. 6). Copyright © 1929 by The Frank A. Munsey Company. Copyright renewed © 1956 and assigned to Steeger Properties, LLC. All rights reserved.

"The Death Spell of Nong Chik" originally appeared in the May 10, 1930 issue of *Argosy* magazine (Vol. 212, No. 2). Copyright © 1930 by The Frank A. Munsey Company. Copyright renewed © 1957 and assigned to Steeger Properties, LLC. All rights reserved.

"The Nine Red Gods Decide" originally appeared in the October 4, 11, and 18, 1930 issues of *Argosy* magazine (Vol. 215, No. 5–Vol. 216, No. 1). Copyright © 1930 by The Frank A. Munsey Company. Copyright renewed © 1957 and assigned to Steeger Properties, LLC. All rights reserved.

"About the Author" originally appeared in the September 8, 1928 issue of *Argosy All-Story Weekly* magazine (Vol. 197, No. 5). Copyright © 1928 by The Frank A. Munsey Company. Copyright renewed © 1955 and assigned to Steeger Properties, LLC. All rights reserved.

Visit steegerbooks.com for more books like this.

TABLE OF CONTENTS

"I'm Shootin' Vely Good" 1

The River Lies in Front 35

"What Kept You? 59

The Death Spell of Nong Chik 105

The Nine Red Gods Decide 147

About the Author 236

"I'M SHOOTIN' VELY GOOD"

Jimmie Cordie, Red Dolan, and their swashbuckling band of gay cool adventurers, shoot their way into a merry fracas with Chinese waterfront pirates and ruthless war lords

CHAPTER I

HONGKONG RIVER PIRATES

"**SHE DRAWS TOO** much water, Red. What you should get is a—are you listening to me, you ape or are you taking a nap?" Jimmie Cordie demanded.

"Sure I'm listening to you, Jimmie," answered Red Dolan. "I thought I heard a yell from that junk beyant."

They were standing on one of the wharves in Tytam Bay, Hongkong. It was in a part of Hongkong where few "foreign devils" were ever seen and those few would be under strong escort. That fact had not made the slightest difference to Jimmie Cordie and Red Dolan. They always went where they pleased, regardless of time, place or inhabitants. Red was two hundred and twenty pounds of Irishman, blue-eyed, red-headed, all bone and muscle. Jimmie Cordie was slighter, black-eyed, generally smiling and moved with the quickness and ease of a black panther.

"If you are going to stop and listen to all the yells you hear in this neck of the woods, we'll— Hot damn!"

There was a row of junks, bow to stern, tied up to the wharf on either side, the length of it. From the junk at the stern of the one they were looking at, came a series of shouts. As Red and Jimmie whirled, over the side and onto the wharf jumped a girl. She was a very pretty girl, with black eyes, set straight, denoting her Manchu blood, and her little feet had not been bound. Her hair was blue-black and the bedraggled, torn silks she wore could not hide the perfect little form. In her right hand she held a short sword which was red on the point.

Jimmie and Red were near enough to see the expression on her face and in her eyes. It most distinctly was not one of fear, but of anger and defiance.

As she hit the wharf, four white men came over the side of the junk after her, followed by three or four Chinese. One of the white men, as big as Red Dolan, had a splotch of red on the shoulder of his very dirty white cotton shirt.

The girl hesitated a minute, as if undecided whether to stay and give battle or retreat. The desire to fight was so strong that she actually took a step in their direction. Then, having evidently decided that discretion was the better part of valor for the moment, anyway, she turned and ran up the wharf.

From where the junk lay, it must have been about a hundred yards to land and there were twenty odd junks on either side. From all of them poured Chinese, men, women and children. All the men had weapons and not a few of the women. The Sang Shu wharf was known as home by bay and river pirates, and pirates who did not confine their efforts to either.

The girl started up the narrow, rapidly closing open space in the middle. It became like running the gantlet. As she came level with Jimmie and Red, she flashed a quick glance at them as she swung out a little. The second she saw them, she swung in to them. "Help me fight them!" she commanded. Not begged—commanded, as she slipped between the two, then whirled around, her pretty little head coming about to Red's elbow.

" 'Tis us that will do that little thing," answered Red, promptly. "Stay behind us, alanna."

Jimmie Cordie laughed. "We'll do the fighting, Miss Manchu Princess. You hang onto our coat-tails."

THE TWO white men leading the pursuit, the one with the cut in his shoulder and a tall, lanky, dissipated-looking man with a sneeringly cruel face, came swaggering up.

Her desire to fight was so strong that she actually took a step toward them

Behind them came the other two, who looked what they were, degenerate, fat, bloated beach combers.

"All right, you two," the big man barked. "Hop it before you get hurt. That girl is crazy and we're taking her to an asylum. Go on, get the hell out of here."

He and the lanky man had committed a grave tactical error in coming so close. They might just as well have opened a cage door and stepped inside to talk to a grizzly bear with the toothache and a wolverine that has just been disappointed in a kill.

Red Dolan's one idea as to how to start and also settle any matter at hand was to "slap 'em outa the way."

Jimmie Cordie was equally as prompt as far as the slapping thing went, and it may be a little prompter. But at times he would talk a little in giving warning. Red believed that all talk should be done afterward—if the one being addressed was in condition to hear it. If not, it was all the same with Red.

Now Red took a step forward. Before the big man, who was fairly fast himself, could do more than raise an arm that Red brushed aside, he found himself in the grip of what felt like several octopi. Red was, and still is, for that matter, what is known as a mean fighter in a rough-house. He applied a hold learned in the Foreign Legion and added to it for good measure part of another hold that is popular in Dublin.

The big man rose swiftly to Red's shoulder, then down across his hip, and then sailed gracefully out into the water between two of the junks. The way his body relaxed it could be seen that he was "out." By the time he started on his flight, the lanky man had tried to draw a gun from under his dirty shirt.

"Way too slow," said Jimmie, reprovingly, as his Colt barrel crashed against the man's head just above the ear. The lanky man slowly slumped to the floor of the wharf.

As he did, the pretty little girl laughed and called a taunt in Chinese, then turned to the two men who were hanging back, added in English—very good English save for the r's: "You pigs! Why don't you come and get me? You don't dale, cowalds!"

By this time the two beach combers were within ten feet and on three sides forming half a circle that ran from junk to junk were the Chinese, swords and daggers out. The two had seen what had happened to the others and now they saw the blued steel Colt .45s.

The girl stuck her little head out between Red's right elbow and side and made a regular little girl's face at the native white men and the Chinese. Jimmie Cordie could see it out of the corner of his eye and laughed. "Stick your tongue out. That makes it better!"

The two beach combers didn't like the layout at all—the guns, or the cold fighting light in the eyes of the men who stood there with little frozen smiles on their lips, as unconcerned as if they were not on the most dangerous wharf in Hongkong, surrounded on three sides by animal-like killers. The promptness with which their two leaders had been passed out of the picture would have made better men hesitate. But in the last analysis, these beach combers were of a fighting breed, and they had the Chinese with them. They also knew what would happen to them afterward, if they didn't make an effort.

As Jimmie finished speaking, they started.

"Hi s'y," began one. "You better give the girl hup, hand git hout."

It may have been in his mind to hold Jimmie's and Red's attention until the Chinese could close in. If it was, it was a wasted effort. The only way out was to shoot it out and both Jimmie and Red knew it.

"Take that advice to yourself," answered Jimmie, "and be quick about it. I don't want to kill a white man."

THE CHINESE surged forward and the two men were pushed ahead. Red Dolan shot the nearest through the heart. When guns began to do the talking Red's only idea was to kill. He fired three times more directly in the faces of the Chinese.

Jimmie shot the other through the shoulder and, as the man reeled back against the Chinese, shot twice more. This time Jimmie also shot to kill. The circle stopped and widened out a little. Here was no easy prey; these were not men who drew guns but did not use them.

"Onto the junk, Red," said Jimmie, calmly. "We can stand 'em off better." As he spoke he was reloading his Colt from shells carried loose in the side pocket of his coat. The entire wharf was now crowded with Chinese and more were trying to get on it from the land. In front was a space about fifteen feet to where the Chinese milled back and forth.

As Jimmie spoke, a knife whizzed by Red's throat, missing him by the breadth of a playing card, and buried itself in the side of the junk behind them. As they backed the two steps necessary to gain the side of the junk, there was another rush forward. Both Jimmie and Red poured out lead to stop it. Red picking the girl up under his left arm and holding her back of him, much to her disgust and indignation. She wriggled and kicked to get free, but she might as well have tried to get out of the embrace of a polar bear.

The firing was so fast that it sounded like a drum roll and when they stopped, the Chinese had retreated again, except ten on the wharf that couldn't.

Red stepped over the side of the junk, carrying the girl. He put her down as soon as he saw there were no Chinese in sight, reloaded, and turned to cover Jimmie Cordie. As Jimmie came on board, Red's Colt discouraged any attempt to attack. But the wharf was full of Chinese and from the native quarter back on the land came a hum that was like a swarm of angered bees.

On either side of the wharf, junks were being cast off from their moorings. The pirates had no intention in the world of letting the foreign devils get away with this. They were going to close in from all sides.

"Now what, Jimmie, darlin'?" demanded Red. He had the utmost confidence in Jimmie's ability.

Two Chinamen came running up from the stern of the junk, but promptly stopped and dived headfirst into the waist for cover as the two menacing guns swung to meet them.

"Cast off and join the navy," answered Jimmie. "Get to the bow, Red. I'll take the stern. Keep your head down, sis," he added to the girl as he started. "Be a good girl now—and act like a girl, not a darned young wild cat."

The ropes were easily loosened and the junk fell away on the outgoing tide, helped by the shove Red gave it with a pole he had found on the bow. As it did, the junk that had been tied behind scraped alongside and several Chinese jumped on board. Red came down from the bow with a wild Irish yell, the heavy pole held in both hands.

It was like a tiger landing in a pack of jackals who were around his kill. He swung once to the right, then once to the left. Most of the Chinese were still bunched together. The first man that received the force of the blow was literally hurled against the next and they went down like pins in a bowling alley. The

Chinese were slight, compared to Red, who was all of six feet three and broad in proportion. The two on the receiving end at the left joined their companions on the deck.

There were three left on their feet. One dropped his sword and turned to run back to the junk. As he turned, the girl standing by Jimmie raised her arm and the short sword flashed through the air. It struck the Chinaman in the neck and he pitched forward, dead before he hit the deck.

The other two jumped at Red, their swords up. His pole was at the end of the swing and they were past and in before he could get it back. Red dropped the pole and stepped back. As he did he heard Jimmie's Colt go *pow!* just back of his ear it seemed to Red and he saw the face of the Chinaman on the right suddenly become curtained in blood. The other slashed viciously at Red, but was too far out and to the left to reach him. As the sword whistled by, Red leaped in and one steel hand closed on the man's throat, the other on the sword wrist, and Red's knee came up. When he let go, the man went down like a wet rag doll.

"THE OTHER junk!" shouted Jimmie. "Get on her, Red!"

" 'Tis what I had in mind, ye shrimp," answered Red, as they started across to the side of the junk that had scraped them. The girl stopped as she ran lightly across the deck and picked up one of the swords.

"Put that down," ordered Jimmie without being obeyed at all.

"Get behind me, darlin'," Red said, as the girl went a little ahead of them.

"I won't!" she answered. "Boost me up, Led."

Jimmie and Red both laughed and Red once more reached out and tucked her under his arm, sword and all.

Two or three Chinese who had been looking over the side of this junk promptly unloaded into the water as the two white men came over the rail with the girl.

As Red stood her up on the deck she sputtered: "You stop that! I can fight with—"

"With your grandma," interrupted Jimmie. "We'll do the fighting for the family, Miss Amazon. Get that sail up, Red. I'll be quartermaster on this warship. Hot damn, the water front is up, no foolin'."

"What do we care?" demanded Red. "We'll sail this boat to—"

"Nowhere, if you don't get that sail up."

By now there were several junks closing in, some smaller, but two or three much larger, crowded with men. Jimmie went back to the stern to the steering oar, the girl with him.

"Let me take the little gun," she said, the simon-pure fighting gleam of the Manchu in her eyes. There was a smile on her face, a smile she was trying hard to make cold and wintry like the smiles on the lips of the two big white men who had miraculously appeared to fight not for, but with her.

"What?" demanded Jimmie. "My gun? My gosh, be content with the sword. My gun is as big as you are, Miss Iron Hat."

"I am not Miss Ilon Hat. I am Princess Chi Huan of the nine clans in Shantung, and—"

"No 'ands' about it," said Jimmie, firmly. "You sit down between me and this post. Do it or I'll take that sword away from you and you can't fight at all."

The pretty girl looked at him for a second and saw that he really meant it; and much to Jimmie's secret surprise, she obeyed him that time. Red had got the mat sail up and the junk began to answer to the steering oar. Several of the other junks were close now, so close that one captain was already shouting orders for his men to board. Red came back and stood by Jimmie.

"Knock 'em off as they come over, Red," Jimmie commanded. "I'll give you all the help I can, but this darn oar takes two hands."

The girl stood up. "Red—give me the little gun. Take him away flom him. I can shoot."

"Sure now, acushla," coaxed Red, his eyes on the fast nearing junk. "Leave old Red to do the shootin'. 'Tis a fine play ye can have wid the sword do they come aboard."

"Look what's coming," said Jimmie, with a laugh. "Now you won't get a chance to play with the sword, Missee Plincess."

Coming calmly through the welter of junks and motley sampans was a big war junk, flying a flag that had a single character in the middle. It bumped and scraped and nosed the rest out of the way, paying absolutely no attention to any of them and not trying to get out of the way at all. The same thing happened in each case. The crew of the junk touched would line the rail with yells and curses—which were shut off like the turning of a radio dial the second they saw the flag or the grim, scarred faces of the men on the war junk who stood looking down on them. Two or three sampans were run down and pushed under the water, but their crews either swam to the nearest boat or went down in the bay without a yell. There was a frantic effort to get out of the way. The crowded wharf was now still as death.

No Chinaman in his sane senses would ever think of getting in the way of the T'aip'ing. It was their flag that was flying from the war junk, and the men on her were of the most dreaded, powerful and relentless secret society in the Orient, bar none. The Chinese knew that to interfere with the T'aip'ing was the same as baring their bodies to the strike of a king cobra.

"Shoot them," ordered the girl. "Shoot that man at the wheel. Led—Jimmie! Shoot! Oh, I wish I had a—"

"They're friends of mine," answered Jimmie, with a grin. "Don't be so darn bloodthirsty."

THE JUNK won alongside and a dozen or more swordsmen jumped aboard them. This was no disorderly, bunched rush. Each man was two feet away from the next in line, and they covered the junk from bow to stern.

A foot in front of the line was a young man, his high cheek bones and straight-set eyes showing he came of Manchu blood. His face was seamed and cut with old scars and his lips tight, his eyes cold. But as he looked at the two men at the stern, his face lighted up and the tight lips smiled. He turned and snarled an order to the fighting men of the T'aip'ing behind him, and they came across the deck to the rail, their swords flashing in the sun as they lined it. It served notice on the junks and the wharf that the T'aip'ing had the matter in hand, and that it would be very wise for any one who had business to attend to, to get about it.

The young man sheathed his sword and came up to Red and Jimmie. His eyes widened a little as he saw the girl, but he paid no attention to her, bowing low before Jimmie Cordie.

"Lord," he said, in English, "I saw the fight from far away. Had I known that it was you, elder brother of much honor, I would have arrived sooner. Is it your wish that I give a lesson to these curs who had dared to snap at your heels?"

"I'm glad you arrived at any old time," grinned Jimmie. "No, Shih-kai, I guess we did about all the biting ourselves."

"You will bear witness to the magnificent Head?"

"Yeah, boy, just as soon as we land. I think we better come on board your cruiser, Shih-kai."

"You honor us far above our station in deigning to accept us as a guard of honor," and the young war captain of the T'aip'ing, who had been with Jimmie and Red on two or three occasions before, bowed once more. "We will land you wherever you will condescend to mention."

"The wharf of Fragrant and Delightful Sensations will do," Jimmie grinned amiably. "I'm going to take the Princess Chi Huan to a place where she'll be safe."

The girl had stood by, gravely watching and listening. Now she looked up at the T'aip'ing flag, then at the young war captain and spoke two curt sentences in Mandarin Chinese. Shih-kai, his young, hard face impassive, bowed low to her and answered in the same language.

"I told him," said the girl in English, "that you both wele under my plotection and that he is to tly no T'aip'ing tlicks."

"Sure now, darlin'," answered Red, " 'Tis a nice girl ye are to be tellin' this scut of the world that, ain't she, Jimmie?"

"Darn right she is," said Jimmie, positively. "You fully understand that, Shih-kai? That we are under the protection of the Princess Chi Huan?"

"Yes, O resplendent elder brother, I fully understand and the T'aip'ing will—try no tricks," and the pretty little Manchu princess, who had jumped from a dirty little junk onto a pirates' wharf in the worst quarter of Hongkong, nodded gravely, as if backed by a thousand swords, which incidentally wouldn't have made a ripple against the might of the T'aip'ing.

"If you will pardon me," went on Shih-kai, "I will attend to this miserable, unimportant matter." He stepped to the side of the junk and called to the one nearest. The crew on that craft didn't seem at all anxious to come in closer, but did so quickly. Shih-kai pointed at Jimmie and Red, at the junks, at the wharf and at the shore.

Then his lips curled like a snarling dog, showing his even white teeth and he spoke a single sentence in Chinese. It wasn't a long one but the effect was magical. The junk sheered off as fast as it could and before the war junk of the T'aip'ing was under way, the wharf was cleared, the junks had started back to their places, and by the time the native police had arrived, no one within a radius of a mile had seen nor heard a single thing.

An old Chinaman, whose grandson was one of the police, took him to one side and casually mentioned the fact that a T'aip'ing war junk had been seen, about the time that the police thought there had been some shooting. He loved his grandson and he didn't care at all to picture the young man in a kettle of oil which was being slowly heated to boiling point.

The grandfather promptly mentioned this news to the leader of the police party, and the investigation at once became thoroughly superficial. The two wounded white men and the man that Red had tossed off the wharf were not even sought for. Red's man had come to in the water and had clung to the side of a sampan until pulled on board. The one Red had killed had long since gone down the bay.

The whites lay in the hold of the junk that had come in with the girl, unmolested and unsought. A white man "gone native" is held in absolute contempt; even by the natives he works with, or for.

CHAPTER II

A PRIVATE WAR

IT WAS DUSK when they landed at the wharf of Fragrant and Delightful Sensations and a jinrickisha took the girl, Jimmie, and Red to George Grigsby's apartment on a quiet street in the European quarter. The Princess Chi Huan sat between Red and Jimmie, perfectly content. She snuggled down a little, and Jimmie's left arm went around her as he glanced down at her pretty, tired little face. Now that the fighting was over, she seemed to be just a very weary little girl. That she had completely accepted them as her fighting men and had also perfect confidence in them was self-evident.

As they entered the apartment they were met by Grigsby and Putney, the two other members of the quartet that had served in the Foreign Legion, the A.E.F., and for years afterward fighting in the places where the strongest man made and enforced the law. They were all dead shots with either rifle or revolver, and Jimmie Cordie could make a machine gun sing a death song for anything within range. All of chilled steel nerve, any of them would have gone singing to his death for the others, collectively or individually. Grigsby and Putney were both big men, lean and hard-bitten; quiet, soft-spoken, and just about as dangerous to cross as a wounded grizzly.

"This young lady," announced Jimmie, gravely, as both men rose, "is the Princess Chi Huan, of the nine clans, Shantung."

Grigsby bowed. "We are more than honored by the presence of the Princess Chi Huan. I am George Grigsby and this is Arthur Putney. Will you please be friends with us also?"

The girl looked at them calmly, first Grigsby, then Putney; after that she smiled. She wasn't fifteen years old, but she carried herself proudly, and as she was a fighter herself, she felt her heart go out to fighting men.

"I will," she said. "Light now, I want a hot bath and soap and towels and clean clothes and—and everything. When I—when I get clean, I will tell you about me."

Her English, except for her troubles with "r," was as good as theirs. Grigsby called his houseboy, who was about seventy years old. The boy took a quick glance at the little princess, nodded his head, and said: "Can do," when ordered to go out and get a complete outfit of clothes after preparing a bath.

"Come and sit down by me, darlin'," coaxed Red. "Would ye like something to drink now, after all the fighting? 'Tis pale around the gills ye do be looking, machree."

"No, I do not want to sit down yet, until I'm clean. Then I will, Led. Light now, all I want is to be clean and—"

"Everything," interrupted Jimmie Cordie. "All right, Missee Plincess. Only when you do come back, please sit by me instead of that red-headed Irisher, who is of no account."

"It is velly lude to intellupt a pelson," stated the Princess Chi Huan sternly, glaring at the offending Mr. Cordie. But she couldn't help her lips curving up a little in a smile as the much-tanned, black-eyed Jimmie grinned impudently at her.

"It is," agreed Grigsby, "very rude, indeed, and I will have to apologize for Mr. Cordie. His early education was sadly neglected along those lines. Being born a fool, he has—"

"He is not a fool! Jimmie is my fliend and—" She stopped, remembering what she had just told Jimmie.

The four big men laughed, and after a moment the Princess Chi Huan joined in. From that time on she had arrived home where there were four big brothers to serve and protect her.

The boy came in "Catchee bath—plenty evelything."

"The bathroom is the last door down the hall to the right, princess," said Grigsby.

"Tell the boy when he comes with my clothes to put them by the door," she ordered. "Then knock and go away." When the "r" came at the end of a word she could usually handle it.

After they heard the door close behind her Putney said: "Isn't she a bear-cat? Where did you birds find her?"

YEN YUAN rose from the carved chair heavily inlaid with mother-of-pearl and gold, as Jimmie Cordie was ushered into his presence. He was the head of the most powerful, dreaded and merciless secret society in the Orient, the T'aip'ing.

Several years before his only son had been taken suddenly ill at a New England university. Jimmie, a student himself, had felt sorry for the quiet, well-educated young Chinaman, who was sick in a strange, and to him, cold and hostile country. Jimmie had nursed and "kidded" him along, explaining the ways that seemed strange, until Wong Li had been able to rejoin his classes.

After France, Jimmie had come to China and there had met Wong Li, now a member of the powerful Board of Pardons. The young Chinaman had taken him to Yen Yuan. The old man, whose word was law and judgments final over four million Chinese, had risen and bowed low before the young American, who, he was firmly convinced, had saved his only son's life. Word had gone out through the T'aip'ing, through all its countless branches and ramifications, that Jimmie Cordie, the smiling, black-eyed one, was Yen Yuan's most honorable elder brother—and to be treated as such by all T'aip'ing who wished to continue living.

Now, after being served with tea and little frosted cakes, with the bowls of candied ginger on the inlaid table, Jimmie told Yen Yuan of the girl.

"She is the daughter of Chieh-yu, a Manchu prince who holds part of Shantung. He was in Washington for some years as one of the secretaries of the embassy and she went to private school in Chevy Chase. These men that kidnaped her were fighting for her father against some bird that's trying to take all Shantung. We are going to take her back to her father, and

I thought that you would help me figure the best way, O wise and venerable one, father of my friend."

"There are many ways, honorable elder brother. It is true the Prince Chieh-yu fights for Shantung against Tseng Tzu, who was once a general in the army of the North. This Tseng Tzu is also head of the White Lily society, with whom the T'aip'ing are at war."

The old Chinaman calmly spoke of a private war going on inside of a nation, as if it were not a matter of much importance. "We hold the ports and most of the cities, but the White Lily is strong in the provinces. See, elder brother, who saved the life of my not-to-be-mentioned-in-the-same-breath son, to win through to Chieh-yu, one must go past Tseng Tzu, who holds from Kiao Chow Bay to Chi-nan. If we could get there, strike a blow at the heart of the White Lily, much honor would come to the T'aip'ing. But it will require careful planning. It may be, illustrious one, that the White Lily already know of the rescue of the Princess Chi Huan—and of the part played by the T'aip'ing and be on guard."

"That's right," agreed Jimmie, "but he may figure on letting us get in that far, like walking into a trap. Once in, we'll take it from there. It's dollars to doughnuts that we can make delivery of the Princess Chi Huan, anyway."

"Then," answered Yen Yuan, with a smile at the American slang, "let us plan."

WHEN JIMMIE returned to the apartment he found the Fighting Yid and the Boston Bean had arrived to pay a little social call. The Yid was a soldier of fortune, as Jimmy said, "neither pure nor simple." He had fought in Jimmie's machine gun company in France and, before and after, all over the Orient wherever law and order most distinctly was not.

The Boston Bean, whose right name was Winthrop, was tall, lanky and sorrowful looking. He had three or four millions, yachts, country houses, and town apartments scattered all over the world, and he let them lie idle most of the time.

His one idea of a perfectly good time was to be with Jimmie Cordie and Red Dolan, behind a machine gun, dirty-faced, a cigarette hanging out of the corner of his mouth, in a tight place. As far as the tightness of the place went, it may be stated here, he almost always had his desire in that respect more than filled. Failing the chance to be with that pair, he and the Yid teamed up, as they had done on John Norcross's expedition into Chinese Turkestan. His sorrowful face hid a gay, reckless, undaunted heart and both he and the Yid had the same kind of chilled steel nerve. He had served in France in Jimmie's company also, and as Jimmie had complained, "stuck closer than nine dollars in bad money" ever since.

"My gosh," Jimmie said as he came in and saw the Yid and the Bean, both pretending to have fallen desperately in love with the little Princess Chi Huan, much to her delight.

Jimmie told them of what had been arranged with Yen Yuan, and after he had finished Putney said: "It doesn't sound good to me, James, me lad. Too much put in Lady Luck's lap. Tseng Tzu, who is scrapping with the princess's pa, may fall for the first of it, and we may get by as far as Chow Fuo by going up the Grand Canal, if he does. We can also get up the branch of the Hwang Ho as far as Chi-nan—granted he is still sweet. But, young feller, did it ever occur to you that once we have seen the princess safe in her pa's arms that we have a few miles to come back to home, sweet home. How about that part of it, James?"

"Ain't that something?" demanded Red. "How about that, Jimmie, darlin'?"

"That seems to be the sore point, Jimmie," Grigsby said. "You get us up there in the middle of twenty million Chinese who, by your own account, are at each other's throats. The minute we horn in, they'll stop all private feuds and jump us. No doubt we can make contact with Chieh-yu the way you have it set—but I'm with Put; get us home, old kid."

"No good general plans a retreat," said Jimmie loftily, "until he has to. I got you in—get yourselves out. Codfish, where is that young ocean liner of yours?"

"In the harbor," answered the Bean promptly. "She doesn't draw much water, Jimmie. We can get up the Grand Canal all right. I don't know about the Hwang Ho." The fact that the beautiful yacht had cost half a million dollars and the furnishings almost as much more made no difference to the Bean.

"All right, well take it. Yid, are you in?"

"Vy, Jimmie, vot a question! Sure, am I in, mit bells on."

Putney laughed. "I guess we better go along, George, to pull these damn fools out of the lion's jaw."

"Suits me," said Grigsby with a smile. "When our number is up we might as well be in Shantung as anywhere else." And that completely expressed the way they all felt about it.

CHAPTER III

SIEGE ON THE RIVER

THE GRACEFUL WHITE yacht lay headed downstream in shallow water on the right side of the Hwang Ho River above Chi-nan. It had a bad list to port and the bow was torn almost away. She was almost broadside to the shore line and about a hundred feet away from it. On the starboard side the broad Hwang Ho stretched away to the opposite shore about a mile distant.

Tseng Tzu had been notified that the daughter of his enemy was in the hands of some soldiers of fortune in Hongkong who would turn her over to him on the payment of a certain sum of money. That they would deliver her at Chi-nan and afterward fight for him if desired.

The idea being to get that far unmolested, send word to Chieh-yu to come and get his daughter, deliver her, mop up as much as they could on Tseng Tzu with the T'aip'ing furnished by Yen Yuan, turn and come back. The crux of the plan was to get in without exhausting their fighting strength and also the moral effect it would have for the T'aip'ing to attack the White Lily in its home town, of Chi-nan.

The word had been passed to Tseng Tzu easily enough, through sources not known to be T'aip'ing, by word of mouth up the coast and inland. He had promptly sent down word to Kiao Chow Bay, where he had been told they would await an answer, that he agreed to all terms, offered the soldiers of fortune commissions in his army and guaranteed safe passage.

But, on the Hongkong wharf that day there had been a White Lily man. He had reported what had happened, and the news had arrived to Tseng Tzu about the same time as the offer. Being an old hand at the game himself, he had not taken more than a second to figure it out. Then he smiled and began to issue orders.

The yacht had come up to Chi-nan without any trouble, except for the usual putting out from shore of various piratical gentlemen who fought for themselves. After one good look at the white men, who promptly lined the rail, they all decided to sheer off.

On coming opposite Chi-nan, the yacht had turned in from the middle of the river toward the shore, where they could see a small party of Chinese waiting for them.

But if Tseng Tzu was an old hand at many games so were the men on the bridge of the yacht. There were too many junks on the river on the starboard side and the town was altogether too quiet. Tseng Tzu had mounted a battery on a hill beyond the town and not concealed it very well. He should have left it open as if part of his defense of the city. But he had tried to camouflage it, and as a result it was picked up by eyes that had been on the Western front.

"Keep right on, Codfish," Grigsby said calmly, as he lowered his glasses. "Jimmie's sucker is all hooked up for us."

The Bean gave an order to the slim, blue-eyed young captain, who had taken the wheel himself, and the yacht picked up speed and went by Chi-nan. A half mile above, just as the battery on the hill opened fire, a mine exploded at the bow. It was a home-made affair, this mine, manufactured by a couple of Germans in Tseng Tzu's army, but it worked. They had made several and strung them across the river. The yacht would have sunk in five minutes if the captain hadn't beached her, bow pointing down-stream.

The minute after she was hit the sides of her deck houses slid back, piles of innocent looking stores on deck forward and aft were tumbled down and she became what she really was, a fighting ship fully equipped. Up came the muzzles of one and two pounders; out of concealed nests came the machine guns; and from below came one hundred of the best fighting men of the T'aip'ing, led by Shih-kai and armed with thirty-thirty rifles in addition to their swords.

The two-pounders on the bow manned by Jimmie Cordie, the Fighting Yid, and Putney, hammered the battery on the hill with a merciless rain of steel. The Chinese gunmen were still aiming too high. There were no high shots from the ship; one shot to get the range, another for elevation, then squarely on the target.

Red Dolan, Grigsby, and the Bean handled the stern two-pounders. Machine guns lining each side amidships were manned by the members of the crew, fourteen men, counting the black gang, all of whom had seen service in the American or English armies. There were no Tseng Tzu men in sight on the land side as yet.

FROM THE shore on the other, starboard side, came junks, rafts, sampans, and every kind of craft that would float, loaded to the gunwales with men. The T'aip'ing lay along the deck close to the rail, their eyes gleaming with the joy of the fight that was coming.

The Princess Chi Huan stood by Jimmie Cordie, with the air of an expert, watching the effect of the shots landing on top of the battery. Jimmie was using explosive shells and the explosions came so close together that it sounded like one continual roar.

There was a feeble response at first, then silence, and after two minutes of rapid fire, Jimmie stopped and straightened up. As he did, the Yid and Putney ceased firing also.

"And that's that," Jimmie said. "Those birds are through. Say, for Pete's sake, you get below!" He had caught sight of the Princess Chi Huan.

"What? I go below? Well, I—" she was so angry at the suggestion that she didn't finish her sentence, but started along the sloping deck toward the stern where Red was.

"I will help *you,* Led," she announced as she squatted down beside him.

"Sure now, darlin'," protested Red. " 'Tis no place—" He didn't have time to finish before the starboard guns went into action.

Tseng Tzu had figured on trapping them, but he had figured on a small yacht and five or six men who would not, or rather could not, put up any resistance to speak of. The promptness with which the attack of the battery had been met, the uncovering of the guns on board, the line-up that he could see through his glasses convinced him that he was in the position of the man who had the bear by the tail. But lives were cheap in Shantung and he was certain that one or two—at the most, three—waves of men would be sufficient to sweep over the yacht and then on board of her.

The fire that met the oncoming boats was a withering, deadly one. The range was point-blank and the men behind the guns all veterans. Junk after junk yawed and fell away, her deck covered with dead and dying men. The one and two pound rifles put many of the smaller boats out of commission with one shot through the sides. But there were too many of them to stop that way, and junk after junk, both at bow and stern as well as amidships, scraped along the yacht's side. As they did, men jumped down on the slanting deck, to be met always by the swords of the T'aip'ing who dropped their rifles for the weapon they were more familiar with.

Jimmie Cordie, the Yid, Putney, and the slim, blue-eyed

English captain were together at the pilot house, using thirty-thirty rifles. No Chinaman who jumped on deck at the bow lived to fight.

Red let the princess think she was fighting the gun with him until the minute of contact with the first junk, then he had picked her up and put her behind a pile of boxes with: "Stay there, darlin', I'll see that no wan comes near ye." Then he picked up the sword of one of the T'aip'ing who had been hit by a stray bullet. Red would let go a gun any time for a sword and the chance of using it at close quarters.

Grigsby, the Boston Bean, and the crew still fought their machine guns, covered by the T'aip'ing. Junk after junk would come up, sometimes two or three at a time; men would come over the sides, their swords flashing in the sun, to be met and cut down by the T'aip'ing or shot down by the guns of the white men. There was little shooting on the part of the Chinese. Ammunition is hard to get in the interior and what guns Tseng Tzu had were mostly in the hands of his trained regiments at the front engaged in holding Chieh-yu and others. Here and there a rifle or revolver was fired from a junk, but they did little damage.

Twice from the hill that the battery had been on came a rush of men carrying bamboo rafts and one-man and two-man sampans, but it was more a disorderly mob than a disciplined attack by trained troops. Each time it was swept out of existence by one or two of the machine guns on the stern.

IT WAS a hard, fast, merciless fight, in which quarter was not given nor asked. The T'aip'ing closed with the Chinese that the guns had left alive, there was a flash and ring of sword blades, and one or the other went down.

Jimmie Cordie had dropped his thirty-thirty and was using his Colt .45. Red was now beside Shih-kai, who had greeted him with a smile, and their two swords promptly cleared that part of the deck. As Jimmie stepped a little to one side to get a shot at the oarsman on a junk coming in, he brushed against soft silk, and as he looked down to see what it was, a .45 went off at his elbow.

The Princess Chi Huan was in the fight, very much so, with a big, blued-steel army model .45—not an automatic, but a revolver.

She had picked it up on the deck where it had been dropped by one of the crew when hit. She was holding it with both her little hands, straight out, firing as fast as she could pull the trigger with both her forefingers making the pull. Her pretty little face was dirty in streaks where she had touched it with her powder-and-grease-blackened hands. A belt of cartridges was wound twice around her waist and she was patently having the time of her life. As Jimmie looked at her she smiled delightedly.

"I'm shootin' vely good, Jimmie."

"I see you are," Jimmie returned with a chuckle. "Why don't you take my thirty-thirty? It will be easier for you to hold down."

"I like this—"

Two big junks hit the bow at the same time, and in the mad whirl of the fight that followed Jimmie didn't hear what she liked. He tried to keep her back of him as much as possible, but she didn't want to stay in back of any one, and he momentarily lost sight of her.

The attack at the stern and along the side had fallen away, and Red, Shih-kai, and what was left of the T'aip'ing came up, their swords red. The Yid and Putney dropped their guns and, picking up swords, charged with them, and the bow was cleared. Red would have kept right on going into the junks if Putney hadn't got in front of him.

The junks shoved off with what men they had left. As they did, Jimmie heard a Colt roar over his head.

The Princess Chi Huan had climbed up on the pilot house and was standing there, straight as an arrow, her little heels together, shooting the six shots she had just put in the chambers as fast as she could at the junks.

The first wave of Tseng Tzu was broken and thrown back. All

craft in sight was fleeing to the other side and on the land there were no troops in sight except the wounded and dead.

On the yacht Red had a sword cut in the left arm above the elbow, the Bean had a bullet in his shoulder, Putney in the last charge hadn't quite been fast enough in turning a slash at his head and had received a bad head wound in consequence. Grigsby, Jimmie Cordie, the Yid and the yacht's captain were untouched, as was the fighting lady of the expedition. Of the crew six were dead, three wounded with sword cuts. The T'aip'ing had thirty men left on their feet, the rest were dead or badly wounded, mostly dead. Shih-kai had a cut across his chest, not deep, but all the way across.

Putney looked at Jimmie Cordie and grinned. "Now, all we have to do is to escort the princess to her pa and then go home, isn't it, James?"

"That's all, Archibald," answered Jimmie cheerfully. "We ought to be home by four o'clock."

"Look over at the hill, ladders," said Grigsby. "You may have to wait a few minutes and talk to the gents coming to see us."

From over the top and around the sides poured hundreds of Chinese armed with all kinds of weapons. Tseng Tzu's second wave had started.

"TWO OF your men to the other side, Shih-kai," commanded Jimmie calmly, "to give warning if the navy starts over. We'll damn soon stop this afternoon calling stuff so late in the day."

They did, with the machine guns. It was over level ground, and the Chinese were massed. The fire of four machine guns stopped the charge within five minutes. The Chinese, those who could, turned and ran.

"Ain't that something?" demanded Red. "Why the hell couldn't some of them come on wid their swords and—"

"You'll get plenty of swords before we go home," Putney said. "What now, General Cordie?"

"Council of war," Jimmie answered. "First aid before that,

then clearing the decks. Something tells me that we are going to be here a little while longer."

An hour later Tseng Tzu sent another wave, this time from both land and river. The land attack was the same as before and was stopped as easily, but the river attack was different this time. The junks spread out more and came across in twos and threes. It was an easier attack to handle because the two pounders took care of most of them, but it kept steadily up for a long time.

The junks would start, get to within five hundred yards, the guns would open, manned now by Jimmie Cordie and the Yid, Red, and the captain and the crew. The junks would come steadily on for a moment or so, then fall away and go down the river. It may have been Tseng Tzu's idea to have them exhaust their ammunition; he had plenty of men to swap for it.

Finally the junks stopped coming, and it looked through glasses trained on the shore as if a first class mutiny was in progress.

The T'aip'ing went ashore under Red Dolan's supervision and dug trenches. Grigsby had pointed out the fact that if Tseng Tzu brought up some heavier guns, which he most certainly would do, the yacht would be no place to use as a fort; so the trenches were dug.

The council of war brought no results except a grim determination to make it a costly operation to remove them from the scene. Any thought of cutting their way through to Chieh-yu was abandoned. All knew that Tseng Tzu had too many men concentrated around them.

The Princess Chi Huan had sat in the council, but never said a word. Jimmie had tried to get her started by teasing her, but only got a smile in return.

That night about eight o'clock she sat down beside Red, who was on the bow. He had been looking at the damage done, the yacht's searchlight playing as low as it could for him. The mine had been strong enough to tear a big hole in the bow, but had not hurt the engine room amidships.

"Led," she commenced, as she came willingly into the crook of the big Irishman's arm and snuggled against him. "Let's you and I go and get my father. We can put on some clothes and you can take a swold. I'll take the little gun and—"

"What?" demanded Red, who had not been paying much attention when she started. "Sure now, darlin'—'tis ravin' ye are."

"No, I am not, Led. It's only fifty miles flom this place to my father. We can slip over the side and—you can cally me, Led, if we can find some holses. He will come and lescue Jimmie and evely one."

"Wait a minute, alanna; could we now? Tell it slow to old Red. Ye know the way?"

CHAPTER IV

THE LAST ATTACK

THE NEXT MORNING when Red and the princess were missed, Jimmie Cordie cursed viciously for one of the few times in his life, the smile gone from his face. "That blanked red-headed fool will get himself killed and the princess along with him, damn his—"

"Hold it, Jimmie," answered Grigsby, "They have gone for help somewhere. Red probably figured he might as well be killed one place as the other. I'll back the Princess Chi Huan to get through anywhere. Did you see that little monkey shooting that Colt yesterday?"

"Yeah, she was beside me most of the time. It isn't that—but Red is so damn big and red-headed to boot, he hasn't a chance to get through. I could have passed as a—"

"So that's where the shoe pinches our fair James," scoffed Putney. "He wanted to go himself!"

"Darn right," grinned Cordie, suddenly returned to good humor.

"Well, you—hey, *hit the deck!*"

The attack came again from both land and river, but it lacked pep. It could be seen from the yacht that the men were being driven to it. The assault was beaten off without much trouble, neither junk nor land force getting to within a hundred yards of the yacht.

After it was over, the Yid did a little investigating and later handed a list to Jimmie. "Dot's all de ammunition left, Mr. General," he announced with a snappy salute. "Enough to last five minutes, ain't it?"

"You are too optimistic, Yid," grinned Jimmie grimly, after one look. "Make it three."

All that day and the following night there was no attack. The T'aip'ing went on shore and made a quick sortie around the hill. They promptly came back, and it took some of the precious two-pound shells to cover their retreat. They reported that some heavy guns were being brought up and that Tseng Tzu was evidently massing troops for a final push. Anyway, they found plenty of resistance, more than they could handle.

"We better get to the trench, Jimmie," Grigsby said with a grin. "We can hold 'em longer."

They transferred the guns, what ammunition was left, stores, and whatever else they thought necessary. The small boats were used in the transfer, but the launch was left on deck. They know that no small boat could get down the river, no matter how well manned.

As they were shoving off with the last load the Yid said:

"Vate. If ve leave her like dis, dey can get on her and fire direct into de trenches. Vich is not so good, ain't it, Jimmie?"

"Double not good, old settler, and for that reason, the Bean and I have arranged that the navy is blown up at the right minute. Notice those two wires, Yid? Well, at the other end is an electric firing box."

"Oi, Jimmie, tell me ven it goes off. It is so close dot it rains yachts all over us."

"What do you care? Get in your funk hole. Think of the Bean-eater seeing his yacht go flooey to save you."

The Bean laughed. "I never liked her anyway."

TSENG TZU'S new battery was finally placed, back on a hill out of range of the two-pounders, and began firing. The first shots went high, the next few low and on the side, then the range was found, and the defenders promptly dived for cover. One or two of the shells hit the yacht, the rest landing in front of or behind the trenches, all that didn't land fairly in them. But every man was so far below ground that no one was hit.

The shelling stopped in a little while and the men came up like badgers from their holes.

"I say," remarked the young English captain cheerfully, after taking one look. "The beggars are coming both ways again, what?"

They were, from across the river and from behind the hill. The trench had been extended around now so as to face the yacht also, and machine guns placed.

"The Bean and I will take the river side," announced Jimmie with a grin. "When we stop shootin' you birds duck, she's going to cut loose."

The land attack came on slowly, the men more spread out this time. They weren't any too anxious to charge, either, and as soon as the machine guns started a great many of them turned and ran, to be driven forward again by Tseng's swordsmen.

The junks came across faster, being manned by a different breed, mostly pirates.

They came alongside the yacht and swarmed over it like ants. Many of them stopped fighting then and there and began looking for loot.

Five big junks were alongside the craft when all firing from that side of the trench stopped. The men in the front line took time enough to see that no Chinese were close enough to reach the trench for at least three minutes, even if they did come on after the explosion, and then promptly took cover.

The Bean worked the handle of the firing machine up and down twice, then shoved it home.

There was a roar that seemed to split the skies and suck all the air out of the world, then a crash, then another roar; and a big parachutelike mass of red and yellow topped with black went whirling up in the blue, carrying with it all kinds of wreckage, also human bodies.

When it subsided there were no junks, nor yacht either, nothing but falling and sinking fragments. The Bean and Jimmie had used all the dynamite on board.

Two thousand pounds of seventy per cent gelatin, which is nitro-glycerin mixed with guncotton as a base, will make quite an effort if properly placed. It nearly obliterated the trenches, let alone the junks. It certainly stopped any further advance by the army or navy of Tseng Tzu's forces that could get as far away as possible from the scene.

For the rest of the day there was no attack, but the defenders could see with the glasses that troops were being moved up across the river and every now and then a shell would come from the hill.

Jimmie Cordie, the Yid, and Grigsby were sitting just back of the first line trench, Putney and the Bean were down at the shore. All wounds were healing rapidly, owing to the prompt first-aid and the hard, clean living of the men.

The T'aip'ing and the crew of the yacht were strung out near the guns.

"I'm getting darn fussed up about Red," said Jimmie. "If they got through he ought to be—"

The *"wh-e-e-e-e"* of a shell coming to say howdy met their ears, and with one movement, like well-trained weasels, they dived into the trench and rolled into the nearest holes.

Putney and the Bean were caught farther out from safety, but made it in before the bombardment became heavy.

It kept up, steadily getting worse. Shell after shell hit along the trench, one or two landing squarely. But the trenches had been laid out by men who had built trenches before, and no man was hit.

"Not so good," Jimmie said to Grigsby, who was in the same hole. "The old boy is advancing troops this time, no foolin'. When it stops they'll be right smack on top of us."

"What of it?" answered Grigsby indifferently. "They'll stop before the said troops— Up and out, Jimmie, old kid!" The shell-fire had stopped, but there were no Chinese within a hundred yards of the trench. Beyond that there were plenty, but they were halted, looking back.

"It sounds as if Red had arrived," said Jimmie as he stood up from his machine gun. A moment later around the hill charged a compact body of Chinese in khaki uniforms with bayoneted rifles.

They were led by a white-haired officer; and by his side, Colt in hand, came Red Dolan. Alongside Red trotted the Princess Chi Huan, this time without a gun, but very much present.

With one accord the remainder of the yachting party jumped up on the top of the trench and let out a yell that made the fleeing Chinese let out another link of speed that nobody thought they had in them.

"We lescued you, Jimmie," the Princess Chi Huan announced breathlessly as they arrived.

"My gosh!" answered Jimmie, gravely, "I'm glad you did. We sure needed rescuing."

TEN DAYS later Jimmie and Red stood at the eastern gate of Wu-chen, the city of Chi Huan's father, Chieh-yu. The rest of the party with a strong escort had already passed through en route to the coast. With their help Chieh-yu had effectively quenched any further opposition to his being top man in Shantung, having followed Tseng Tzu's broken army through the city gates of Chi-nan. Tseng Tzu was dead, killed in the defense of his city and the rest of the contenders widely scattered or dead also.

The way to the coast was clear for Jimmie's party, and there a war junk awaited them.

The Princess Chi Huan stood with Jimmie and Red.

"I am solly you go, Led and Jimmie," she said, bravely trying to wink back the tears. "You are my honolable big blother, and I—" She could not hold the tears back.

"Why, darlin'," and Red lifted the proud little princess in his brawny arms and held her tight. "See now, didn't your pa promise he'd bring ye to Hongkong soon? We'll be waitin' for ye, acushla. Won't we, Jimmie?"

"Yeah, boy," answered Jimmie. "And if we need you to rescue us, Missie Plincess, we'll send for you right away."

"All light, Jimmie. If you send, I will come and lescue you—any time."

THE RIVER LIES IN FRONT

Chinese greed and lust run afoul of Jimmie Cordie and his swashbuckling crew of gay adventurers in the Orient

T'SENG CHU SAT in the garden of the little stone mission house just outside of his city of Lao Kai, in Yunnan, China. The war lord looked at the flowers, at the two graceful, pretty girls who were sitting on the wall of the compound, at the two young men who were idly oiling and cleaning a pair of shotguns over under a tree, then at the Reverend Thomas Wilson, former All-American football player and A.E.F. chaplain.

"I regret," the Chinaman stated courteously, in very good English, "that I no longer find myself in a position to be able to extend you my protection. The dogs from the south have been victorious in Peking, and the army of the north is in full retreat. A good many of the northern war lords will undoubtedly pass this way, and it will take all of my men to protect my city."

"I see," answered the Reverend Wilson calmly. "It is, of course, rather unfortunate, as far as we go. When the chance came for us to go down the river in safety you assured us that there was no need, that you could fully protect your territory. Now, when going is impossible, you tell us that you can no longer protect us."

"I am very unfortunate myself," answered T'seng Chu, his cruel, hard young face impassive, "in that you misunderstood me. My command of English is very poor, although I spent four years in London. What I meant to say was that I could not protect you here against the bandits of the north. If you will come with your family into my city of Lao Kai, I will protect you to the extent of my ability."

As he spoke he looked at the younger of the two girls.

The Reverend Wilson saw it, and the fingers of his right hand spread out a little. It was an involuntary thing, this finger-spreading, and belonged in the old days, when he was Tommy Wilson, of the Deer Gap Wilsons, in Breathitt County, Kentucky, member of one of the most famous "feudin'" families, in the days before he "saw the light."

He sensed rather than felt what he had done, and his lips tightened. He, a minister of God, to do a thing like that! He must pray and fast, that the hot blood that he thought cooled be really cooled by grace.

T'seng Chu was speaking again, his eyes still on the girl Kathleen. "If you stay here," he was saying, "there is no question but some war lord will see your flowers, and want them."

The Reverend Wilson knew that if he took his family into the city of Lao Kai they would simply disappear. In the mission house they were a unit to be accounted for, or at least a rescue would be attempted later by the church. If the house was found empty, who would tell of their going into Lao Kai, or where they went from there? There was only one thing to do, and he did it.

"No, T'seng Chu. We will stay right here. If you cannot protect us, as you agreed, then we must try to protect ourselves until help comes, which it will. My church is very powerful, and soon marines and sailors will be landed who can drive off any war lords who may lose their minds enough to attack a mission."

T'seng Chu smiled, a tight-lipped, amused smile. "You think so? But where from? The foreign dev—the foreigners have plenty to do, in taking care of themselves." He rose and suddenly the mask fell away from his impassive face. "You will come to my city," he snarled, "quietly, bringing all your family with you, or—"

"Don't finish it, T'seng Chu," drawled Wilson, also rising. "I may not be able to remember much longer that I am a man of peace. I know what you want; you want my daughter Kathleen. You will never get her. I and mine will stay here, in our house. Even a man of God is allowed to defend his house and his loved

Cordie swept the deck of the junk with steel-jacketed death

ones. Go to your city of Lao Kai and defend it against all that come against you—as I will defend mine, which is the house of God, against all that come."

"I will go—and await your coming," T'seng Chu answered; "and if you do not come, I will send for you. After which you and your sons will die, very slowly."

He bowed low, then turned and walked back to where his bodyguard of swordsmen awaited him.

AS HE went through the gate of the I compound, a man came out of the house, waved to the girls, and joined Wilson. He was a tall, well-built man, dressed in very expensive white flannel clothes, buckskin shoes, silk shirt and tie. He looked more like a Long Islander at a country club than any one connected with a mission in China.

His face was a handsome one, with clear-cut features, but his lips were a little too full, and his eyes were set just a mite too close together. He gave the impression of being a rich man, selfish and arrogant. His name was Payton, and he had gone up country against the advice of friends to see if he could buy some Ming china. Caught in the sweeping backflow of the revolution, his bearers and hired guard had promptly deserted just beyond Lao Kai, and he had just barely made the mission house on the hill.

He sat down beside Wilson.

"Well," he demanded, "did you tell him that I would pay well for a guard to take me to Peking?"

"Yes," answered Wilson shortly. He did not like this man, who bragged about his money and social position back in the States. "I told him—and he asked me if you had the money with you. I have tried to explain to you that he is not to be trusted. If you had money with you, he would take it—then his men would kill you once out of his sight. China is not as America, Mr. Payton. There is no more law and order here, unless enforced by guns."

"That's applesauce," sneered Payton. "Money talks, anywhere. I suppose you want to do the rescue stunt yourself, and collect some from me? I'll see him myself, and—"

"Do you see those woods at the bottom of the hill?" asked Wilson coldly. "You would not live to get to them, let alone to Lao Kai. You do not seem to realize your position—or ours. We are surrounded by millions of hostile Chinese, in direct danger of being attacked any minute. No money can save us, Mr. Payton. It would be taken away, and we would be killed just the same.

"The reason that the attack has not come before is that T'seng Chu has waited, hoping to get me into the city with my family, where," and the Reverend Thomas Wilson smiled grimly, "he could attend to the matter with less publicity or investigation later."

"You mean," asked Payton, his face white, "that we are in actual danger of being killed? Why, why that is absurd. I am Charles Payton, of New York, and worth millions. Do you mean to say that I am in danger of—"

"I haven't time to argue it, Mr. Payton. You are in the same danger my wife and daughters are in, no more and certainly no less. You brought a rifle with you—I suggest you get it ready for auction. T'seng Chu said that he was coming to get us," and the Reverend Wilson smiled grimly. It started out to be a joyful smile, but he remembered, and devoutly shut the joy off.

"WHY SHOULD he?" persisted Payton. "He could protect us easily enough."

"He wants Kathleen," answered Wilson calmly. "If I would let him have her, he would protect us—for a time."

"You mean he wants to marry her? Well, if that is all, and it would save our lives, I should think—"

The rich man from New York stopped. There was a cold, frozen smile beginning in Wilson's eyes and on his lips.

"Of course," Payton finished lamely, "it wouldn't do at all."

"That's plumb right," drawled Wilson. "No, suh, I reckon it wouldn't do a-tall." He was one of the "feudin'" Wilsons for a moment. As he finished he walked away from Payton, who looked at him for a minute with a little sneer, then went over to where the two pretty girls were sitting. Both of the pretty Kentucky girls looked up, but neither smiled a welcome to the rich man. They both sensed his lack of courage. His looks, his millions, his social standing made no difference to them. He lacked what their "men folks" had, and so was outside the pale.

"Your father has been telling me that we are in danger of attack from the Chinese," he said as he sat down. "You girls don't look very frightened."

"Well, suh," drawled Kathleen, very much like her father, "I don't reckon we are. We got us three men folks right here to take it to the end of the row for us."

Payton frowned a little as he figured that out. Wilson and his two sons—one and two made three. Evidently they didn't count him in at all. Which was wise of them, as he was certainly going to get away if he could. He smoothed out the little frown and laughed. "I think your father is unduly alarmed," he said. "They will think twice about attacking white people."

Nancy, the elder of the two girls, laughed. "Not missionary people," she said. "Reckon they attack them any time. If you want me to show you that stitch, sugar, we better be getting in. Will you excuse us, Mr. Payton?"

"Certainly," answered Payton.

These people didn't seem to realize just who he was. After the girls left, he sat on the wall, staring down at the woods and the tops of the houses he could see through the trees. He'd go and see this Chinaman himself, damn shortly.

WILSON HAD gone around to the rear, where the hill fell away shortly in a steep little precipice. From where he stood he could see the passes leading into the hills. Suddenly he gazed more intently, then went into the house to come out with a pair of glasses—and both girls, who seemed to have learned that stitch very quickly. He leveled the glasses on one of the passes.

"Two men," he announced, "and several bearers. They are fighting something off—using their rifles—two of the bearers are down." Then he thought of the two girls. "Here," he said, handing out the glasses, "you look, Nance, then let Kathy."

"No, daddy," answered Nancy. "I'll get our glasses. You look and tell Katrinka till I get here."

"You look and fell me, honey," said Wilson.

Kathleen took the glasses. "Oh, my goodness gracious, there is only one bearer left! Men are coming out of the pass, daddy. The two men are kneeling and shooting! Oh, they have killed them all! The bearer is running—"

Nancy arrived with two pairs of glasses, and Wilson took his back, but now all he could see was the two men and the bearer running toward the mission. "I hope they are white men, and fighters," he said as he lowered his glasses. "We need fighters—not more mouths to feed."

Half an hour later his two sons, whom he had sent to the foot of the precipice to meet the men and show them the path up, came into the living room with the newcomers. The bearer had been sent to the Chinese quarters.

Wilson looked at the men, who grinned cheerfully at him. Both the girls and their still prettier mother were there. And a strange thing happened. Both girls and their mother took one look at the two very ragged gentlemen with weapons that were spotlessly clean and efficient-looking, and then all three of them smiled. Kathleen said: "Daddy, reckon you've got two more fightin' men, no foolin'."

Both of the men grinned at her, and the tall, lanky one with a sorrowful face that hid a reckless, gay, dauntless heart, said mournfully: "There are times that I would rather fight than eat—but at the moment I could do rather well at eating."

He was the Boston Bean, a soldier of fortune known by that title all over the Orient, instead of by his right name of Winthrop. He had the misfortune—or it may be the fortune—of being born in Boston, hence the name—both names.

The man with him was the Fighting Yid, a roly-poly Jew whose eyes always looked surprised as if asking: "Well, what do you know about that?" But the Fighting Yid was never surprised at anything, and was, like the Boston Bean, a soldier of fortune. Both of them had served in the A.E.F., and since then for many war lords and other gentlemen who required very, very expert handlers of machine guns or men.

They had calmly gone into the hills on a little private business of their own, and the fact that they had been chased out, losing all their bearers and very near losing their lives, didn't affect them in the slightest.

Winthrop, who was a millionaire with town and country houses, yachts and all that goes with them at his command, would and did drop them all and go on any kind of expedition at any time.

"Well," dimpled Kathleen, "I'll go and get something for you-all right away."

AN HOUR later they sat with Wilson and his two sons on the wall. Payton was not in sight.

"Vell," said the Yid, "maybeso ve can hold 'em mit de rifles. Oi, vat vould I gif for a Brownin', mit plenty of shells! Den ve vip de whole army of the north for you, ain't it, Beaneater?"

"It ain't," answered the Beaneater firmly. "No fair wishing, Yid. Why not wish for the old Thirty-First Division? We can make it darn interesting for these lads right now."

The attack came, earlier than they expected, but it was met with a withering fire from modern rifles. The Reverend Wilson had, with the arrival of his sons, received a half dozen 30-30 Winchesters and several cases of ammunition. Some of the Wilsons back in the Kentucky' hills had not been quite so sure about the power of prayer as they were about the persuasiveness of a 30-30, and had insisted on including the rifles and ammunition in the shipment that went over "for the good of the cause."

Wilson had grinned cheerfully as he came upon these while unpacking and had lovingly cuddled one to his cheek for a moment. Sometimes it was hard for him to remember that he had seen the light.

T'seng Chu sent his men up the hill, expecting to lose a few men in the killing of Wilson and his sons, but it had not been nearly as easy as it had looked, the taking and looting and killing he had anticipated. The first uphill charge had been stopped by the accurate fire of modern rifles in the hands of men who were all "dead" shots. Before the charge broke there were twenty-odd bodies lying on the hill, and the rush had not reached the wall.

Now the Chinese officers were trying to get the men worked up for another try. There was no discipline to speak of. T'seng Chu's men were not under the control of the officers like the men in the far northeastern provinces. It was too easy to desert and join another war lord.

"These foreign devils," shouted an officer, "take your children and drink their blood! They are up there waiting for you to come and give them the slicing death. You may have all the women save one to play with. I will lead you. Their bullets cannot last long. They stopped shooting as soon as we retreated. They would not do that if they had plenty. Come and punish these poisoners and blood-drinkers. Come with us!"

This time the charge did not break, but swept up the hill to the wall, in spite of the fire that met it.

"Call the boys from the rear, Kathy," called Wilson to the girl who knelt behind on the pillars of the veranda with a rifle in her pretty little hands. "We need them here."

"Ve do," said the Yid, reloading, "und den some."

"They're spreading out," called the Bean from the corner of the wall.

The two young men came around the corner of the house. "No attack from the rear, dad," one of them said cheerfully as he raised his rifle. "The mountain's holdin''em back, I reckon."

The charge was within a hundred feet of the wall. It was a charge of swordsmen now; those that had guns had fired them at the start, then dropped them and took to the sword.

"Get back, Buck," said the Reverend Wilson calmly, "and when we go down, do what I told you."

"Yes, suh," answered Buck, starting to where his mother and sisters were. "I will, yes, suh."

"Vait!" shouted the Yid. "Oi, don't do it. Von Vinchester less und maybe ve don't hold 'em. Vait till ve see!"

It didn't look as if they were going to hold them, even with Buck's Winchester. The swordsmen came steadily on, their long curved blades flickering in the hot sun.

CHAPTER II

THE JUNK FLOATED idly down the Yuen-kiang River, the current carrying it along at two or three miles an hour. In true Chinese style, the four men on the deck aft made no effort to help it along. One of them was sitting by the steering oar, the rest sprawled out on deck, their big straw hats over their faces, their cotton blouses and loose trousers flapping in the breeze.

The junk was an old one, the sail torn and almost black with age and dirt.

One of the men turned, and the hat fell away from his face.

"Keep that red head of yours covered, you big ape," charged the man who was sitting up. "Who ever saw a Chinaman with a mop like that?"

"What the hell now?" demanded another, sitting up and blinking his eyes. "Jimmie, ye pup, what did you want to wake me up for? I was just getting in line for chow and—"

Jimmie Cordie laughed and turned a little, so that he could reach his cigarettes. As he did he glanced back up the river. "You're in line for a chunk of lead right now," he commented cheerfully; "here comes a war junk."

The other two men promptly sat up.

"And a big one, at that!" one said. "Wonder if they've spotted us?"

"You'll know in a minute or so, old kid," grinned Cordie. "One of you grab this oar while I get my baby out of the cradle."

"Ain't that somepin'?" demanded Red Dolan, the red-headed man. "Here we are almost to the Gulf and along comes this big hooker."

"What do you care?" asked Cordie, as he started for an innocent-looking pile of bags and boxes. "You and me, Red, we can lick the Chinese navy, can't we?"

"And the army. I didn't want to be gettin' my vase broke, that's all."

The four men all laughed. They had fought together in the Foreign Legion, then on the Western front, and for the years afterward in places where law and order most distinctly were not. From the Malay Peninsula to northern Manchuria they had fought and laughed at the death that always seemed to be reaching out for them. Now, coming back to the Gulf of Tonkin, with some almost priceless vases and jades in the old junk they had commandeered, they looked at the big war junk crowded with men that was coming up, and laughed.

"You and your vases!" jeered Putney. "Go sit on them, Red."

"You better go and sit near that Browning," said Grigsby. "They won't do any talking. Ease her out in the middle, Putt, and let her drift. Here they are!"

The war junk swerved in toward the easy-looking prey and a brass cannon roared from the bow, but the ball went way high and over.

"The next one hits your vase smack in the middle, Red," chuckled Cordie, as he slid the muzzle of a Browning machine gun over a couple of boxes. "Feed me, boy."

Grigsby and Putney laughed and raised their 30-30 Winchesters. Cordie swept the deck of the junk with a steel-jacketed death, as coldly and accurately as if on the target range. It was a merciless fire, delivered by men all of whom could wear the distinguished marksman badge.

The men on the deck of the junk were literally blotted out and the junk yawed and fell away, drifting by the stern of the little craft that looked so helpless. Dead and wounded men hung over the war junk's sides. The fire ceased and the four white men stood watching her.

"NOW, THE moral of that is," said Jimmie Cordie gravely, "look before you leap; or, all things are not what they seem; or—"

"There's a guy going to do some leaping," said Red. "Look!"

At the stern of the junk stood a man, a white man, poised ready to jump into the water, but he seemed afraid to do it. As they watched him, a wounded Chinaman staggered to his feet, raised his long sword and lurched forward. Red Dolan drew his Colt .45 and fired once. The Chinaman sank to the deck, his sword dropping almost at the feet of the white man, who yelled in absolute terror, then jumped into the river and began swimming toward the little junk.

"Something tells me," said Jimmie Cordie, "that your friend on his way to visit you, Red, don't care for this kind of a party."

"Yeah?" Grigsby answered. "And maybe those gents he's been playing with had something to do with it. Wait till they catch you, James, me lad. You'll get the slicing death and the hot egg treatment, right after."

"Bet you it will make me good and mad," grinned Jimmie, going to the side to help Red pull the man up.

He stood there before them, a wretched, shivering sight, dressed only in torn and bloody silk underwear. That he was beside himself with fear was evident, and he made no attempt to control it.

"Quick," he chattered. "Get started! There's two more right behind. Oh, my God! Ten thousand dollars if you will get me to safety! I am—"

"Two or twenty," interrupted Red Dolan, his blue eyes like steel. "What the hell do you think we are?"

"Can't you understand? They are coming, I tell you! I'm Payton, of New York and worth millions. I'll give you twenty—fifty thousand to get away!"

"You may be worth millions in money, ye scut," Red snarled. "But in nerve ye are not worth a—"

"Hold it, Red," interrupted Grigsby. "Get to that oar, Jimmie. We are drifting in to the bank. Now, Mr. Payton, of New York, worth millions, sit down and take it easy. We can handle any attack two junks can bring us. How did you come on the junk?"

"Before the attack came I bribed one of the house boys who told me that his cousin had a boat and would take me to safety. Instead he took me to this devil T'seng Chu, who said he would cut me up in small pieces unless I paid him—"

"Wait a minute. You said: 'when the attack came.' Came where?"

"On the mission where I was staying."

"What mission?"

"The Lao Kai mission. What difference does it make?" The presence of armed white men had begun to give him back some of his arrogance and confidence his money engendered, and a note of it crept into his voice. "I will pay you men—"

"When did this attack start and who was there to defend it? What men, I mean—besides yourself?"

"My God! Here I stand cold and wet and hungry and you ask questions. You can't help them any—there's too many Chinese. Soldiers from—"

Red Dolan's big fist clenched. Payton saw it and stepped back.

"STEADY, RED," Grigsby said icily. "When I want any help from you I will ask for it. When did the attack start, and who was there to defend it?"

"It started right after I left. I could hear the guns. Yesterday noon. The Rev. Thomas Wilson and his two sons and two men that came down from the hills are there. Why do you stand there asking questions for? Get me some dry clothes and—"

"Who else is there?"

"His wife and two daughters. They have nothing to do with me, I tell you, and—"

"You thought that you could get in the clear, so you ran. Is that it?"

"I just told you they were nothing to me," the burly Payton tried to bluster. "Oh, I know how it looks to men who make their living by fighting as you men do, but I—"

"It will be something to you," Grigsby said quietly, "because you are going back, or over the side, I don't care which.

"Swing her around, Jimmie!"

"She's been swung for three minutes, nitwit," called back Cordie. "Me and the red-headed terror from Cork swung her. Look at the sail, gents."

"You are going to certain death!" squealed Payton. "I'll give you a hundred thousand dollars if you will turn this boat around and get me to my yacht in the gulf."

"Wid women and kids behind us?" said Red. "What the hell kind of a thing are ye, I dunno?"

"Put him on the port sweep, Grig," called down Jimmie Cordie, "and tell him he's hit a place where nerve is worth more than money. Come up here, you hunk of jelly, and give me a hand. What do you think you are, a first class passenger on this liner?"

"Ain't that somepin'?" demanded Red, as he came up. "What the hell's the matter wid that canary bird, Jimmie, darlin'?"

"No sand in his craw. Lots of people that way. This lad has been living where there was a copper on every corner to holler for. None of the Dolans ever had any sand in their craws either until the Cordies came along and lent 'em some."

"What?" yelled Red, his two hundred and thirty pounds of bone and muscle stiffening. "Why, ye cross between a shrimp an' a small size' polecat! The Dolans—and no sand! Wan Dolan can lick any nine Cordies wid wan hand tied be—"

"Pipe down! Pipe down!" called Putney. "What are you trying to do, tell all China about something?"

"Don't pay any attention to Putt, Red. Go ahead and tell me how good the Dolans are—and incidentally, quit riding on this oar and do a little work for a change."

"Now," grieved Red, "I bet me fine vase goes to hell."

"Why? We'll beach this junk, go and get 'em, come back, and yorricks and away," grinned Jimmie, who had hunted in England.

"That is," he added, "if you decided to quit riding and do some pulling."

"Me? I'm pullin' the oar and ye along wid it!"

CHAPTER III

THE YID WAS right about holding. Almost at the wall, the charge broke and those that could, ran down the hill once more. There was no more for the rest of the day, except continual sniping from the woods, which was too wild to do any harm. All that night there was a constant watch maintained, but no attack came—until dawn, when a weak charge was beaten back. It was not a "carry through" attack, but more in the nature of a feeler.

T'seng Chu was waiting for some of his more disciplined troops to come up, having realized what a hard job he had on hand. About noon they arrived and he began throwing them up the long hill, company after company, in a steady assault.

The five white men held them, grim, hard, and cold. No wasted shots: fill the magazine, empty it, refill—over and over again. No pause, nothing but line a man up between the sights, pull trigger, and do it again.

"Oi," gasped the Yid, as he reached for some more cartridges, "ain't I got it any? I vish dot—"

"Cease wishing, Yid," said a cheerful new voice behind him. "Get out of the way and let a good man in. Gimme room, according to my size and disposition," and Jimmie Cordie threw himself down beside the Yid, his 30-30 already at his cheek.

"Oi!" yelled the Yid like a battle-cry. "Jimmie Cordie! Vare in hell and south China did you come from? Oi, Jimmie, now ve gif dem vat dey need!"

The Fighting Yid seemed torn between a desire to dance and shoot—but his rifle never got cold. Red Dolan, Grigsby, and Putney came running around the house, and knelt alongside Jimmie, their guns already busy.

After a few rounds, the redhead, still panting, gasped to his commander: "How the hell ye ever climbed that mountain, I dunno, Jimmie, ye shrimp. But here we are, and a swate time we'll be havin'—aw, hell, they ain't runnin' already, are they? Sure now I've just come and had no fun at all. The yellow scuts!"

The Chinese were indeed running, for the moment anyway. The sudden addition of four white men, whose rifles were even more deadly than the others, was too much and the charge went back to cover.

"Look at that now," went on Red, in deep disgust. "What the—" He saw the Yid, who grinned at him. "For the love of all the good saints! Look who's here, Jimmie darlin'. 'Tis the pride of Hester Street! Yid, ye devil, the last time I saw you—"

"Where's the gat?" demanded Cordie. "If you've dropped any part, the Yid and I will climb your big frame."

"You two and what other six?" asked Red, promptly.

"Ve don't need six," said the Yid with a smirk, "four vill plenty. Oi, I'm glad to see you gents," and the little fighting Jew who had been in Jimmie's machine gun company in France, smiled and began patting Red's big arm. "Red, und Jimmie! My, but I am glad."

"Hey, Yid," asked Red, in a coaxing tone, "ye have been around here longer than me. Is there anything to drink, now? Answer me truthful, ye scut!"

THE REV. Thomas Wilson came up then, from the post he and his sons had been valiantly holding. He looked at the four newcomers, and they looked at him, then they all smiled, seeing in each other that which good men look for first, the world around. Wilson said no word of thanks, nor had need to; his glance and handclasp spoke louder than oratory.

"And is there a drink, now, reverend darlin'?" Red queried.

"We have a few glass jars of corn likker, to be used only in case of sickness," answered Wilson sternly. "Are you men sick? I am frank to say that I feel right ailin', myself."

"No wan could be sicker than me," Red said, firmly.

"Where is the Browning, Putt?" Jimmie asked.

"I left my part with the piece Mr. Payton-of-New-York-worth-millions was carrying. It's all there, Jimmie. Don't bother me, I'm sicker than Red."

"Go ahead, you birds. Yid and I will get 'er set up. I don't want any likker right now. We'll hold the far-flung battle line, won't we, Abie, old kid?"

"Yea, boy," answered the Yid happily. "You und me und de Beaneater can vip all de Chinks in China."

Jimmie shouted: "Who? The Boston Bean? Is he here? By

gosh, I see him now! Hey, Codfish, come on over here. That wall will stand alone for a few minutes!"

After the rest had gone into the house, the Beaneater asked: "How come you birds jazzin' along at the right minute?"

"Easy," answered Jimmie, sitting down by the machine gun. "We were going along down the Yuen-kiang, tending strictly to our own business with some stuff one of the priests in a temple had presented to us, when a war junk gets fussy at our being on the river. We argued with them, and after they agreed that we had all the right in the world to be there, a gent named Payton jumps off what's left of the junk and comes to see us. He tells us about you apes being here—so we beach our junk in a little cove, get our party clothes on, and come across country. There were some few yellow brothers in the way here and there, but we smacked 'em out of it."

"Short, sweet, and to the point," grinned the Beaneater. "As a story teller, you are a fine machine gunner."

When Wilson, with Putney, Grigsby, and Red entered the house, Payton was already there. He was dressed in the Chinese clothes that Jimmie Cordie had taken off. He was saying to the pretty, calm-eyed women: "So I thought that I would go and see if I could bring help."

Kathleen answered in her soft, lovely drawl: "Yes, Wu Chuen, the house-boy that you bribed, has told us about it." The rest smiled.

A WHIRLWIND attack came in about an hour. Not one company at a time, but all the men that could crowd on the hill, wherever a man could walk. But it was beaten back without trouble. Jimmie Cordie started at one side with the Browning and swept the front like a gardener playing a hose on a flower bed. All the way across, then back, then across. The rifles took care of those he missed.

The Chinese didn't get halfway up the hill before they broke and ran, this time for keeps. Tseng Chu had tried to force the issue because a large force was coming up from the south according to his spies, and he knew that he was due to hole up in his city very quickly, if he wanted to keep it. He staked all he had on this last attempt, and then gave up the idea, for the time being anyway.

"Well," Grigsby said, as the white men talked it over, "we can't stay here, sooner or later they will gang up the neighbors' children on us from all over. I think the best way to go out is to go back to the junk, then down the river. If we go back over the mountain they will think we are scared and running. The other route right past the city of this bird, who evidently has got plenty of fighting for a little while, is the one to take, in my estimation."

"Well," said Jimmie, with a grin, "I wouldn't climb that mountain again for nine million dollars, let alone a few yellow perils. Red, the Yid and I will shoot a road through for you—if our little boy friend from New York didn't get lazy and throw all the belts away. We've about fifty left or ought to have."

"Mit Jimmie at the trigger und me und de Bean und Red, vot could stop us?"

"Any cripple with a crutch," answered Grigsby. "He didn't throw anything away. I was behind him. If it is satisfactory, Mr. Wilson, we will get started?"

"It is," answered Wilson, his eyes shining. "Very."

The compact little column marched slowly down the hill, Jimmie Cordie and the Yid with the machine gun, then the Bean and one of the Wilson boys. Then came the women in the center with Payton, who was carrying ammunition, then Wilson, Grigsby and Putney, with the other boy.

The few Chinese in sight outside of T'seng Chu's little walled city promptly scuttled for cover and there was no attack from the city. The river was ten miles away and they started for it, down along the left bank of an old dry canal.

About halfway to the river and almost up to a grove of trees that extended on both sides of the canal, Jimmie stopped and raised his right hand above his head. "No likee," he said, as the rest came up. "I caught a glint of steel in the woods."

"Yeah?" Grigsby answered slowly, as he came to a halt beside Jimmie. "Maybe-so allee same ambush. You and the Bean go and flush them out, James."

"Vy not flush dem out mit de Browning?" asked the Yid.

"Because, dumb-bell," answered Jimmie, "we only have a few rounds left and we want to be shooting at men, not trees. Come on, Brown Bread."

They had not got twenty feet when an orderly body of native troops filed out of the woods, about a full company of two hundred and fifty men. The officers were dressed in spotless whites and one of them was a European.

"Oh, my goodness!" Kathleen said. "Look behind us!"

One hundred yards behind them was another company about the same strength.

"How about that, Jimmie?" asked Red, as Cordie and the Bean came back.

"If you see what I see," said Jimmie with a grin, "not so good. No Winchesters are going to hold this bunch. We better get down in the canal bed."

"Hey, Jimmie," Red said, drawing his Colt .45, "I got five dollars that says I can make cold meat out of the little lad in front wid my Colt."

"You want easy money. So could I, for a ten-spot, with my—"

"Hold it, you damn fools," Grigsby interrupted. "Here he comes with a white handkerchief out."

THE YOUNG, slim officer walked calmly up to them, his keen bold eyes taking it all in—the men, the machine gun, the rifles.

He looked at them all, from the Rev. Wilson to the three lovely women. When he got to Jimmie Cordie, Jimmie grinned and after a moment the young officer grinned back. They knew who he was without being told. He was a French officer of French Tonkin, China.

After calmly taking in the entire outfit, he snapped his heels together, bowed and said: "Major Irene de la Montaigne, Fifth

Colonial Regiment, Republic of France," in very good English. Then he removed his white cap and bowed low again, this time to the women, his eyes lighting up with admiration as he looked at Kathleen, who smiled at him.

"You are now on French territory," he announced, "and I am desolate to the heart of me to have to tell you that you are under arrest. Not you, monsieur, of whom I know," he turned to Wilson, "or your so brave family. You are my guests and the guests of France. But these Americans—there is a little matter of the firing on a junk, that is to be explained, also a junk that is beached in the so quiet bay with jade and vases that—"

His eye caught the flash of a little metal badge in Jimmie's coat lapel. "But yet? You have fought for France, in the Legion?"

"Four years," answered Jimmie, cheerfully in French. "I was one of Captain Biroux's sergeants, M. le Major. We all have been in the legion, except this gentleman here," and he poked the Yid in the ribs, "and he's a monkey beneath notice."

"Then," said the major, in a troubled tone, "it is of the double hardship that I must—"

The Rev. Thomas Wilson stepped forward. He was a carrier of the Word to the far places, and a fighting Kentuckian to boot.

"Major, when my women-folks and my sons and I were almost down to our last bullet, when water and food were almost exhausted, when the bandits were almost to the wall and I had sent my son in—to do what you would want done to your loved ones—these men came down from the hills in the rear and saved these women for me. I put it to you, who are of the race that counts death as nothing in the defense of women. If these men are the men you want, they had got well away to safety down the river when they turned and came back. But—follow me closely, major: they came down from the mountains in the rear of the mission and—the river lies in front."

The gallant young officer looked at the towering mountain, back to the river, then at the pretty Kentucky girls and at the little button on Jimmie Cordie—then he smiled.

"Of a certainty! It would have been impossible for them to have come from the river. It is with the great regret that I have the so big mistake made. If you will allow me, I will act as escort for you to the river and there find a junk so that you may proceed in safety. The junk of the so bad men, that I must further search for, has been sent to Haip-ong." He bowed again and went over to kiss the pretty hand held out to him by Kathleen.

"Jimmie," said Red, as they went toward the river, "could we have licked 'em?"

"We could have tried 'er," answered Jimmie, with a grin. "But if we had, I have a feeling that there would have been some new faces in the angel chorus right after."

"And me pretty vase goes to hell, just as I thought," said Red, bitterly.

"Never mind, Red," soothed the Yid. "Me und Bean got it a bag full of jewels. You safed us—und so now ve split 'em. Fair enough, ain't it?"

"What? Ye have? And where would the likes of ye be gettin' all them jewels?"

"Who vants to know?" said the Yid. "Anyvay, ve got 'em."

"Oh, ye dirty robber," said Red virtuously, "walk close to papa, Abie, darlin'."

"WHAT KEPT YOU?"

Gayly daring a Chinese War Lord,
Jimmie Cordie and his soldier of fortune
comrades find action aplenty

CHAPTER I

IN THE CHINESE FOOTHILLS

CUTHBERT PAGET ETHERINGTON, English mining engineer, lay dying on the narrow little path that ran zigzag down one of the foothills in the In-Shan mountains on the border of Shan-si, China.

A girl, not more than eighteen, blond, lovely, with slim, dainty little body and the pure white skin that goes with the perfection of English girlhood, was with him. She was as yet unwounded. On the path, a little back from where he lay, the bodies of two Chinese bearers were huddled together. Kneeling by the engineer, holding his head up, was another Chinese, hardly more than a boy.

"I'm going—West, Kathy," Etherington said weakly, between moments when the blood did not seep through his lips. "Carry on. If you—see that you are—to be taken—" (a long pause here)—"Kill yourself with—" His head sank.

"Oh!" stammered the girl, one hand to her heart. "Don't! Uncle Bert! I—oh, please! Please! I'm—I'm afraid!"

The dying Englishman raised his head and for a moment came back to put her on the right path. "You are a Neville," he said, slowly and sternly. "Live—and die like one. You are not afraid. No Neville or Etherington for a thousand years has been a coward. You will go with Li Tung here as far as you can." This time his head sank back, for the last time.

The Chinaman eased him down and stood up. "May the Celestial Dlagon, smoothly as a swan, cally youl honolable spilit on high," he said, then turned to the girl. "We must hully, missie. No can stay alound—honolable uncle vely dead. Come click!"

"Oh! I—I can't leave him this way. We must—bury him, Li Tung." The tears came as she looked down on what had been her ever-gallant, courtly uncle, who had taken her and guarded her and cared for her ever since the death of her own father and mother twelve years before.

"Stay, and Chow-yang catch," announced the boy, very firmly. "No can do. Lun like helle, raakee Kotan—plenty fliends Kotan."

The sound of rifle fire came from a path that crossed the one they were on a little above.

"Guns! Why, it may be some relief column," she cried, her tear-stained little face lighting up.

"Maybe-so—maybe-so not," and Li Tung tugged at her sleeve. "Hide! Hide! Behind these locks—maybe-so China-man get guns! No can lun now, too close. Hide!"

KATHERINE NEVILLE allowed him to hurry her behind a rock alongside the path. As they crouched down, two men came along the path and at the crossing, turned down toward the bodies. They both were armed with 30-30 Winchesters and round their waists were belts full of .45 cartridges and from each belt swung a holstered Colt.

The pockets of their khaki uniforms bulged out with shells for the Winchesters. Outside of that they both carried packs and one man had four canteens hooked on various places.

One was tall, thin, with an aristocratic, solemn face, which disguised his gay, reckless, laughing spirit, and a general air of "you be damned."

The other was short, fat and roly-poly, with a good-natured face in which the big blue eyes seemed to be popping out with surprise at what was going on. The eyes were misleading; the Fighting Yid, soldier of fortune, was never surprised at anything. His real name was Abraham Cohen, but he was the Fighting Yid to any one in the A.E.F., or in the Orient where since the war he had been cheerfully wildcatting, selling his uncanny skill with a rifle or machine gun to whatever War Lord was most in need

The Bean and the Fighting Yid gave the bowmen their attention

of it. And if he couldn't sell it, he would go off on an expedition on his own or with any kindred spirit. It never made any difference to the Yid. All was fish that came to his net.

The tall man was the Boston Bean, real name was John Cabot Winthrop. Born in Boston, Massachusetts, of course. Millionaire several times over, with yachts, country houses, town apartments scattered all over the world; A.E.F., Foreign Legion, and like the Yid, a soldier of fortune. He left his yachts and other impedimenta in the hands of hired men while he "fussed around" wherever the fussing was good. To make the Bean perfectly happy, all that was needed at any time was a machine gun to fight, enough cigarettes to smoke, and the dirtier he was, the better, while the fighting lasted.

The two had come up in the hills with plenty of bearers, who had to be able to fight as well as bear, if they wanted to go with the Yid and the Bean. Their objective was an old shrine where they thought there would be some rare jades. But they had found between them and the said objective, a War Lord who didn't see any special reason for allowing two foreign devils an opportunity to look over shrines uninvited, at least in his neck of the woods.

They argued the point with him, the argument on their side being conducted with 30-30 rifles, and on his part with what old trade guns he had, swords, lances and what-not. What he had that turned the argument in his favor was a thousand or so men that he didn't mind having killed off. He threw them at the Yid and the Bean in a ceaseless stream. The Yid, the Bean and the bearers all did "noble," as the Bean said afterward, but before long there were no bearers left; and the Bean and the Yid began to execute one of those famous rearward movements commonly called a retreat.

The War Lord, after counting what noses he had left, decided he'd had about enough, himself, and was content with detailing a party to stick along and harry the retiring forces, which consisted of the two above-mentioned gentlemen. The War Lord cherished the pleasant hope that they would run out of ammunition.

The Bean and the Yid, however, weren't packing much else besides ammunition, and so couldn't oblige the War Lord. The pursuing swordsmen soon learned that to show themselves meant death for the careless one, or a wound in the part that showed, and they contented themselves with tagging along, as much out of sight as possible. Every once in awhile, one or two of them would get full of opium and would test their luck, which was always bad.

AS THE Bean and the Yid saw the bodies, two Chinese came down the path, full speed ahead, their swords out and ready.

"Somebody has been handing that hop around again," said the Bean mournfully, as his 30-30 cuddled against his cheek.

"Here is a pill to go vid it," said the Yid with a smirk, as his rifle came up also. There were two whiplash cracks, and the two Chinamen pitched forward on their faces, their swords glimmering in the hot sun. The Bean and the Yid stood there, their rifles ready, but no more came around the bend of the path.

"I guess that's all this time," said the Bean finally as he lowered his rifle.

"Und two more makes—vat is de count, Beaneater?"

"I lost track. What do you care, you won't ever be able to publish it, and no one would believe you anyway."

They both laughed. The fact that they were on foot, in a territory teeming with men who would try to kill them on sight, and with at least three hundred miles separating them from any place where there was a semblance of law and order, didn't appear to worry them in the least; and as a matter of fact, it didn't.

"Go down and take a look-see," said the Bean. "I'll wait for a minute and see if any more are coming."

The Yid went down, his eyes seeming to pop out further as he stared down at Etherington.

"Oi! Beaneater!" he called. "Vite man! Englisher! Colder than a vagon tire. Come on down und—vat de hell!"

The girl and the Chinese boy rose from behind the rock. The Bean promptly came down, ignoring the chance of any further attack.

"You—you are white men!" gasped Katherine. She swayed back, then forward.

"Steady," said the Bean, putting a long arm around her. "Steady goes it. You are all right—we are white men. Americans."

"On de fire!" yelled the Yid. "Comin' up de hill. Kvick!"

He knelt, almost beside the body of Etherington, and his rifle began to spit a steel-jacketed death at the body of Chinese who were charging straight up the hill at them, not more than two hundred yards below. As the Bean released the girl, she stiffened as, never again to leave her, the blood of the fighting Nevilles came surging through her dainty body. Her proud little head went up and she drew the small automatic at her belt. As the Bean's rifle joined in, her little gun did also.

It was a silent charge and a deadly one, led by a young officer in a natty uniform. It was not a large party, some twenty odd men, but it started out and came up like a very efficient one. As the guns began to stop it, a small group of Chinese came around the bend. They were all that was left of the outfit that had been following the Bean and the Yid. They took one look at the men coming up the hill, recognized who they were, and promptly started for home. One look had told them they had been playing tag with the Bean and the Yid a little too long and it behooved them to get out of that territory as fast as possible if they wanted to live any longer. They all loved life better than their War Lord's revenge, so they left rapidly.

The efficient-looking fighters were climbing the hill under the fire of men who were just as efficient and dead shots also. Man after man went down, the young officer among the first; and when the charge reached within fifty yards, the survivors had got plenty. It was like running squarely into the face of death. They broke and ran, on both sides. As they reached the bottom of the hill, a much larger body came into sight.

"Oi," said the Yid, as he stood up, "dot vos only de advance guard. Here it comes de army."

The troops made no attempt to charge at once. They stood there, waiting the command of an officer who was mounted. This man sat on his horse, looking at the men who were now fleeing toward him.

"Two—four—maybe-so four-fifty yards," counted the Yid, raising the sight on his Winchester. "I got it ten smackers dot says I can knock him off de pony in von shot, ain't it, Beany?"

"Let him alone. He may withdraw the army. We better be hunting a place to hole up—and make it snappy, also. This is no place for us. Come on."

"Vare—oi, I see it. Could ve get up dare mitoudt vings, ve stands off de army, no foolin'."

"It's up to us to grow some feathers then," answered the Bean grimly. "Come on, talk about it later." He led the way up what looked like a crevice along the side of a towering rock. From where they stood, the top looked level for a space about as big as a billiard table.

"Vait," said the Yid. "I get it these canteens—our vater is almost nix." He stooped and unhooked the two canteens that were on Etherington and snapped them on his own belt. As they started up the crevice, the Bean helping Katherine, the officer on the horse far below shouted an order and one company trotted briskly forward.

"Dey is caming," announced the Yid, who had looked back for a moment. "Make it snappy, Beaneater."

THEY MADE the top, about one hundred feet, as the company reached the bottom of the little slope that led to the rock. It was just about what it looked like from below: a flat top, about ten by six feet. No vegetation, no water, no dirt, nothing but bare rock. The whole rock was like an immense silo with a flat top. There was no way up it except by the crevice, and that was so narrow that two persons at a time, even if thin, would have a hard time making it.

"My, vat a fine place," said the Yid, as they reached it. "De only vay dot dey gets us, is by bombin' vid planes. Already dey is going back to tell popper about it."

"They'll try us out," answered the Bean, "and then do that siege thing. But at that, we couldn't take all the fight they'd bring us in the open. Are you all right, Miss—?"

"My name is Katherine Neville," she answered. "I am so glad that you came. That was my uncle." The tears came in the hyacinth blue eyes and the exquisite lips quivered a little in spite of her efforts.

"Tell us about it later," said the Bean hastily. "You are quite all right now, Miss Neville," and he smiled at her. Few people could resist the homely Beaneater's smile, and the girl, after looking at him for a moment, smiled bravely back.

"Popper has sent dem back to bring us to him," announced the Yid, who was lying face down, looking over the edge.

"Yeah?" answered the Bean, "We haven't much time then. Here, you, what is your name?" to the Chinese boy.

"Li Tung," he answered promptly. "Top-side boy for Captain Ethelington."

"Fair enough," said the Bean gravely. "His spirit is now watching you from on high to see how much top-side boy you are. This, his spirit tells me to order that you do. Go down the rock and run, hide, run, hide until you reach Chi-kow on the Gulf of Chih-li. You know Chi-kow?"

Katherine spoke: "It is where we started from, sir."

"I know," answered Li Tung, "plenty good. I lun, I hide. I lun—what do aftel gettee Chi-kow?"

"You will find there four white men. Ask for a man named Jimmie Cordie—say that name."

"Jimmie Coldie," repeated Li Tung, with a smile. He was clever, this young Chinese boy, and Etherington had taught him much in the four years Li Tung had been with him.

"Right," went on the Bean. "With him will be Red Dolan—say that."

"Led Dolan," Li Tung answered.

"With them will be Grigsby and Putney—say those names."

"Gligsby and Plutney."

"If any of them are there, give them this message. Come here, Yid. Never mind the neighbors' children for a minute—they can't get here for a little while. I want to frame a message for Jimmie."

JUST AS the first of the advancing men reached the slope, the boy wiggled down and out of the crevice into the brush like a snake. As he started, the Bean said, "Remember, Li Tung—the spirit of Captain Etherington gives you five days to make it."

If the boy was seen, which is doubtful, there was no attempt at pursuit. It may have been that they thought that one Chinaman wasn't worth chasing in the face of better game.

The Yid and the Bean let the men of the company get up to the crevice and then, with only their rifles and forehead and eyes showing over the edge, killed the first two men that started up.

Several guns were promptly discharged at them, but as is mostly the case in that part of China, or in any part away from the coast, the arms carried were mostly swords and lances with quite a few bows and arrows. The gunfire did not even come close and after one or two arrows had come nearer than was pleasant, the Yid and the Bean gave the bowmen their exclusive attention for a few minutes, with the result that when they turned again to the crevice, there were no more arrows to trouble them. The Chinese tried the crevice, two by two, then in a continual stream, but none lived to get halfway. It was suicide, that was all, and very soon the Chinese recognized it as such and quit trying. Those that were left went back to the main body. The three on top of the rock watched them until they merged with the rest, then in a little while, saw a circle, well out of accurate firing range, form around the rock.

"Vell," said the Yid with a grin, "from vat I see, it looks like ve stay avile, ain't it, Beany?"

"At least long enough for us to introduce ourselves to Miss Neville," gravely answered the Bean. "The gentleman on your left who has just spoken, Miss Neville, is Mr. Abraham Cohen, late of New York City in the vicinity of Hester Street, then the A.E.F. and points east and west. I am John Winthrop from Boston—"

"Vich is de home of de codfish und de bean, Miss Neville," interrupted the Yid. "Und dot is vy ve call it Beaneater, or Codfish, or Beany."

"Mr. Cohen will answer much more readily to the name Yid," the Bean solemnly added, "and I will recommend him highly as a simon-pure specimen of a fighting Yid—and what could be fightinger than a fighting Yid?"

"I esk you?" grinned the Yid.

Katherine sensed that they were talking to keep her spirits up, and she smiled at both of them. With the unerring intuition of a woman, she knew that she had found two men who were as big brothers to her and who would both die before any harm could reach her.

"How long do you think it will be before the men you sent for can get here, Mr. Winthrop!"

"That question is a hard one to answer. Given that Li Tung makes it, and our friends are still there—I would say roughly ten, twelve days, Miss Neville."

"Twelve days! Must we stay up here on this rock for twelve days? Why, what will we eat and drink and everything? Why, how can we last that long?"

"Well," answered the Bean, just as gravely, although there was a twinkle in his eye, "any one that gets tired of staying up here can go down at any time. Personally, after looking at the reception committee, I am going to stay here. And that starts us off. Yid, open up the packs and see how much we have left of the old iron rations. There's four, no, six canteens of water. Miss Neville, you will have to go on an allowance, I'm afraid."

"I am—my father was Colonel Neville, Mr. Winthrop, and after his death I was with my uncle, Captain Etherington, all over the world. I can go on short rations. Oh, Uncle Bertie—I—I am a soldier's daughter and I am not going to cry—at least not while we are on the fi—firing line," she announced sternly.

"Oi, vat a business," said the Yid, from where he was parceling out the cans and packages. "Und vy not cry? Go ahead und cry all you vant. Me und de Bean cry, lots of times, don't ve, Beaneater? Cry, und den you feel it better, ain't it? Maybe-so dot your Uncle Bertie from vare he is sittin' on high, he see you cry und den he feel better, knowin' dot de cry vill make it better for you, likevise. Go ahead und cry, like a nice girl," the Yid encouraged.

"Why, I—I know you will take care of me and—" The tears came and she turned away, burying her proud little head in her arms.

THE SOBS gradually died away and she raised her head. Her eyes opened wide as she saw the little tent the Yid and the Bean had made right in the middle of the top. It wasn't much of a tent, being made by the two rifles as poles, the packs as weights and two blankets and two clean white suits, some clean B.V.D.s, and anything else usable that had been in the two packs. It looked like a pile of fallen family washing, but it gave some privacy at least.

"Your apartment," said the Bean, with a flourish of his hand. "You will note that it is in the middle of the building. The one I will occupy is on one side of you, Mr. Cohen's will be on the other side. So in case you do any sleep-walking, you will not fall off the roof. In case the apartment suddenly falls in on you, it will be because we are reaching for the poles in a hurry."

She saw what they had done for her and now, feeling better after her cry, she really smiled. "Why, thank you, Mr. Winthrop and Mr. Cohen. It is a very nice apartment, indeed."

"I really wish," said the Bean, "that you could find it possible to drop that Mr. Winthrop thing and I am quite sure that Mr. Cohen feels the same. Frankly, if you could use the names that we are more used to hearing, it would make us feel much more at home."

"My goodness, yes," assured the Yid. "I haven't heard dot Mr. Cohen for so long; und dare is so many Cohens, ain't it?"

"But only one Fighting Yid," said Katherine, with a smile. "Of course I will—Beaneater, and Yid."

"Dot's de girl," answered the Yid. "Und now, listen to popper. Dare is, mit care, enough to eat for eight days; mit extra care, ten; und on a starvation ration—two veeks. Vich do ve go on?"

"I think," announced the Bean, "that we better take the extra care one. Which do you suggest, Miss Neville?"

"Katherine, please," answered Miss Neville. "I think the extra care one, also."

"Suits me," agreed the Yid. "Und now the vater? Dare is four full canteens und"—he reached for the two he had taken from Etherington—"von is full, und dis von"—he shook it—"not so good. Maybe-so a little."

"Half a cupful morning and night, then," said the Bean. "All set?"

"All set," answered Katherine.

"Jake mit me," grinned the Yid. "I take it de first vatch," and eased over to the edge.

CHAPTER II

HUNGRY FOR TROUBLE

THE FOUR BIG, lean, bronzed Americans sat in the scented gardens of Feng-cheng in Chi-kow. They had been on a mission for Yen Yuan, head of the dreaded T'aip'ing secret society, a mission that only white men could accomplish, and now they were ready to return to Hongkong. A T'aip'ing war junk was in the harbor, awaiting their pleasure. Feng-cheng, who had graduated from Boston Tech in the same class as Jimmie Cordie, one of the four, had persuaded them to stay over a couple of days with him. If he hadn't, they would have missed the worn and ragged Chinese boy who now stood in front of them.

They were all big men: Red Dolan, the biggest, was two hundred and thirty pounds of living steel, surmounted by a flaming red topknot of hair. Jimmie Cordie was the slightest of the four, with black eyes, a thin face, a smile almost always on his lips and in his eyes. George Grigsby, a dark chap from the Kentucky hills, had a hawklike nose, tight lips, and a body as lithe and quick as a panther. Arthur Putney, from Vermont, was as tall and broad as Grigsby, silent, slow to speak and fast to move, with the steady eyes of his New England ancestors. All of them had served in the Foreign Legion, the A.E.F., and after the war had been together continually, in the places where the only law was how far you could make men obey your orders. Any one of the four would have cheerfully died for the rest, and all of them could make a machine gun hold on a mark as closely as a rifle. Of the four, Jimmie Cordie was the best shot, if a best could be picked out. Big Red Dolan loved Jimmie Cordie better than he did his patron saint.

The Bean had known the four were going on a mission for the T'aip'ing. He had invited himself to go along, as he did on every possible occasion; and having been refused with friendly jeers, he had gone with the Yid, who had a little private enterprise, as stated. The Bean and the Yid had not been needed on the T'aip'ing affair.

"Ye have a message from the Boston Bean and the Fighting Yid?" Red demanded of the Chinese youth. "And what do they mean by sendin' a message by the likes of ye?"

The boy, Li Tung, met the cold gleam in the frosty blue eyes with a smile. A look of intense concentration came on his face and he drew a long breath; then, as if beginning a lesson taught him—he was, for that matter—he began, in a singsong voice:

"Boston Bean an' Fightin' Lid say, come vely click to big lock—Shang-si—lescue them flom bad men—allee same lescue—"

"What?" shouted Red. "We are to go to Shang-si and rescue those apes? Why the hell don't they stay at home, the monkey-faced gibboons?"

"Put a jaw tackle on that flannel mouth of yours for a minute," said Jimmie Cordie. "Listen, little brother: If the men you call the Boston Bean and the Fighting Yid did not send you—or if they have been in any way compelled to send this message—or if they are not in trouble—then it will be much better for you that you turn and walk away, now."

"It will," added Red, "whilst ye are still all in wan piece."

"It is tlue," said the boy. "My mis'ble head will pay if not so."

"It will," answered Red with the deepest conviction, "wid or widout your permission, me bucko."

"Shut up, Red," Cordie said, his eyes on the Chinese boy. "Go ahead with the message, little brother."

Li Tung drew another breath, and the effort came back into his voice as he started to chant, all in one breath:

"Boston Bean tell me, sing to Jimmie Coldie: 'Beans an' blown blead Slat'day night, an' fish balls Slunday molning'—an' Fightin' Lid say tell Led Dolan, 'Big Ilish bum come an' get Liddish beatin' up.'"

He finished gasping for breath, but with a smile of triumph, well pleased with himself—and he had a right to be, at that.

"'Tis them," announced Red firmly, "and when I get the two hands of me on that Yid ape, I will—"

"Tell *him* about it," drawled Grigsby. "Let's get at it."

"BETTER LET me handle things," said Jimmie Cordie, rising. As he did, he said: "You have done well, O honorable little brother. This," he took a handful of money out of a pocket and handed it to Li Tung, "is not pay for what you have done—but a present from one man to another."

Li Tung bowed and took the money, his eyes shining. There

was enough there to give him ease and luxury for a long time; and even more he appreciated the honor paid him.

"Come with me, and eat and drink," Jimmie went on. "I'll be back as soon as I get the dope," he said to the rest as he started with the boy.

In about half an hour, he came back, Li Tung with him. Their host had acted as interpreter.

"Here it is," Jimmie said, "as close as I can get it, with Feng-cheng's help." He told of the meeting of Katherine Neville with the Yid and the Bean and where they had holed up. "That was five days ago. Now it seems that this Captain Etherington was looking at some mines in Shan-si for an English syndicate. The top cutter of the town agreed to furnish protection for Etherington's party, which included his niece and a couple of young engineers; and he did that little thing until another War Lord by the name of Chow-yang came along and started a fight. Etherington's outfit got off to a flying start, but it seems that before the scrapping started, the new War Lord had caught a good look-see at Miss Neville and wanted to add her to his collection. He sent a party out after them as soon as he mopped up on the city, evidently. They caught up and in the running fight that followed, the two young engineers and all but one of the bearers, this young gent, Li Tung, got killed. Just as the Yid and the Bean appear on the scene from the good Lord knows where, Etherington goes West. The Yid and the Bean stand off the pursuit, and make it to the top of a big rock which they were going to hold against all comers. They send the kid here out with an S.O.S. to us. Now that you know all about it, let's go."

"Wait a minute, Jeems," said Putney. "Go how. Do you think that all we got to do is to start and walk through Shang-si? If you do, young feller, me lad, take two more thinks. Did it ever occur to you that in the province of Shang-si there are some fifty million gents, any one of whom would cheerfully give us the hot egg treatment?"

"If ye are afraid to go, ye lily-livered old lady," announced Red, with deep disgust, "me and Jimmie will go by ourselves."

"I'll go anywhere you will go, you red-headed ape from the north of Ireland," grinned Putney, "only I'd like to take a look-see first."

"And well I know ye would, ye black-muzzled scut," conceded Red. "Do ye mean to tell me that we can't take a couple of machine guns and slap all the Chinks between here and them lads outta the way?"

"Why take any?" answered Putney. "Take a sword, Red."

"Listen, kidders," Jimmie Cordie broke in, "while we are sitting here, the Yid and the Bean and Miss Neville may be starving to death."

"Not the Yid," asserted Red, "he's got too much fat."

"All kidding to one side, Jimmie," Grigsby interrupted, "have you got any idea how to go in—outside of doing as Red says?"

"Yeah, boy. Feng-cheng tells me that there is an English flyer in Pei-ho that has been working for some darn War Lord or what not. He says that this bird has an old army bomber of some kind, big enough to hold five or six. He's off now to see if the said flyer is open to do a little high and lively flying on the side."

"Yeah? If he is, then what?"

"Why, we'll take my little brother here, Li Tung, load 'er up with all the ammunition she can carry, plus a couple of Brownings, plus ourselves, and then fly to the rock. Simple, isn't it?"

"Darn simple," said Putney, with a grin. "Only, Jeems me lad, continue from there. We fly to the rock—then what?"

"My gosh, have I got to take you by the hand all the way? We land and—"

"But do we? Is there a landing place up there? Given that we do, how can we pack three more people back? Also—"

"Ask the flyer," grinned Jimmie. "Let's get to the rock, first."

FENG-CHENG CAME back from Pei-ho late that afternoon and brought with him a lean, tanned young Englishman, who, after one keen look at the four men who arose to meet him, smiled cheerfully and became one of the outfit. After they told him what they wanted, he still smiled. "Well, if we can land, and if your people are still there, we can make room for them by unloading most of the ammunition. I've carried eight in the old bus before now. She's a stanch old thing. I say, we can mount the blooming machine guns on the scarf yoke and turn her into a battle wagon, what?"

Red had been looking the young English flyer over and, having decided that he was "there," produced his cigarettes and handed them over. " 'Tis a good idea. Wid the likes of ye at the stick and me and Jimmie at the gats, we can go from here to hell and back." Which was admitting John Cecil Mowbray to the fellowship.

They had Brownings and ammunition with them, having brought them up from Hong Kong to use in their little affair; but it had been compromised after a pitifully easy fight.

The young flyer brought the plane down, and all the useful load, besides their own weight, food, water, gas, and oil, they made up in ammunition and guns. The flyer took off easily, went a little way out in the Gulf of Chih-li, so as to satisfy the curious that they were bound for Port Arthur, then turned and headed for the border of Shan-si.

Red was sitting by Jimmie Cordie and leaned over to shout in Jimmie's ear, "Hey, Jimmie, this beats walkin', don't it?"

"It do—except that if anything goes wrong you can't get out and fix it, old kid."

"Who would want to get out, ye scut? Step over the side, count three and pull the cord and—"

"And land smack in some War Lord's back yard. This is the province where they are always glad to see foreign devils—to give 'em the slicing treatment."

"Not me," said Red firmly. "Do I land, I have me Colt in me fist, first, last, and all the time."

They flew steadily and nothing went wrong. Hour after

hour, due east. From Pei-ho to the rock was roughly some four hundred miles.

"At ninety miles an hour," said Jimmie, "we ought to be picking the rock up any minute."

Li Tung heard him and answered, "Velly soon now, honolable eldel blothel."

CHAPTER III

BRAVE DEFENSE

THE FIRST NIGHT on the top of the rock had been one that allowed neither the Yid, the Bean or Katherine any sleep. As soon as it got dark, there began a slow, steady dribble of Chinese, sometimes one, sometimes two, up the slope and then up the crevice. But always to meet them was the beam of the Bean's flashlight, and the *Pow!* of the Yid's .45 Colt.

In the morning a party had advanced under a flag of truce and halted at the start of the crevice. The Yid stuck his head over the edge and conducted the negotiations for the besieged.

The Chinese officer sat on his horse, an interpreter stood beside him. The officer looked up at the smirking Yid, then down at the interpreter, and snarled a sentence. The interpreter looked up and shouted:

"The Lord Chow-yang, who is War Lord of all Shang-si, demands your surrender." This interpreter must have been educated in England, as he did not slip on the "r" that is fatal to most Chinese.

"Gif de Var Lord de compliments of de Boston Bean und de Yid, und tell him dot he could go to hell vid all Shang-si vid him. Tell him likevise dot ve double-dare *him* to come up de crack. Ve are some Var Lords ourselves, ain't it?"

The interpreter translated this to the best of his ability, and the officer dictated another order.

"The lieutenant of Chow-yang, who is here before you, says that you are very foolish. You cannot escape. The Lord Chow-yang wishes the maiden that you have with you. If you will give her to him, he will send you to the coast with an escort and much gold. If you do not, he will send his men against you until you are out of ammunition and then, when he takes you, you will both receive Ling'ith or will be boiled alive in oil. The lieutenant of Chow-yang says for you to choose."

"Tell de Var Lord dot first he must catch de rabbit before it starts dot boiling in de pot. Ve is comfortable up here und don't vant to meet no Var Lords. Besides, de Lenox Avenue Tigers und de Navy und de Marines dot alvays land first is coming up de creek to rescue us as soon as dey gets through lunch. Here ve are un here ve stay. If de Var Lord don't like it dot ve liff on top of de rock, tell him to come and put us out. Go back und tell him dot de Boston Bean und de Yid say he is a piece of cheese—"

"Katherine Neville also," came a clear voice from behind the Yid.

The Fighting Yid grinned and added, "Und also Miss Katherine Neville say dot de cheese is limberger."

The officer, on getting the translation, snarled a short sentence, whirled his horse, then pulled up and spat out a few words more. The interpreter called, "The War Lord Chow-yang will come. The request is made that the wounded and dead may be removed."

"Go ahead," answered the Yid, agreeably. "Take 'em avay if you vant 'em. Ve don't."

The officer and his escort trotted back, and a little later a burial party came out.

Twice that day the Chinese tried massed attacks, but no man lived to get even close to the crevice. The Yid and the Bean began shooting long before the bowmen could get within arrow range and what few guns the Chinese had were negligible factors. To reach the rock under fire of two marksmen would be hard enough for any outfit without heavy loss and to climb up a narrow crevice one by one and live to get to the top was impossible as long as the defenders could pull trigger—and these two men most certainly could do that thing.

No more came that day, but at night the dribble commenced once more. The Yid and the Bean didn't mind; the nights were fairly warm and now the moon was out, making the flashlight unnecessary. They spelled each other or stood the watch together.

If any two men in the world had to be on top of a rock in Eastern China and the hardest to "draw" had to be chosen, there is no question but what the Yid and the Bean would be among those seriously considered. Both of them looked upon life as a huge joke; both fatalistically believed that when their number was up they would pass out, and not before. Both were expert marksmen and neither of them feared any living thing—or things.

And Katherine Neville slept soundly at night in "her apartment," undisturbed by the occasional *crack* of a Colt .45. During the day she would keep watch and the Yid and the Bean would sleep. Just where the crevice reached the top she had found a little opening in the rock that made a small cave, and when the men were awake, she would go there to get out of the sun, which didn't seem to affect the Yid and the Bean at all.

ALL IN all, as the Yid announced as they sucked on some beef cubes, the fifth morning, "Ve got it all de comforts of a home, ain't it?"

"We'll have to break the lease, though," answered the Bean, as he poured out the water allowance. "The water is running low. I'll speak to the janitor about the low pressure. If Li Tung made it to Chi-kow, he is there by now. Give Jimmie and the rest six days to make it there—ladies and gentlemen, I regret to announce that from now on, the water will be doled out by the spoonful."

"Oi, Beaneater," protested the Yid, "dare is enough und—"

"Enough to last us seven days, yes. But, my distinguished friend from Jerusalem, if James doesn't come—what then?"

"Easy. Ve gif him until de seventh day und by den if dey are not here, ve sneak down de crack in de moonlight und starts out to meet 'em."

The Bean, from where he sat, looked at the far-away circle of Chinese, thought of the four hundred miles between them and anything that even faintly resembled safety for a woman—and grinned. "Fair enough."

"Und right over dare is plenty of vater," continued the Yid. "Vat ve do is dis, ain't it? Right now, ve all take von good drink und den go back to de ration stuff for seven days."

"Suits me," answered the Bean. "How about you, Katherine?"

"Well," she confessed, "I really would like a real drink, you know. I'm awfully thirsty."

"Dot settles it," said the Yid, getting up, "I'll get it."

He went over to where the canteens lay in the shade of the "apartment" and came back with a full one. Katherine looked at it. "Why, that's one of Uncle Bertie's. There was very good water where we camped."

"We'll sample it," the Yid said, as he reached for a cup.

Both the Bean and Katherine held their cups out and the Yid filled all three.

"Happy days," he said, as he lifted his to his lips. They laughed and all three drained the cups of water. As the Bean put his down he made a wry face. "I don't think much of that good water of your Uncle Bert—." He pitched forward on his face, his body over Katherine Neville's feet.

The Yid's eyes almost popped out as he got to his feet. "Dot vater! Drugged! Kvick—get—." He swayed and fell across the Bean. As he got up, Katherine Neville had worked her feet loose and tried to rise also. She couldn't make it before the powerful drug got her. As if in a mist, she saw the Yid come forward, then she felt herself sinking in the darkness that had come. She went down, her proud little head finding a resting-place on the Bean's shoulder.

KATHERINE NEVILLE awoke to find the darkness gone.

As she did, she was conscious of a bad zinc-like taste in her mouth, and her head ached badly. She groped with one little hand to touch some familiar thing—then sat up. She was in a room, hung with heavy satin curtains for walls, the front of which was open to a little ornate balcony. From where she sat, in the silken bed, she could see out over the roofs of houses and temples. Her clothes had been taken from her and in their place she wore a sheer Silk robe.

Beside the bed sat an old Chinese woman. A little further away were seated two young Chinese girls. Katherine Neville did not have to be told where she was. She knew in the first glance that she had been captured by some Chinese War Lord.

Her lovely face went white and her lips trembled for a moment, then her head went up and her lips became tight. She remembered what her uncle had said, "You are a Neville. Live—and die like one." There must be some way that she could kill herself; and whatever that way was, she would take it.

The old woman spoke to her in Chinese. Katherine shook her head; she did not understand Chinese, save for a few words. The woman said something to one of the girls who bowed and left the room. The other girl rose and came to the bed with a little porcelain jar of water. Katherine took it and drank, rinsing her mouth as best she could. As she handed back the jar, the girl who had gone out came back with a man. It was the interpreter who had been at the rock.

He bowed low, then straightened up and stood near the bed. Katherine reached down and pulled one of the silk covers up over her shoulders as far as she could. The little silk robe exposed her white flesh more than it hid it.

The Chinaman had not looked at her. He knew that was for Chow-yang.

"I regret to have to disturb you, Miss Neville," he said blandly, "but orders have been given that I was to see you at once, on your return."

The thought that she must get a sword or a knife beat against her brain and with it came strength to play a part.

"I am very glad to see some one," and she smiled. The Neville blood was in action now. "Outside of those two white beasts that held me prisoner."

In spite of his training the man's eyes widened a little. "You mean the two men that met you as your uncle passed on high?"

"Yes. They made me go to the top of the rock with them."

"You went with them unwillingly?"

"What else could I do? Just as I went with my uncle—unwillingly."

"I am afraid that my poor brain cannot grasp it, Miss Neville. You went with your uncle against your wishes?"

"Very much so," she answered with a smile. "I did not wish to leave the city. I am tired of ceaseless traveling and would rest—with the Lord Chow-yang, whom I saw before my uncle fled."

The young Chinese interpreter, who had spent several years in England and America, smiled. "Your words are as fair and scented as a flower," he said, "and they will warm the heart of the Lord Chow-yang." He knew she was lying. He had had enough contact with English and American women to know how they felt about the yellow race. That this English girl would willingly come to the arms of a Chinese was preposterous, but, like all Chinese, he admired bravery.

"In that case," he went on smoothly, "you will receive the administrations of the slaves here, in preparing you for the happiness that awaits you. The Lord Chow-yang had ordered that you be made ready—for him."

Katherine felt suddenly cold, all over. There was something more deadly than force in the bland, polite tones. She wondered, even as she answered, whether or not she could leap from the bed and draw the short sword from his sash, before she was stopped. "Why, of course I will be glad to be prepared for the Lord Chow-yang." As she said it, the Chinaman must have read in her eyes what she wanted to do, because he smiled and stepped back two steps.

"The men that held me on the rock? Are they dead?" she went on.

"No, they are not dead. Yet. The Lord Chow-yang has them in a safe place," and he smiled once more. "You may discuss with him their disposal."

"Tell the Lord Chow-yang that I await him."

The Chinaman was by now frankly puzzled. That any Anglo-Saxon girl would take things so calmly, he could not understand. He knew she lied about the compulsion, and knew that she must have some plan; but he thought it concerned escape. That she could talk calmly, awaiting her chance to kill herself, hoping to disarm watchfulness by doing it, never occurred to him.

"I will tell the Lord Chow-yang," he said, then bowed and left the room. Katherine let the silk cover fall and got out of the bed. She stood straight, as straight as if at attention, her shoulders back and her head up. "I am ready."

The old woman sensed rather than understood her, and rose. Seated on a three-legged stool, she was offered tea and sweetmeats and little chopped pieces of meat in rice. All the time the hand-maidens were scenting and massaging her lovely body, Katherine had tried to see something with which she could kill herself—a long hairpin, anything; but she had failed. The Lord Chow-yang's "mother of the maidens" had prepared maidens, unwilling maidens, before, and knew how little a thing, properly used, was needed to cause death.

That the Yid and the Bean were still alive Katherine knew. That they would in some way be used by Chow-yang to compel her surrender to him, she also knew. No Chinese wants to take a woman by force—he wants the woman to yield to him, by what means matters not.

Finally the summons came, "The Lord Chow-yang is ready to receive the Lady Neville."

Katherine rose and with a bodyguard that seemed to her to

have materialized out of thin air, she walked proudly out on the balcony and along it to a door that was held open by low-bowing slaves.

Chow-yang rose as she entered the room. He was young, not more than twenty-six or seven; an educated Chinese, a fighter who had won his way to an overlordship in the Army of the North, then had taken his men and gone to his home province. He was cruel, hard, and typically Chinese. Lord of as many men as he could recruit to his standard, lord of as many peasants as the district be controlled reached, lord of life and death as far as his might carried.

He was not bad-looking, although his face was scarred with sword cuts. He claimed Manchu blood and probably had it, as his eyes did not slant up. His eyes lighted up as the lovely English girl entered the room. He could not speak very much English. A little, learned in Peking and Hongkong. Now he tried it. "It—gives me—plea—ples—I cannot say it—"

Katherine Neville, of the house that had been noble in England since the days of William the Conqueror, smiled gayly. "Your English, my Lord Chow-yang, is as bad as my Chinese." She saw the hilt of a sword, gem-incrusted, at his side. If she could reach it—perhaps she could if she got close enough to him—she would sway in toward him and then—

Chow-yang smiled. "It is—true—I make—I hear better than speak. Come to the window and see—" He gave up trying to talk English and motioned. Katherine walked to the window. He stood beside her, but on her left. Unless she gained his left or got in front of him, she could not reach the sword hilt.

She looked down on the top of two wooden cages, hung about ten feet below the windows from iron hooks set in the wall. The hooks were some five feet below the windows, the cages, at the end of two-inch ropes about twelve feet in length, were about fifteen feet from the ground. Between the wall and the temple across the square, not more than two hundred yards was the gardens of Chow-yang, rich with many colored flowers.

"The men who—dared—defied me," he said blandly, with a wave of his hand down toward the cages. "Tomorrow, in the—" He did not know the English word for square, so he waved his hand around it. "They die—by Ling'ith."

He looked at the lovely face of the girl beside him. The sun had gone behind the hills and the soft velvety dusk had come, but it was still light enough to allow him to see that her lips had quivered for an instant.

"It may be," he went on, blandly, "that if you—asked—begged of me—in the morning, that their death—could be made—sudden."

Katherine Neville's proud little head went back and there was no quiver to her lips now, She stepped away from him, then in front, between him and the window. "The Fighting Yid," she said, slowly and distinctly, "and the Boston Bean are gentlemen, and would not allow me to do anything to save them at the expense of—"

She swayed in, as if from weakness and her little hand darted to his sword hilt. But Chow-yang had not won his War Lordship by being unalert or slow. Before her hand touched it, his left had closed over her wrist in a grip of steel, He raised her hand and arm as high as her shoulder, then his right hand closed on the white firm forearm and pressed in.

For an instant Katherine Neville stood there, then as the pain swept through her body, she screamed.

Chow-yang laughed. "You do—not like? I will tea—lesson you. See, I tighten once—again and then—"

CHAPTER IV

TOO LATE

LI TUNG STOOD up and shouted, "Lock! Lock! See! Lock!"

He pointed to the right. Jimmie Cordie raised his glasses. "I see a rock, but no one on it."

"They may be down at the side," said Grigsby, raising his own glasses. "It looks as bare as Mother Hubbard's cupboard, at that. No one around in the valley, either. Looks as if the relief expedition arrived after the show was over."

The little valley that led up to the slope made a perfect landing place, no bumps or cracks and the pilot brought the plane down and taxied almost up to the rock.

"There may be some of the enemy holed up," Grigsby announced. "It's a cinch they could have seen us coming. Jimmie, you and Red get up there. Putt and I will cover you. Go with them, Li Tung, and make sure that is the rock."

"It's the right rock, all right," said Jimmie Cordie, as he and Red started with Li Tung. "The Bean and the Yid have left some markers."

They had, in the shape of several dead Chinese, who had been in the last rush. When the would-be rescuers reached the top, they looked down on the mute evidences of occupancy. The Chinese, when the first soldier had gained the top and waved them up, had taken everything that took their fancy, but had left empty cartridge shells, some beef cubes and rations. The Chinese had let them severely alone, fearing poison; also there were three or four canteens. The Chinese, not being fools, had seen at once what had happened. Just what had poisoned or drugged the three whites, they didn't know or care. They had their prisoners, so they only stayed long enough to pick up the 30-30s, the clothes, and other valuables.

"If there had been a fight," Jimmie Cordie said, slowly, as he looked around, "there would be blood around and dead men. The Yid and the Bean would have bitten some of them, if they were out of ammunition. There was no fight up here, that's one sure thing."

"Maybe-so they got tired of waiting," supplied Red, "and started to meet us. I thought we ought to have come in on the ground—"

"Write a letter about it," answered Jimmie, a puzzled frown on his face. "Would they leave without the canteens, dumb-bell?"

"And that reminds me," said Red. " 'Tis thirsty I've been since morning. While ye are dopin' it out, Jimmie darlin', I'll get me a drink, if them scuts has left any."

"They couldn't have decoyed the Yid and the Bean down," went on Jimmie, to himself. "Those birds are too wise and they had a woman with them. They might have left this rock for a better place to stick around in till we came, but why in hell did they—"

He was interrupted by a curse from Red, who had tasted the water sparingly to see if it was foul.

" 'Tis quare-tastin' stuff, Jimmie. Tastes like—like—now what in the name of all the saints does it taste like?"

Li Tung sprang forward, and touched the canteen to his lips, then spat carefully. "Dlugged! Dlugged!" He spoke some unfamiliar Chinese name.

"Drugged? How?" Jimmie Cordie snapped. "Was it drugged when you were here?"

"No, no!" The Chinese boy held his head in his hands. "We not dlink from that befole I leave. That one of Captain Ethelington's canteens. I think—maybe-so—"

"Well, spit it out—what do ye think, ye scut?" Red growled.

"Easy does it," Jimmie warned. "What do you think, little brother?"

"I think maybe-so that Chi-sha put dlug in it. Chi-sha one of Captain Ethelington's boys. Captain find Chi-sha spoiling guns when we lun flom Wal Lold Chow-yang. Captain dlive Chi-sha flom camp—think Chi-sha in pay of Chow-yang. Maybe-so he put dlug in watel, tly to makee Captain Ethelington go vely dead long time. Chow-yang catchee."

"You're right, Li Tung," Jimmie said slowly. "Red, that's how it was. One of the bearers was in this War Lord's pay, and tried to drug the crowd with knockout drops as they ran away. When the Bean and the Yid got to this canteen—blotto! Along comes the War Lord and carts them away."

THEY WENT down the crevice, Jimmie carrying the canteen, and told Grigsby, Putney and the flyer, Mowbray, what Li Tung had told up on the rock.

"Who was this War Lord who was attacking you when you left, Li Tung?" asked Jimmie.

"Chow-yang," answered the boy promptly.

"Do you know where this Chow-yang's city is?"

"Flive—flifty miles—plenty know. That way—up and dlown—all the way."

"That's close; five or fifty miles. After Captain Etherington ran, Li Tung, how long was it before he got here to this rock?"

"One night. Maybe-so after sun come up, thlee owls."

"Three owls?" interrupted Red. "What time keepin' is that, I dunno. Come on, what's the use of wah-wahin' here? The Yid and the Bean may be still—"

"Hold it a minute, Red," Putney interrupted. "This is bad country to go bull-rushing through. If we could land near the city it would be a darn sight better for us, and for the Yid and the Bean also, if this bird is saving them for anything."

"How much gas have you, Mowbray?" asked Jimmie.

"Not enough to do any jazzing around, I'm afraid. I figured eight hundred miles and a little over. I gave you all the weight I could for ammunition, you know. We've come four twenty-five right now."

"All right, that ends any figuring about the plane taking us.

We can't all go and leave the plane. Red and I will go with Li Tung."

"Not so good, Jimmie. If you got in, what could you do, the two of you?"

"Darned if I know. Something might turn up. Red and I have been in places before and messed around, haven't we, Red?"

"We have. Come on. I'll pack gats for the Yid and Beany. Wid the four of us, what Chink can stop us?"

"No one Chink, ape," answered Putney, with a grin, "but a million might."

"I say," said Mowbray, "I can do this, if I can find a place to land you. I can take you as close as I can, then go back and get some petrol. I'll be much lighter, you know. If you lads can get in and make it back to where I drop you off, in ten hours, say, I'll be back. That way you can all four go."

"Boy," said Jimmie Cordie, with a grin, "step on the gas or whatever it is you do, and make it snappy."

Mowbray took them some ten miles in the hills and when Li Tung pointed out a mountain ahead and shouted, "City Yungning ovel hill," he made a smooth three-point landing on a level space not much bigger than a pocket handkerchief.

"Well," said Jimmie, as they unloaded machine guns and ammunition, "ten miles is much better than a kick in the neck, carrying this load. If we are not here, young feller, look for us on top of the rock."

Mowbray grinned and waved his hand as he took off.

"Li Tung," said Jimmie, "can you go ahead and get into the city without being stopped?"

"Can do. Plenty Chinaboy come and go."

"All right; you go ahead and find out if the girl and the white men are there and where they are, if you can. Is it a walled city?"

"Not on hill side. In flont, plenty wall."

"Can we get in or close up without being seen?"

"Maybe-so, come night—same way Captain Ethelington got out."

"This path leads to the city?"

"Yes, to livel, then down livel to little hill, then into city."

"Follow the river? Fair enough," grinned Jimmie Cordie. "Get going, little brother, and if you can, come back to us."

"I come," answered Li Tung firmly.

"Ain't that somepin'?" demanded Red, as Li Tung ran up the path. "We will walk in, get the Yid and Beany and the girl and walk out to the bus widout a fight at all. Why the hell don't we go in the front way and slap them outta their nightgowns?" To Red, the thought of going anywhere and not getting a fight was very displeasing.

"I have a feelin', Red, old settler," answered Grigsby, "that while we may walk in, on the way out we are going to get all the fight we want handed to us; so stick around."

CHAPTER V

CAGED

THE YID AND the Boston Bean came to about the same time. They were in Chinese punishment cages. These are built so that the persons in them can neither stand up straight, lie down or sit down without doubling up somewhere. It doesn't sound like anything very bad, but in a few short hours, the muscular pain becomes almost unbearable.

The cages were side by side, open affairs with bars of bamboo about three inches apart.

The Yid stirred and tried to stand up, only to rap his head on the roof of the cage. On the way in, he had moved in the arms of his captors and had been promptly rapped over the head with a sword hilt. The wound had bled a lot and the blood had run down and dried on his linen underwear, which was all the clothing he had been left. Even his shoes and stockings were gone. The Yid was short and roly-poly, seeming about four feet broad across the shoulders; but at that, most of him was muscle instead of fat.

He touched his head, felt around the cage, felt of the bars, tried to sit down, couldn't, without bending his very sore head, and then said, "Vell, how in hell I got in here in de monkey cage, is vay beyond me." He wiggled around and surveyed another cage within three feet of his.

"Hey, Beaneater," he said, with firm conviction, "ve drank it de doped vater, und ve vake up in de cage. Beany? Vake up! Time for anodder drink." The Yid's nerve was intact, steady as ever.

"I don't have to wake up," answered the Bean, through the bars of his cage. "I am already awake, thank you. You're all dressed up, in your B.V.D.s. Glad they left me my pants."

"Vare is Miss Neville?"

"That's what is worrying me," answered the Bean. "If we are somewhere in cages, where is she?"

"If I could answer dot kvestion, I could—ouch, oi, my back it already feels like dot it is full of red-hot needles—hey, vot de hell?"

"Oh, my God," whispered the Bean, and he fought the bars of his cage. Katherine Neville's scream had reached them.

The Bean was a strong man, strong in every muscle and like steel wire, but the cage he was in was a new one and he could not, on account of his height, get any kind of leverage. He did loosen one bar before he sank as best he could to the floor, a huddled heap, every bit of his strength gone. He had put it all in the effort.

The Yid, even as the scream lasted, was turned into a raging dynamo of fury. He literally went crazy. The Yid, when he saw any child or woman in pain, would do anything to stop it. As the face of the lovely girl who had smiled at him and called him Mr. Cohen, and who was, as the Yid had announced to the Bean, "von game kid," came to his bloodshot eyes, the Yid went berserk.

The cage he was in was an old one, although it was still strong enough to hold a Chinese prisoner, who, strangely enough, would never try to burst out, but would bear the pain until death, as stoically as an Indian.

The Yid crouched, his broad back against the back of the cage, and put his big feet against two of the bars. The cage was built for just such a pry, also. He straightened out and the bars and all in front went flying out, the Yid almost going with them. He never waited an instant. Like a great cat he was out, on top of the cage, and swarming up the rope. From the hook, he could stand out and reach the low-cut window sill. As his hands closed on it and he drew himself up, Katherine Neville screamed again. This time the scream stopped with a gurgle. She had seen the Yid coming in. At least, she saw the bulk of him coming through the window, as the moon was now faintly shining.

AS SHE stopped, Chow-yang saw by her eyes that she had seen something and he dropped her arm, turning to face whatever it was.

It was plenty for any one man to face, or any two. The Yid came down on him, arms outstretched, fingers bent, great shoulders hunched. The Yid's face in repose was a handsome one, but now he looked very much like some great prehistoric ape.

Chow-yang was no coward, but his face went gray as his hand flashed to the sword hilt that Katherine Neville had tried for. His hand reached it, and the shimmering blade was a foot out of the sheath, when the Yid reached him.

Katherine Neville, her back to the wall by the window, saw Chow-yang, War Lord of the city of Yung-ning, bend slowly back, one of the Yid's great arms around the small of his back, one hand at his face, covering it. The Yid's body seemed to sway forward and then she heard a snap, as if a tree limb had broken.

The Yid released Chow-yang, who crumpled to the floor, his back broken. As he went down, the Yid drew the sword from the silken sash and cut down, once. The War Lord Chow-yang, from his room in the heart of his palace where he was surrounded by guards and swordsmen, went on high to join his ancestors. Those on guard outside may have heard some unusual noise, must have heard the screams; but until their master called or signaled, they would have no more gone in than they would enter the cage of a tiger.

The Yid, as he raised the sword from the heart of Chow-yang came back from berserkland. He looked at Katherine Neville and grinned.

"Und dot is dot. Vare do ve go from here?"

"Well," said a voice from the window, a critical voice at that. "If I were you, Yid, I'd go and get some clothes on. Double shame on you."

The Yid whirled around. "Oi! Jimmie! Now ve is rescued und everything!"

"You are counting your chickens a long time before they're out of the incubator," answered Jimmie Cordie, sternly. "Come on, through the window. You are Miss Neville?"

"Yes, I—oh, are we—"

"You are. Talk about it later."

A burst of machine gun fire came from under the window, one round, two, three, and the *bang-bang-bang* of Winchesters. Then silence for a moment, as far as gunfire went. There were shouts and the sound of running feet. As Jimmie lowered Katherine Neville down to the hook, where the Yid, who had gone first, was waiting to help her down on top of the Bean's cage, the door of the room opened.

"Catch her, Yid," Jimmie called. He had one leg over the window sill. As he let go her wrists he drew his Colt.

The swordsmen coming in hesitated a minute, then, urged on from behind, charged across the room. It was their last charge, this running with naked swords into soft-nosed lead bullets that hit with the force of a ton and more. Jimmie Cordie sat there, half in and half out of the window and killed the first four with bullets squarely between the eyes. As they fell, the others behind them turned and ran back, out of the door.

"Oi, Jimmie," yelled the Yid from below. "Hand me down de pig sticker till I cut de Beaneater loose."

Jimmie Cordie laughed, drew his other leg up and calmly stepped into the room, picked up the sword and went back to the window.

"Tell Jimmie to hurry up," called Grigsby, from under the cages. "They are ganging up for a rush and—hop to it, Red!"

THE MACHINE gun opened fire once more as Jimmie slid down the rope from the hook. Katherine Neville had been held down at arm's-length by the Yid and dropped the rest of the way, to be caught in Red Dolan's brawny arms and landed without a jar. The Yid had the sword between the bars of Bean's cage and was prying and cutting at the same time.

Jimmie Cordie leaned over and tried to reach the hilt to give a hand. As he did, the already much tried rope gave way and, as in the old song, down came cage, Beaneater and all. When they reached the ground there was no more need to pry the Bean loose. The cage was a wreck and the Bean was out of it. He picked himself up and began feeling tenderly of several places. The Yid and Jimmie Cordie had ridden it down and were not badly bruised.

"All right, Codfish," said Grigsby. "Latch on to a gun and get busy. Feel of yourself after the battle."

The Bean grinned and picked up a 30-30. "I'm not hurt—except in my feelings," he said, as the butt went against his cheek.

"Come on, Yid," shouted Jimmie, "get on this gun with me. Putt, take the other with George, Red, you and the Bean cover us. In here, Miss Neville. Straight out! Beside me, Li Tung! Which way?"

"Lite! Lite!" shouted the boy. "To the wall gate."

There was a fast, silent charge of swordsmen across the square and from the palace. It came in front and both sides, right and left. The moon was much brighter now and it was almost as light as day. Chow-yang's men were fighting men, born and bred in a hard school. They had fought with him in the south, and with him had looted many cities. They had no machine guns and not many rifles, but they knew what they were; and they knew also that they numbered a hundred to one against the white men who stood with their backs to the wall. But they were charging against men who were also veterans, men who could serve a machine gun in the face of overwhelming odds and laugh as they did it.

Jimmie Cordie picked up Grigsby's line of fire and sent a cross-stream of steel over it. The Bean and Red Dolan, back to back, stopped the thinner rush from the sides with their Winchesters.

The charge in front wavered, steadied, then came on, wavered again and then broke, and those who still could ran for cover on either side. Two machine guns properly handled, can, as the Yid said, "do a lot of dirty vork at de crossroads, ain't it?"

"All right," shouted Jimmie Cordie. "Let's go! We'll take the rear, George."

They went slowly to the right across the square. First Grigsby and Putney with a machine gun, then the Bean with Katherine Neville, then Jimmie Cordie and the Yid with the other gun, and with them Red Dolan, thoroughly in his element. Twice, as they crossed, a rush came, only to be wiped out and beaten back; and now, from the palace windows came gunfire. Jimmie Cordie raised the muzzle of the Browning and swept the windows clear, as calmly and coldly as a surgeon would probe for a bullet.

They reached the gate and Li Tung opened it. When they got through, he closed it after them. No hurry, no slamming it, just a leisurely closing. This Chinese boy Li Tung had fighting blood in him from some ancestor. There was a good deal of noise in the city behind them, but as they walked toward the hills, there seemed to be no pursuit.

CHAPTER VI

PURSUED

GRIGSBY HAD A slug of some kind in the fleshy part of his left arm, near the elbow. Red Dolan had been neatly cut above the ear by a bullet. Putney had been hit in the right shoulder, high up, but the bullet had gone through. The rest were untouched, except for the bruises the Yid and the Bean had collected.

Katherine Neville walked alongside the Bean. "Let me carry your gun," she said. "I—oh, my goodness!"

"What's the matter?"

"My arm hurt me. It was where he gripped it." She held up her white slender arm like a child, for the Bean to see. There were four black and blue marks. The Bean swore softly under his breath as he looked at them.

"I screamed," she confessed. "I didn't want to, but he hurt me so."

"My gosh," answered the Bean. "Any one would have screamed. I bet I would have screamed two or three times. At that, it was your scream that brought Jimmie and the rest."

Red Dolan dropped back to them. Katherine Neville looked up at the hard, lean face with the cold blue eyes, and then as every woman and child did, she saw the real Red underneath and she smiled.

"I want to thank you," she began, "for coming and—"

"Oi!" yelled the Yid. "Here dey come, mit horses und everything!"

"On that slope," called Grigsby. "Star front; take the point, Jimmie! Red—Beaneater! Take the sides. Half circle, Jimmie!"

The Yid was right about the "and-everything." Men poured out of the gates of the city on three sides as well as the little portal they had come through. Mounted as well as on foot, they had with them two old brass cannon, dragged by gun crews and coolies.

By this time the fleeing party had come about a mile. For the first half of the distance, the Chinese came on slowly. The moon was now bright, and the little group on the top of a gentle slope could see the advancing enemy spread to surround the hill. The two cannon came straight on.

"If you get hit with one of those cannon balls, Yid," said Jimmie Cordie with a laugh, "you needn't mind about any clothes. Those babies throw a ball as big as a washtub, no foolin'."

"Oi, Jimmie! For vy you vish it to me the bad luck? I am still sick from dot vater—"

"Start her off, Jimmie," called Grigsby. "No use in letting them get too close."

"Jimmie," pleaded the Yid, "knock off dem guys mit de big brass poppers first. I esk it as a favor." All of the six reckless, unafraid soldiers of fortune laughed as they began to pull trigger; and Katherine Neville joined in with Jimmie Cordie's 30-30. She could shoot a rifle, this dainty girl, and she was as unafraid as they.

Jimmie Cordie picked up the men at the cannon with the first round and they dropped like leaves blown from a tree. Grigsby poured a sleet of steel into the mounted men who had hardly got started, and Jimmie's gun swung around to pick up the fire from where he had started back.

Already men were running back toward the city. It takes cold nerve, or hot blood, or iron discipline, to charge into machine gun fire. Or an extreme of patriotism—and the Chinese had none of it. Not that they were not brave, for most Chinese are, but they knew that the master they had served and feared was dead. They were mostly mercenaries and this idea of getting themselves killed where there was no prospect of loot or even hand-to-hand fighting didn't appeal to many of them. Those that did come on were the men of the city, led by the interpreter. They numbered about a hundred, and long before they got in close enough for swordplay both machine guns were full on them.

The interpreter was lifted from his horse and hurled to the ground as if hit by a giant hammer, his body almost cut in two. When he went down, a few horsemen turned and fled; the rest couldn't run.

"I think," said Jimmie Cordie, as he stood up, "that will be about all for the moment."

"Moment is right," said Putney, pushing the pack he had made from half his coat and shirt into the wound in his shoulder as far as he could. "Let's get goin', Jimmie. My shoulder is commencing to bother me."

"My gosh," said Jimmie, staring at Grigsby's arm, down which a trickle of blood was running. "Did you shoot that gun with a wounded arm, you big ape?"

"No, young feller," answered Grigsby with a smile. "I shot it with my right hand. What do you think Putt and I were doing, taking pictures?"

"Yeah? I hope I've still got that iodine in my pack. We'll make it back to where we started from and then I'll operate on you two blame fools."

"VAT A nice night for a valk," said the Yid, as they started. "Vait—I get me some clothes, ain't it?" He started down the slope toward the nearest bodies.

"Come back here, ye grave robber," yelled Red, but the Yid paid no attention to him.

"Take the first suit that fits you, Abie," called Jimmie Cordie. "Don't shop around. It looks like—here they come again! Yid! Get back here!"

Whoever it was that had taken command in the city after Chow-yang's death, had stopped the unorganized rushes. Now a body of troops came out of the gates and split up into three columns. One went on a fast dog-trot far out to the right, another to the left. The column in the center came forward slowly, giving the other two plenty of time to get on the left and right of the little group on the slope.

"Not so good," said Grigsby. "They'll box us in. Get going; we can beat 'em to the pass. From now on, gents—and ladies—there will be straight shootin', no foolin'. Here's a chance for Red and Jimmie to do that slapping-out-of-the-way thing."

"Give us room according to our size and disposition, and we'll do that little thing," answered Jimmie, with a grin. "Won't we, Red?"

"All the time," agreed Red.

They made the pass, with but a hundred yards to spare as the three columns converged. And there they stood and did their straight shooting. These Chinese were under officers who drove them forward, and when the attackers finally weakened and drew back out of range, there was no more machine gun ammunition. Jimmie Cordie and Red calmly shattered the firing mechanism with bullets from their Colts.

Little Li Tung regretfully surrendered to Jimmie the Winchester with which he thought he was doing frightful execution, and they started up the pass. It was a slow advance. The Chinese would close in, only to be driven back; the party would advance a hundred yards more and have to make another stand.

It was dawn now and the sun was beginning to be felt. There was little attempt to attack from the sides of the pass. They were too steep to climb, most of the way, and once a man got up there, he had no way to get ahead of the moving party below. The Chinese tried it twice and both times slid down back of the column, to be promptly shot down.

Grigsby's arm was hurting him badly now and Putney's shoulder had stiffened. Both Katherine Neville and Li Tung had fallen heir to rifles now, Grigsby and Putney using their Colts. That left the Bean, the Yid, Jimmie and Red. Four first-rate rifles, in the hands of men who are all dead shots, can hold back a good many men not armed with the same. Katherine

Neville was a good shot, but Li Tung had the universal Chinese habit of pointing his gun in the general direction of the object he wanted to hit, shutting his eyes, and cutting loose.

They fought their way slowly up the pass. No panic, no flurry, just a cold, merciless beating back of attack from wherever it came. But the ammunition was getting low and there seemed to be just as many Chinese as ever.

As they came out in the little valley where Mowbray had left them, they saw that he had not got back.

"He stopped for tea somewhere en route," Jimmie Cordie laughed to Grigsby, who was beside him.

"Let's hope he didn't wait for the jam to be spread on the cakes," answered Grigsby grimly. "Look at our boy-friends behind us."

"Oi," said the Yid, who had joined them. "All Shang-si has come to de party, ain't it, Jimmie?"

"Right now," answered Jimmie Cordie with a grin, "I'd like to be on top of your rock, Yid. Next time you want to be rescued, for Pete's sake stay put."

"Oi, Jimmie! Could I know that the—" The Yid's Winchester drowned the rest. The charge against them this time was the most deadly of all. Putney, his Colt rising and falling with the regularity of clockwork, began crooning an old song. He always did when hard pressed. This time it was, "Oh, my darling Nellie Gray," and every other word was punctuated with a *pow!* Red Dolan stood as if on the rifle range, his eyes the same frosty blue, giving the matter in hand his undivided attention.

The Yid, beside Jimmie Cordie, was talking and shooting at the same time. "Oi, Jimmie, vot lufly shootin'. Knock 'em off, Jimmie. Oi, vot vouldn't I gif for just von little rat-tat baby—oi, vot ve could do to dem. My goodness, dey is almost here, ain't it?"

The Bean sat down, his back to a rock. The drug he had swallowed had about cleared his stomach, but every once in awhile he felt a wave of sickness. He sat there, his lean, aristocratic face as calm and indifferent as if watching a polo game that bored him. The only thing he said was, "Really, Putney, I wish you'd pull over a little. You are blocking my line of fire." Putney didn't pay the slightest attention.

KATHERINE NEVILLE crawled on her hands and knees over to where the Bean sat, dragging a rifle with her. As she sat up beside him, the Bean smiled. "Hullo, Neville, are you still alongside?"

"Yes," she answered, returning the smile, her lovely face powder-grimed, but unafraid. "If we—don't stop them—I—would like to have you the one that killed me," she went on calmly, as she raised her rifle.

"What?" gasped the Bean. "If we—they're stopped already!"

They were; at least, they were wavering and not coming forward as fast. It was a hard charge to carry home, this charging in on men who killed with every shot and who stood so confidently with a never-ending supply of bullets. Some of the Chinese fell purposely as if shot down, others turned and ran. The charge, as a charge, had failed. But it had won, if the Chinese had only known it. The little band of fugitives had not, all told, one hundred rounds left of any kind of cartridges.

"See?" went on the Bean, who was feeling better. "Now all we have to do is to wait and ride home in state."

"Home? Why—I haven't any home, now," and the blue eyes filled with tears. "I—Uncle Bertie took care of me, and—"

"And now I am going to," the Bean concluded, as politely as if he were chatting with a guest on board his yacht at Nice. "I'll be your Uncle Beaneater from Boston."

Katherine Neville looked at him and a real smile appeared behind the tears. "You are too young to be my uncle, John." Up on the rock, the Bean had told her his right name.

"Wait till we get home. I've got it all settled in my own mind. If you'll—" But the Beaneater was interrupted by Jimmie Cordie.

"Come on, you and Miss Neville. We'd better be hiking toward the nearest airport."

As they marched toward the meeting-place, they saw, far off in the sky in the direction of Chi-kow, a black speck that steadily grew larger.

"Well," the Boston Bean said to the girl beside him, "didn't I tell you? Here we are, rescued and all that. Now, as for home—won't you let me—take care of you?"

"Do you want to, really, John?" she inquired, smiling up at him.

"I do," said the Bean, gravely. "Very much indeed—forever—that is, if you—" and John Cabot Winthrop, dead shot, reckless soldier of fortune, and gentleman unafraid, stammered like a schoolboy.

"Go on, John," she encouraged. "Whatever it is, I do." And they both laughed.

A few minutes later Mowbray landed, bumping along over the grass. He had with him another young man and two machine guns.

"Oh, I say," he protested in a disappointed tone as he got out of the plane. "It really isn't all over, is it?"

Jimmie Cordie, who had been watching the Bean and the lovely English girl, grinned. "It's just starting, young feller. Oh, you mean the fighting. Yes, the fighting is all over. What kept you?"

THE DEATH SPELL OF NONG CHIK

Mysterious things happen in the Malay Peninsula—
and not the least weird was the witchcraft plot
that engulfed Jimmie Cordie and his five fellow-
adventurers of the Orient and way stations

CHAPTER I

AN ENCOUNTER WITH MALAYS

JIMMIE CORDIE AND Red Dolan had come ashore from the Boston Bean's yacht which lay off Pahang, Malay Peninsula. The rest of the party on board had been asked to go along and look at a little shrine that was famous all over the Orient for its delicate, intricate carving, but the invitation had been received with scoffs and jeers.

"Vot?" had demanded the Fighting Yid from where he lay stretched out in a deck chair alongside a table that held a little silver pail of cracked ice, soda bottles, and two or three long-necked ones. "Ve should go oudt mit the sun so hot? I ain't lost noddin's on shore dot I should go und hunt for it—ain't it, Beaneater?"

"Quite right," answered the Boston Bean, who was listed in that city's social register as John Cabot Winthrop. "It most decidedly 'ain't,' as far as I go. You and Red have our royal permission to go, though, James."

"Do ye know what ye are and what ye look like, to good men?" demanded Red Dolan, as he glared down on the four men sitting on the quarter-deck of the palatial yacht. His red thatch fairly bristled with indignation.

"No; tell us, Mr. Dolan," George Grigsby answered sleepily in his Kentucky drawl. "Start with Putt; he's sound asleep and won't hear it."

Putney opened his eyes and looked at Red. "I'm going to give you until I count three," he announced with a Vermonter's gravity, "and then if you are still around wah-wahing I'm going to climb your frame, you big red-headed ape. Take him by the hand and lead him away, Jimmie, before I kill him."

Jimmie Cordie laughed. "Come on, Red. We'll go and strut our stuff all by ourselves."

"Go ahead, mit our blessin's," said the Yid generously, as he poured out a whisky and soda. The six lean, hardbitten soldiers of fortune laughed. They had served together in the Foreign Legion and the A.E.F., and after that for whatever War Lord needed the services of expert machine gunners or riflemen. Between times they would go on expeditions of their own for anything they wanted, no matter where it was or how many men stood in between. The Yid had not served in the Legion, but had been with Jimmie Cordie in France.

"Stay here then," Red said with mock contempt, as he and Jimmie started. "Ye lazy scuts! Whatever Jimmie and me find, divil a bit av it do ye get, ye lily-livered crosses between an old ladies' home and a black-and-white kitty."

"Don't shoot!" Cordie yelled just as Red was pulling trigger

"Them's harsh words, Nell," moaned the Bean. "Trade him off for something that will sink, Jimmie."

Red, who weighed two hundred and thirty-odd pounds and every one of them hard, would have stopped and argued the point, but Jimmie had already started, so he followed.

THE LITTLE shrine had not, at least in their estimation, lived up to its reputation, and they were sauntering back toward Pahang. It was hot in the sun, and they felt it in spite of their hard, perfectly conditioned bodies. Red stopped in the shade of a tree and took off his woven straw helmet.

"Ye know what I think? I think that for once the Yid showed that he had good sense. Jimmie, ye shrimp, what the divil do ye mean by draggin' me out in this—"

A compact little column of ten or twelve Malays trotted out of a side path onto the trail where Red and Jimmie were striding along. They were so close that neither had the chance to step back. It is very doubtful—very doubtful indeed—if such an intention would have occurred to Jimmie or Red, anyway.

The Malays, coming from their city, wore fighting dress; and they were in a hurry to get where they were going. They had sleeveless jackets with texts from the Koran written on them; below were short tight drawers reaching to the middle of the thigh. Their *sarongs* were bound tightly around their waists, leaving the hilts of the daggers in their girdles exposed to view. All were armed with *pedangs,* the deadly long sword of the Malay; and in addition, two or three carried the curved *chenangkas.*

The leader of the party brushed Red's sleeve as he passed, they were so close. Now, if there was one thing that Mr. Terrence Aloysius Dolan did not like, it was to be touched by a native. As fast as a big brown bear, he cuffed the Malay with his open hand—just as the bear would slap out of his way anything he didn't like. The slim brown man literally left the path and sailed out into the brush beside it. He lit all spread out, but came to his feet like a cat, spitting like one too. His sword was already out.

The others in the party were almost as fast. They spread out, and before their leader had got to his feet there was a circle around Jimmie and Red, the swords and *creeses* shimmering in the sun.

If they were fast, they met foemen worthy of their steel in Mr. Dolan and Mr. James Norcross Cordie. As Red cuffed, Jimmie's .45 Colt materialized in his hand as if by magic, and he stepped to Red's back. The tree that they had been under was only a small, thin one, and did not offer any protection. Red's hand, coming down from the blow, angled sharply in for a split second, then up, and his Colt came up with it.

Neither he nor Jimmie was under any illusions as to the advisability of striking a Malay. They had both been in the peninsula many times before, and they knew that if a man fusses with a

Malay, that gentleman would better be all ready to take a fight and instantly.

As the leader came to his feet he shouted a command, and the two men close to him who obstructed his path to Red swung out a little. He charged home at the man who had struck him. A Malay running amuck is the hardest living thing to stop. He will keep on coming as long as there is a spark of life left in his body, no matter how many bullets are crashing into him. The leader was not quite amuck, but close to it. He came up with the full intention of killing Red, no matter how many bullets hit him in the meantime.

As he started, the circle started in also. Jimmie and Red raised their Colts and the hammers began to go up. One of the Malays got a look at Jimmie's face and stopped as if halted by a bullet. He shouted an order, and the rest wavered for a moment. He snarled another, and this time was obeyed. Even the leader halted as if frozen in his tracks. The man who had shouted was one of the fighting priests, and the leader, as fight-crazy as he was, knew better than to disobey.

Jimmie caught the hammer of his Colt with his thumb and eased it down.

"Don't shoot!" he called. "Red! Don't shoot!"

Red just had time to flick the muzzle of his Colt up, and the bullet that had been lined with the eyes of the Malay he had cuffed went up in the blue.

"WHAT NOW?" Red demanded. "I had that monkey-face dead center, ye scut." Red's slogan at any and all times was, "Aw, slap 'em outa the way," with anything handy.

Outside of this slogan, Red had two questions he would ask that settled any and all matters as far as he went. One was, "What now, Jimmie?" and the other was, "How about that, Jimmie darlin'?" The answer always satisfied Red.

"Darned if I know," answered Jimmie cheerfully. "Something happened all of a sudden. The bird that yelled recognized me, or you. Stand fast, Red, old-timer, until we see what's up."

The circle broke, and the Malays bunched in front of Jimmie Cordie, listening to the one who had shouted. Red, in spite of Jimmie's order, turned and stared at the Malays, his blue eyes frosty. The fact that they were confronted with a dozen fighting men in a lonely spot made no difference to Red—or to Jimmie Cordie either, for that matter.

Both were firm believers that when their number was up they would pass over the one-way trail, and not before, whether they faced one man or one thousand. He and Red could have stopped most of the Malays before they arrived, but "most," in the case of charging Malays, would not have been enough. It is very likely that if the man had not shouted, both Mr. Cordie and Mr. Dolan would have been climbing the golden stairs in a very few seconds.

"What the hell are they squawkin' about?" asked Red restlessly. "If I get the hands av me on one av them swords I'll run them ragged, Jimmie alannah." Red's one and only love, outside of Jimmie Cordie, was a sword and the play he could get with it.

"Stick around, you may get one yet," grinned Jimmie. "In the meantime ease over toward that knoll. The conference may end in— No, here he comes."

The priest advanced to within two feet, ignoring the leveled Colts. The rest of the Malays followed him, staying about three feet back of him. At the moment there seemed to be no further thought of letting steel settle the matter of the blow.

He began to talk in "Low Malay," which is a medium of speech between the natives and Europeans, made up of regular "High Malay" terms with a mixture of words from other languages.

The priest pointed at Jimmie, then at Red's flaming head of hair, then at the Colts, turned a little and pointed at the hills, at his own stomach, made his hand wave like a snake's head about to strike—all the time talking steadily.

"If 'tis a stomach-ache ye have," Red interrupted once, "then why don't ye go and see a doctor, ye scut av the world?"

"Pipe down," ordered Jimmie. "I can't get him very well as it is, let alone having you stick your bazoo in."

The priest hadn't understood Red, but had stopped as Dolan spoke. He listened gravely as Jimmie spoke to Red, and at the finish he nodded his head several times as if quite sure about something now.

Two of the Malays stepped in closer. They had heard Jimmie's voice. One began to talk in a mixture of Low Malay, Dutch, and English, with a word or two of Spanish for good measure. This time Jimmie got a name, "Nong Chik"; and *"sakit,"* which he knew meant sick, and *"mate,"* which meant to die.

Jimmie's mind was on the name Nong Chik, which he knew he had heard before; but where? Now he caught *"peng-lipor lara,"* which he knew meant soothers of care, and just as Red broke in he had recognized *"ajar-ajar,"* which meant sainted person. But it was all mixed up as far as he went. He knew that they were desperately trying to tell him something, but whether it had happened or was to happen, or to whom, he couldn't make out.

It was Red who solved the problem for him. Red had an uncanny memory for faces, even if seen only once before.

"This scut forninst ye, Jimmie," he said with deep conviction, "is one av them apes that was wid the little banty that George donated the gat to, the time we was up in Trengguan. The wan that got the canoe for us."

As Red spoke, Jimmie's brain clicked with the name Nong Chik, and he grinned: "Nong Chik, *raja*—" Then he touched Red's chest: "Red Dolan"; then his own: "Jimmie Cordie." Now he knelt and went through the movements of firing a machine gun. At the *"rat-tat-tat-tat,"* which he tried to make as realistic as possible, the Malays grunted with approval. Of all the Oriental races, with the exception of the Manchu, the Malay is the quickest to grasp the meaning of sign talk.

"THAT'S IT, Red," Jimmie said, as he stood up. "These birds are telling us that your little banty is sick somewhere, and are asking us to go and see him. They are the outfit that were up in Trengguan with him."

"He was a game little scut," answered Red. "Let's go, Jimmie."

Jimmie grinned and spoke to the priest: "Nong Chik?" and pointed north.

The priest nodded and answered, or tried to answer, but the numeral three was too much for him. He got out the *"tidor,"* which meant sleep, then held up two fingers.

"Holy cats, Red. It's two nights out. Three days' traveling!" Jimmie announced.

"What av it?" demanded Mr. Dolan, who craved action at all times. "Do ye want to go back to that damn' boat av Beaneater's and sit around wid the rest av them omadhauns? Come on, 'tis glad I will be to see that fighting little divil again."

Jimmie laughed: "There's more to it than seeing him, old kid. Are you aware of the fact that we only have two Colt .45s with us and darned few shells? We are not dressed for a party in this neck of the woods, young feller me lad."

"What?" Red answered with real astonishment. "Do you mean to stand there and tell me that you and me can't slap any of these gibboons outa the way do they get in it? Come on, I'll lead ye by the hand, ye delicate shrimp."

"All right, Red," Jimmie said, with a grin. "You do that little thing and I'll be safe. Don't let go my hand, though. *Allons, mes braves!"*

The Malays didn't know what that meant, but they understood the gesture that went with it.

Swords were sheathed, and, with Jimmie and Red in the middle, the little column started for the hills. As they went along Jimmie said:

"Red, you better give some kind of a present to the one you smacked down, to square it. He's dropped his feud for the moment, but it still is with him. If you square it now, it can be done while they think we are going on some kind of a rescue stunt."

"If ye say so, Jimmie. But what the divil will I give him? I have nothin' on me that—"

"Give him your flash light. That will tickle him and make him a topside man. I'll make a speech, and then when I finish, you hand it to him."

Jimmie halted the party, pointed to the man Red had cuffed, and made an impressive speech. He recited very gravely: "The boy stood on the burning deck whence all but he had fled. The deck fell in, and he fell through the bosom of his pants," and as much more as he could remember of that epic.

At the finish he motioned to Red, who produced the flash light. It was fairly dim in the timber, and Red threw the beam into a couple of the darker spots, then handed it to the Malay, who took it with shining eyes. All of the natives knew what Jimmie was doing. It was given in payment for the blow at the command of the slim, black-eyed, always smiling chief.

The Malay tried it out two or three times, grunted with pleasure, and tucked it in his sash. Then he slowly drew his *creese* and held out the blade to Red.

"Touch it, Red," Jimmie said, and Red did so. That signified that a blow had been given, payment made, and Malay steel had touched the one who had given the blow. After Red touched it the *creese* was sheathed, and the party went forward once more, at peace with each other for the time, at least.

CHAPTER II

REMITTANCE MEN

AS THE MALAYS, with Jimmie and Red, disappeared around a bend in the path some distance ahead, a half-caste Chinaman rose from the underbrush about a hundred yards from where the ceremony had been performed. He had been following the Malays, but at the greatest possible distance at which he could still see them. He had no desire at all to get closer, knowing that any one of them would not hesitate a split second in slipping a *creese* into him, any more than he would hesitate to kill a snake in the path. The spy could see that the Malays had taken with them the two white men they had met.

After waiting a few minutes to make sure that the party was really on its way to the hills, the breed went back to Pahang and entered a big straw-thatched hut on the outskirts. As he did, his lips twisted a little into a sneering smile. He would report what he had been ordered to find out, but he would not mention the white men, he decided. It might be that in some way that air could interfere with the plans of Carter and Morton, who made him feel like a dog and of whom he was desperately afraid.

Those two looked up as he entered and walked up to their table. They were both Englishmen of "the remittance man" type—receiving so much a month as long as they stayed away from England and from their families.

They were big men, beefy and with red faces. They looked like former army officers gone to seed. As a matter of fact, both had been cashiered out of the service. On the table there were bottles, glasses, playing cards, and the remains of a lunch. Over in one corner sat two native girls of the class that would enable any one familiar with the Peninsula to place the white men instantly.

The bigger of the two snarled, "Well, come on with it. What the deuce do you mean, you rotter, standing there grinning like a Cheshire cat? Are they on their way home?"

The Eurasian, son of an Englishman and a Chinese mother, smiled insolently. With all his body and soul he hated the two men sitting there, but the Chinese in him prevented him from telling them so to their faces. He worked for them because he had to, but all the time his hate smoldered and he watched for his chance to wipe out countless insults. He smiled with his lips, but in his heart there was engraved the record of even the slightest taunt.

"Yes, *tuan,*" he answered, giving the title "Lord" in hardly concealed mockery, "they are on their way."

The man named Carter rose. "You half-breed rat," he spat from between his thick lips, "how many times have I told you not to take that tone with us? You need a beatin', I see."

"Sit down, Harry," commanded the other. "We know that it is just the Chinese part of him that is snappin'. Let's get at the thing and mop up. You can take a crop to him later."

At the mention of a whip, the breed's hand stole to his blouse and his eyes tightened. Both men saw it, and they both laughed.

"Take your hand away from that knife, you fool," ordered the man who had remained seated. "Your English half wants to draw it, but your Chink half won't let him. Tell us how far you followed—and be quick about it."

The man's hand came away from his blouse, and he answered sullenly: "I followed them until they turned on the path that leads to the hills. They were going straight along and were carrying all they had brought with them."

"Right—that's the way to report. Go and get something to eat."

The man turned on his heel and walked out, trying to swagger a little as he did so.

"He'll bite some day, Morton," Carter said, as he reached for a bottle.

"I don't think so," the elder man answered indifferently. "We will be through with him after this goes over. I'll turn him in for the murder of that Filipino, as soon as we get these stones."

CARTER LAUGHED. "I say, you are rather a rotter, what?"

"Birds of a feather," answered Morton, with a sneer.

"The same," answered Carter shortly. "Get on with it; what's the next move? If we let this superstitious fool Nong Chik die in the hills, how do we get the stones?"

"I do not intend to let him die. We'll give them a chance to grow sufficiently worried over their not finding this medicine man down here. After a week we'll start for the hills and put him over the jumps. His sub-chiefs have weakened or they wouldn't have sent this party down to find and consult old Wan Da of the Bendahara Korish."

"Whom, strange to say, they could not find," Carter added with an evil smile as he thought of the reason for the medicine man's disappearance. "It is a lot of rot, isn't it? Because an image of a Malay is pinned on a tree, that Malay must die and—and he will, too. Sort of mental suicide, what?"

"Pass that bottle over, will you?" Morton interrupted with a bored yawn.

"One thing I've thought of. Will it be safe for us to go up in the hills? They know that you know where the tree is—and they might try torture."

"That's out," answered Morton curtly. "I send word that if they try to force me to tell, the tree will know it, and hide, so that no one can find it."

"My word! Do they believe that?"

"They believed the other, why not that? Superstitious heathens! We'll have the jewels and be on our way in ten days."

"But not to German East Africa," said Carter, who was pretty drunk.

Morton cursed him viciously and with visible horror. "You fool," he ended up, "if you ever mention that again I'll kill you. There is no German East Africa, and we know nothing of that affair, you understand?"

"Two can play at that killing game," snarled Carter, who was not in the least afraid of him. "Keep a civil tongue in your head when you speak to me, or I'll drive it down your throat."

Morton half rose, then laughed and poured out a drink. He would attend to this loose-tongued dog later, he thought grimly.

CHAPTER III

FRIENDLY MAGIC

NONG CHIK, MALAY chief and fighting man, lay on a couch made of skins in his hut built in the middle of his *cheruchuh,* his stockade, far up in the hills. His slim, brown young body seemed perfect as he lay there staring up at the roof. It was perfect, and yet he was dying.

As Jimmie and Red were brought in, Nong Chik sat up and his tight lips smiled as his eyes lighted with friendliness and almost with hope. He held out both arms and began an excited oration in Malay, one hand going to his stomach as he got into the swing of his rapid speech.

Nong Chik knew quite a little English, having been with the British in India when a boy, but at first he couldn't remember any of it.

"So!" boomed Red, kneeling down beside the couch. " 'Tis ye, is it, me fightin' banty! What the divil are ye floppin' on that bed for? See, Jimmie, 'tis our little fightin' banty av the north himself."

Nong Chik held one of Jimmie's hands tightly, and he smiled in spite of the pain he was really suffering—for it was real, even if it was caused primarily by his imagination and his faith in magic.

"O Red War Lord"—he was remembering his English now—"and you, smiling black-eyed chief! Good to see you—before I die. I—" He lapsed into Malay in the excitement of trying to tell what the matter was with him.

Red kept interrupting, and finally Jimmie told him, "For Pete's sake, beat it out of here until I get the straight of it. There is something darn rotten in the State of Denmark. Take our boy-friends out and play around with them until I get it."

Nong Chik understood enough to wave his hand, and every one in the room but he and Jimmie went out. About a half an hour later Jimmie came and sat down beside Red, who was watching some children at play, with a broad grin on his tanned face and in his blue Irish eyes, which were now soft and smiling.

"Well, I got it," Jimmie announced as he lit a cigarette.

"Ye have what, the tummy-ache?" demanded Red lazily. "That little divil over there is as graceful as a swan, Jimmie. Watch her."

"Listen, nitwit, pull yourself together. One of us has got to get to the yacht, darn quick."

"In this weather, 'tis ye that will—I'm shut, Jimmie darlin'."

"Keep that way, then, you big hunk of nothing. Am I to do a lot of Sherlocking, and then have a red-headed chimpanzee like you— Well, anyway, here it is: Nong Chik is going to die unless we can find a tree that has an image of him fastened to it by a sharp point stuck through the belly of the image and driven into the tree until the sap of the tree runs through the hole."

"Ye just told *me* to quit foolin', ye half-baked, peanut-sized idjut," Red snorted. "What is all this about trees?"

"Why," Jimmie answered gravely, "the oozing sap is the life spirit of the victim, who begins to suffer as if from a deadly ulcer, and it can only be cured if a friend secures a piece of wood from the tree."

"Saints above!" Red almost shouted. "And does that little fightin' banty believe that?"

"Listen, dumb-bell, it all depends on how you were brought up, what you believe. The Malays believe that they can be killed by that hokum; and they'll starve and get sick and finally die. They believe that just as much as we believe in what we do. And you can't argue them out of it. Get it?"

Red studied the matter for a minute, then nodded, "I do. 'Tis like the lad who was wid me once in France. If he cut his finger, he thought he was goin' to die av blood-poisoning—and damned if he didn't. The doc said that it was the fright that killed him and divil a thing else."

"That's it, Red. Nong Chik can't reason about it, he doesn't think about it, he just knows that he is going to die; and die he will, no foolin'. It's up to us, old-timer. He was a game little monkey, and don't forget he helped us out once when we needed help darn bad."

"He did," Red answered with deep conviction; "and he gets help by the same token. What now, Jimmie alannah?"

"**WELL, THE** blamed thing is all mixed up. He talked about two Englishmen who wanted some jewels of his; but he couldn't give 'em on account of a family curse being put on the whole tribe if they went out of the possession of the ruling family, and—"

"Hold it," interrupted Red in disgust. "I am getting sunk deeper every minute. You tend to it, Jimmie. Here is a thought—let's you and me go out and bring back a piece av any old tree, and tell him—"

"I thought of that," Jimmie answered with a grin, "but no can do, Red. Some of the tribe would have to go along to see the image, or he would have to be carried there to make sure. It's all mental stuff, Red. I got a line on the medicine man he is sure hung the jinx on him, but it seems that this Wan Da has disappeared. There's only one thing to do: you stick around here, and I'll go back and dig in. He likes you and thinks that red mop of yours is going to help him stand the pain. Kid him along, but don't, whatever you do, laugh at his belief. You hear me?"

"I won't, honest. Sure I'll tell him it is a bad wan he is up against, but wid Jimmie Cordie on it we'll damn soon bring him the whole flamin' tree, or take him to it."

"Thanks for them kind words," grinned Jimmie, rising. "Your confidence in my ability, Mr. Dolan, touches me deeply—you big red-headed, flannel-mouthed ape from the north of Ireland. One Cordie can lick ten Dolans."

"Ye mean, ye poor skinny piece av tripe which a Dublin boardin'-house keeper would turn the pug nose av her up at, that wan Dolan can lick all—"

Jimmie sang mockingly:

"Oh, me Uncle Mick,
He had a big stick,
And the Orangemen couldn't git 'round him."

But his smile told plainly how much he thought of Red—and the red-head's answering grin told the same about Jimmie.

"Come on, Red, let's go in and see if we can put a little pep into Nong Chik before I start. Follow my lead."

"I will, Jimmie. While ye are gone I will get these gibboons to show me some tricks wid the sword."

"And believe me, they have plenty of them to show," Jimmie answered as they entered the hut.

He made a speech to Nong Chik and the headmen that were once more assembled there to find out if Jimmie knew of any more powerful medicine man who could disclose the whereabouts of the tree. Jimmie talked slowly, using all possible words that they would understand.

He said that he knew it was a powerful magic that had been brought to bear, and while he was confident that he could bring much mightier wizardry against it, the matter of getting his magic together would take time—probably six sleeps. He was leaving at once to get his magic, and in the meantime— Here he stopped speaking, to loosen a little Foreign Legion clasp that he was wearing in his buttonhole.

He handed it to Red, who bowed very low over it. Then Jimmie ordered Red to pass the charm to Nong Chik, who took it, his eyes shining once more.

The charm was so powerful, Jimmie went on, that he could not pass it directly to Nong Chik; but the War Lord of the Flaming Hair had absorbed some of the power, which would remain with him until Jimmie's return. The charm was not powerful enough to disclose where the tree was, but it was powerful enough to halt any further sapping of the life spirit for ten days. Nong Chik was to keep it always touching his stomach. As Jimmie said that, the clasp was promptly put on his bare stomach by Nong Chik.

The Malay is a fighting man pure and simple, clever and

resourceful, who can plan and carry through intricate campaigns; and yet these men believed every word Jimmie said, and believed it fully. One thing that helped was that they had seen Jimmie and Red in action, and had seen, heard, and felt some bombs that Red and Jimmie had thrown—which to their minds meant making oranges explode; no mean magic!

When Jimmie left with four of the Malays an hour later, Nong Chik was sitting up, with Red on one side of the couch and several of his pretty little brown-skinned wives on the other, the entire row smiling for the first time in a month.

CHAPTER IV

GOOD "FRAMERS"

JIMMIE MADE THE yacht the second day; which spoke a great deal for his physical condition. The men on board, who had not been in the least worried about where he and Red were, knowing them both full well, listened without interrupting while he told them about his discoveries.

"There's only one thing to do, Jimmie," George Grigsby drawled finally. "Get to Pahang and dig out just who these two Englishmen are. At the same time, try to locate this medicine man your boy-friends couldn't find. If we can get to him, we may be able to get him to lead us to the tree."

"Vell, Oi, George, are you suggesting that ve kidnap the wizard?" smirked the Yid—who would go anywhere at any time and do anything. He was fat and roly-poly, and his big blue eyes always held a childish look of surprise at a naughty world and its doings. That surprised look had fooled several men to their sorrow. The Yid, born Abraham Cohen, and on Hester Street, New York City, was a fighter from the ground up; and as Jimmie had said, "What could be fightin'er than a fightin' Yid?"

"Send the Yid in to hunt for him," the Boston Bean said.

"He's been eating too much meat lately. A good walking trip will cut his comb."

"I'll go in and get a line on the English johnnies," Jimmie agreed. "I can go to some friends I have in Pahang. Yid, that was a good suggestion of the codfish duke's. You can sling a lot of dialects and what-not. Go in and find out what happened to a lad named Wan Da of the Bendahara. And make it snappy."

"Oi, Jimmie! Vat did I effer did to you dot you vant me to melt in de sun?"

"All right, you fat—"

"Vait, Jimmie; sure I go. You und me is pudners, ain't it, old kidt?"

"We are, like hell, you walrus. I don't even know you. Get going—and make it snappy like I told you."

"I'll go and see if Sir Henry Ireton is still in Pahang," announced the Boston Bean. Mr. John Cabot Winthrop was tall and lanky, with a grave, thin, aristocratic face which concealed a gay, reckless spirit and chilled steel nerves. He was a millionaire several times over, with everything at his disposal that money can bring; yet his one idea of perfect happiness was to be with all or any of these five soldiers of fortune, somewhere near the ends of the earth, and preferably where bullets were flying. He had served in the Foreign Legion and the A.E.F. with Jimmie Cordie and the rest and fought a rifle or a machine gun with a bored "you-be-damned" air—and had faced death a hundred times in exactly the same manner.

"Ireton is the British hush-hush gent for this neck of the woods," the Bean went on as he rose. "He'll know about these chaps if any one does."

"All right," Jimmie answered, "let's get at it. George, you and Putt stick close to this hooker until we get back. Get all the shade you can, old kids. I have a hunch that you will soon be *en route* for the hills."

Both of the big, dark, silent men laughed. Lean, lanky, as big-boned and almost as strong as Red without his weight, those quiet men could go into action with the suddenness of detonating TNT—and with very nearly the same destructiveness.

"Mosey along, young fella," Grigsby drawled. "We'll stay in the shade—or go to the hills, either one."

THE YID got back first, then a little later the Bean arrived on board. It was dark when Jimmie Cordie came over the side.

"How fast can you shove this bumboat along?" Jimmie demanded of the yacht-owner as soon as he got to the quarter-deck aft where they were all waiting for him.

"She's rated twenty-eight knots, Jimmie. I have shoved her along at thirty-two—and I think if I gave old Sandy Macintosh's engine room four bells and a jingle, he might get a little more. Why?"

"In about an hour you'll be heading for Hongkong under that four bells and a jingle thing. First—"

"Vat is dot four bells und a jingle bizness?" asked the Yid.

"Give her all you've got," answered the Bean gravely. "Strut your stuff with nothing held back. Four bells and a jingle equals full speed ahead, Mr. Cohen. Plus more speed."

"Tell it to that Yid monkey on the way," interrupted Jimmie. "Time is the well known essence, gents. First, Codfish, how many of your crew can you use as a landing party with rifles and what-not?"

"All of them, except a deck guard," answered the Bean promptly.

"How many is that?"

"Twenty-five or six, counting the stewards. There are plenty of rifles and what-nots, Mr. Cordie."

"Yeah? In Hongkong you get khaki uniforms for all twenty-six of them, and full marching kits. Allee same expedition stuff."

"Wee-wee, mouse's ear. Hearing and obeying, O king; it shall be did as thou orderest. I take the bumboat to Hongkong under four bells and the aforesaid jingle. What then, Gineril?"

"Less wah-wah right now," grinned Jimmie. "What did you find out, Yid?"

"Oi, plenty as far as de vizard goes. De vizard had vent, Jimmie—vent down de bay on de tide, mit his throat cut."

"For Pete's sake! How did you get that dope?"

"Vell, I got it friends here also. Ike Levine has got it a swell store und Jakey Aarons has been here from de early days."

"Write a book about the what's and the from's. Never mind how you got it. What is—"

"Wait a minute, Mr. Cordie," interrupted Putney. "Appears to me that you asked the gentleman how he received his information, and he is being polite enough to try to tell you."

"That's right," Jimmie agreed, with a grin. "Pardon my seeming impatience, Mr. Cohen. Tell it in your own way—but get a move on you, *gondiff!*"

The Yid smirked and bowed, "I accept de apology, mistair. I vent to mine friends und den ve vent odder places und by und by ve finds it a fisherman vot had seen de vizard's body come by his boat von morning. He knew dot it vos de body of de vizard of de Bendahara Korish because he vonce lived by dot tribe. Den ve dig a little deeper by another man, und little by little ve find dot de vizard had been last seen in de company of de two Englishers. Und dot's all dot I vas send to do, ain't it? De vizard has gone to de place vare all good vizards go."

"Tell the Beaneater the rest later. Brownbread, what did you find out from the hush-hush lad?"

"Why, quite a lot, Jimmie. This pair of buzzards have been operating a lot over in what used to be German East Africa. It seems that the last jam they got into was with the Wa-Kerewe."

Jimmie nodded; he had found out something of the sort himself.

"Oi, mine persecuted race," broke in the Yid; "such a business! Vot I don't know about de Wa-Kerewe! Of all de fightin' tribes in dare, de Wa-Kerewe is de vorst und de most bloodthirsty. Once dey—"

"For the love of Mike!" Jimmie interrupted sternly. "Some one put a jaw tackle on that darn Yid. My gosh, have I got to sit here and listen all day?"

"I'm shut mit de mouth, Jimmie. You und me is pudners, ain't it?"

"Like hell we are. Go on, Bean."

"Why, there isn't much to go on with. It seems that they stole the chief's daughter and another girl and had a running fight all the way to the coast and during it they killed the two girls. That's the way Sir Henry Ireton got the story. He's checking up on it and if there is any truth in it the two gentlemen are in for a long trip. The German East is under British control, you know."

"Join with the Yid in writing the history. Well, that fits in with what I got from some of my friends who—"

"Who are T'aip'ing highbinders," Grigsby put in with a grin.

"What do you care? All right—we're set. Bean, you get under way just as soon as you can."

"WHAT'S THE idea of Hongkong, Jimmie?" asked Putney. "You can get plenty of uniforms in Pahang—British or otherwise."

"I know it, Putt. But I want something else besides uniforms. When I heard about the hell these two have been raising in German East, I had a brilliant idea. You rem—"

"That's the boy, James," Putney said. "Tell us about it before we start. Your brilliant ideas have stuck our heads into the lion's jaws before now."

"And also got the said heads out," answered Jimmie, cheerfully.

"Sometimes yes and sometimes no, me good Jeems. Proceed with the brilliant idea," said Putney, who would have gone with Jimmie Cordie anywhere with a smile on his bleak New England face.

" 'Ray for the blue-nosed Vermont Presbyterians," scoffed

Jimmie, who came from Massachusetts like the Boston Bean. "Their war cry is, 'Look before you leap' or—"

"You are taking up time now, Jimmie," Grigsby said. "Get on with it, old kid."

"That's right, I am. I well remembered that in Hongkong I saw a troupe of African natives that were showing the dances of the different tribes, down on the street of—"

"We know where they were showing. You're worse than the Yid."

"Says you. Anyway, the thought struck me to get some of them and chief them up as Wa-Kerewe, and take them—"

"And you called that a brilliant idea! What then?"

"And how the hell do you know what the Wa-Kerewe wear, dumb-bell?" asked Putney.

"If I don't, my old side-kick Yen Yuan of the T'aip'ings will know. Anything he doesn't know, he can darn soon find out about. We get them, chief them up, bring them back here. We find out where these two remittance men are if they are not in Pahang when we get back. Then we—or rather, the Wa-Kerewe—go and get them. Then they start a little of the well-known native ways of—er—making people pay for various things."

"Vell," interrupted the Yid, "vot de hell is all de going to Hongkong for? Vy can't ve do it ourselves?"

"Shut up, Yid," Grigsby commanded. "Jimmie is on the right track, provided we can get the natives to play in his yard."

"I heard in Hongkong that those troupers were not making any more than coffee and cakes, and not that much part of the time. That's the reason I want to hurry and get there before they disband. If they are making money, some of them will come for a few days, for more money."

"All right," the Bean said, "I'll order the anchor on the bow—but damned if I get half of it. What do we do in this Wa-Kerewe play-acting?"

"Get going, Beaneater," Jimmie suggested. "I'll explain it to you *en route* in words of one syllable."

CHAPTER V

JUNGLE JUSTICE

"WELL," SNARLED MORTON, as he came into the hut that had been assigned to them when he and Carter arrived at the stockade of Nong Chik, "he says that to-morrow he will give up the jewels. Why to-morrow, instead of to-day? He acted as if he were very weak and sick, though. Not like his old damn insolence... Brandy all gone?"

"There is some left in the bottle," answered Carter, his voice surly. "I don't like the lay at all."

"I don't give a damn what you like," sneered Morton. "You have been an awful lot of help to me, in this, haven't you?"

"It was my plan in the first place," Carter retorted shortly. They had both been drinking all the way up, and now both were more than jumpy. They realized it and tried to keep their tempers down—until they had the jewels, at least.

"Quite right, it was. Sorry, old thing. Here is what I have arranged for to-morrow. Two of the sub-chiefs will go with me to the tree and—"

"You mean with *us*—not you," interrupted Carter, his voice tense.

"Yes, I mean with us, of course. They will have the jewels, and after I point out the tree and they make sure it is the right one, they will hand over the jewels."

"Then what?"

"Then what? Why, we will go back to Pahang, sell them to a chap I know—and yorricks and away for Hongkong and Pekin, old dear."

Carter sneered as he answered. "Do you think they will let us get to Pahang with the stones—after they have seen the tree?"

"Why not? They think that the jolly old curse won't be lifted until they get back to Nong Chik with the piece of the tree. By the time they do that we can be well ahead of them. The men we brought up will fight for their own lives on the way back, if they wouldn't for ours. We've won, Carter."

"If the tree is far enough away from here," Carter said, as he started for his hammock. "Once they get the piece of wood they'll come after us."

"If you are—er—in any way apprehensive," Morton answered, too silkily, as he got into his hammock, "you might start down from here as I—that is, I mean we—go for the tree."

Carter didn't answer and very soon both men were asleep, aided in that process by the powerful brandy they had been drinking all the way to Nong Chik's.

Carter slept fitfully, waking every now and then and turning to a more comfortable position. It was well toward dawn when he suddenly became wide awake. What woke him up was an arm slipping around his neck and a smell like rancid butter close to his nostrils.

His eyes stared up in a fierce black face that he could just dimly see, in the light of the candle that still sputtered in its pool of wax, stuck in an iron dish on the old box which had served them as table. Neither he nor Morton had put it out when they went to their hammocks.

When Carter saw, surrounding the face, the head-dress of the Wa-Kerewe tribe of German East Africa, he drew a sobbing breath of fear and tried to call Morton.

A hand went over his mouth, he felt as if the heavens had fallen on his head, and everything became black.

Morton could not have helped him, because at the moment that Carter called, Morton himself was in what he thought was a frightful nightmare. He dreamed that he was back in Africa and that the body of the chief's daughter, whom he had slain in a drunken frenzy, was tied around his neck; and he couldn't get ride of it despite his efforts to run faster.

Then the dream changed and the body became an arm. His eyes opened and saw what Carter had seen—a black merciless face with the feathered headdress that framed it. He smelled the fat which the Wa-Kerewe rub on their bodies when they go on the vengeance trail. Then the sky crashed down on him also.

WHEN MORTON next opened his eyes he was sitting on the ground, his back to a tree. He was not tied in any way but his head was so sore that he could hardly bear to move it. He did not need to move it to see Carter sitting at a tree some five feet in front; and he could see that both he and Carter were in the middle of a circle of Wa-Kerewe warriors who sat cross-legged on the ground, their big broad-bladed spears beside them, the oxhide shields at their backs. They saw that Morton was conscious, but not a man of them moved, neither did the impassive faces change in the slightest.

Morton, for all his crookedness, had good blood in him and his eyes did not show fear as he looked at them. He stared at man after man, trying to remember him. He knew they must be Wa-Kerewe. He knew the distinctive head-dress and anklets of leopard skin and the tribal marks. He also knew why they wanted Carter and himself—and knew, too, what they would do to them.

But what his brain, jarred by the blow that had put him out, could not figure out, or connect up, was the fact that he had gone to sleep in a stockade high up in the Malay hills—and woke up in the hands of Wa-Kerewe warriors of German East Africa. That he had been, there was no doubt; but how?

His mind absolutely refused to function and he shut his eyes. How long they were shut he didn't know, but he opened them again on hearing Carter yell, "No! No! Not that! For God's sake, don't! Morton! Do something to stop them!"

Carter was flat on his back, stripped to the waist. One of the Wa-Kerewe was holding his feet at the ankles, another was holding his wrists. His arms were stretched as far over his head as they could go without being torn from the sockets. A third Wa-Kerewe was calmly and slowly breaking up little twigs and laying them carefully on his naked chest. Near him on the ground there had been built a little fire.

Morton's brain was clearer now and he started to get up. A spearpoint went about a half an inch into the calf of his leg from the side of the tree, and he sat down again. Even as he did so, he made up his mind to try for a quick death from the spears as soon as he got strength enough to put up a fight. Utterly selfish, he did not try to plan anything that would help Carter. He knew what was going to happen, having seen the Wa-Kerewe before as they administered what they thought was justice.

Carter yelled again as one of the Wa-Kerewe picked up a burning brand from the little fire. As he did, Morton's brain worked a little more. He remembered that there were few offenses that could not be paid for in blood-money among the African tribes.

"Wait!" he shouted in the *lingua franca* of the Coast. "Who is the leader of this war party?"

A big brawny savage who had been standing by Carter, looking down at him with an expression of uttermost scorn, stared at Morton. "I am, white dog who kills women. Bark no more—you will need your voice for screaming when it comes your turn to go under the fire."

Morton knew better than to try any of that "We are Englishmen and our country will punish you" stuff. It might go in civilized parts of Africa, but here in the Malay jungle, it would be like trying to stop the charge of a wounded tiger by saving, "Down, Fido."

"When I slew the woman," Morton answered, "the strong drink of the Germans had stolen my spirit away and a devil had come instead."

"The devils are still there," answered the Wa-Kerewe leader with a grim smile. All African natives have a sardonic sense of humor. "We will burn them out of you—and out of this jackal that cried 'Ow! Ow!' before he was hurt."

Morton came to the point at once. "I will pay you many times the value of the woman and of the men that were also slain if you will be friends. You will all be great men in the Wa-Kerewe, and the Ba-Ganda and the W'a-Sinja will look up to you—not sneer down at you as they do now."

The savage grunted, "We look down on the Wa-Sinja and the Ba-Ganda now, white man who kills. The orders are to follow and burn. Sit and watch—it may be that you will see the devils leave this whining puppy."

MORTON KNEW he had lost, as the savage motioned the man forward with the brand. His strength was coming back fast now and his one thought was to get to a spear or take one in his heart. Of Carter, who was yelling now in earnest as the top twigs of the pile on his chest caught fire, he did not think at all. He had always been for Morton, first, last and all the time.

Forgotten were Nong Chik, jewels, the mystery of how the Wa-Kerewe had got there, and all else. The most priceless jewel he could get was a quick death, and he tensed himself for the spring that would land him close to the savage nearest to him.

The savages were now standing in their circle. As Morton made ready to win death, one savage shouted and seized his shield, turning around as he did so.

The rest promptly followed suit, then stood still, surrounded. An outer circle of men closed in from the heavy matted jungle that surrounded the little dry knoll.

The savages who had hold of Carter let go and stood up. He frantically brushed the twigs off himself and got to his feet. Morton got up also.

There were five white men together, all in heavy marching order; and their circle consisted of men dressed in khaki with packs and bayoneted rifles. The savages, at a shout from the one who answered Morton, suddenly went into a wedge formation, the oval shields overlapping, the spear blades out. The Wa-Kerewe were evidently going to cut their way through.

The leading white man called an order and the rifles went to the shoulders of the men in the outer circle. All of the five men, in unison, drew Colt .45s.

Jimmie Cordie, who had given the order, stepped forward a pace and held up his right hand, transferring his Colt to his left.

"Hold!" he shouted. "There is no war between the Wa-Kerewe and me. Why do my brothers show me only shield fronts and spear points? And what do the warriors of the mighty Wa-Kerewe do here in the jungle, so far from their home in Mashenge?"

The leader stepped out from the point of the wedge. He had the natural dignity and proud bearing of the African chief he was.

"We have come far from our home, on the trail, O great white chief whom I do not know. These dogs whom we are about to burn, have slain our women. If you are a friend of the Wa-Kerewe, sit and watch. We have traveled far, in a great canoe with white wings, to take these men."

"You certainly have," answered Jimmie, in English; then went back to the *lingua franca*. "White men do not sit and watch other white men burn, O chief. Tell us what they have done and it may be that you can take them back with you to your home far away and turn them over to the British to try. There will be no burning. I say it, I, a friend of the Wa-Kerewe. See the rifles that back up my talk? The Wa-Kerewe are brave, but they cannot eat the bullets that will pour out when I command."

"Better that, white man who speaks of friendship, than to go home without putting a finish to these dogs who betrayed friendship."

"That is true. It is hard to decide which is better for you to do. If you charge, you meet death which ends all. Wait! The Wa-Kerewe do not lie to their friends, that is well known. Is it true, sub-chief of the Wa-Kerewe?"

"Yes, it is true. The Wa-Kerewe do not lie to their friends. Are you a friend, white man? If you are, sit and watch."

"I am a friend yet I cannot do that. It is my taboo that will not let me. This I will do: We will hold court here, and if the crimes of these men warrant it, you may take them back with you—once you have given the word of the Wa-Kerewe that they will not be harmed until they reach Africa, and that once there, they will be given to the British to punish."

The savage looked at Jimmie Cordie, at the other four men standing beside him, then at the circle of rifles. Finally he said, "It is a treaty, white man. Listen and I will tell you what they have done."

MORTON CAME up. "What the hell is the meaning of all this nonsense?" he blustered. "You're not English, but by gad you're white men. Shoot these black dogs down!"

"We're Yanks," answered Jimmie, "and we're likely to do most anything. Keep quiet, both of you. You must be the two white men I heard about over in German East."

Carter had come up to Morton.

"I say," he started, "don't you see that they will—"

"I know what we'll do in another minute," interrupted Jimmie curtly. "And that is, march right on. So put a jaw tackle on yourself."

The Wa-Kerewe began a long rambling tale of how the two white men had come into the Wa-Kerewe country hungry and exhausted; and how, after they had been fed and cared for, they had run away with the chief's daughter and another maiden.

They had been followed and a small party had caught up to them. In the fight that ensued, several warriors had been killed. Later another party had come across the bodies of the kidnaped maidens, who had also been killed. The Wa-Kerewe had held a council swearing the vengeance oath and had trailed the men to the coast. They had almost succeeded in capturing them there—and Morton's shudder attested the truth of this.

But they escaped; and two of the Wa-Kerewe who had once

sailed on the great water in the canoes with white wings had searched further. In the Far East they had found the trail, and the war party that had been left on the African coast, had come in a canoe manned by friendly white men who were not dogs. They trailed the dogs who had stolen and slain to a Malay stockade, and had taken them.

That was the gist of it. There was a lot more about how they arrived and what they had gone through to get there and how they had put on their war dress after they got in the hills and so forth. Neither Morton nor Carter interrupted, and the subchief ended with:

"Now, friend of the Wa-Kerewe—show us that you are a friend."

The Boston Bean said, "Really, Jimmie, I think that we will be justified in marching past and letting the Wa-Karewe have them to play with. That little girl thing does not sound good to me at all."

"I think so, too, Jimmie," Grigsby said, and Putney nodded as he adjusted his pack which he had eased off his shoulders. "They are not worth our putting up any objections."

Several things at once interrupted Putney. There was a crashing in the thick undergrowth at the right, and Red Dolan burst into the cleared space, a sword in his hand, followed by a column of Malays, their swords out and ready.

The two men with rifles had just started to turn when Red went between them. He cut at one who very luckily for himself was able to get his rifle barrel between his body and the edge of the sword before he fell over backward. Red was on his way to headquarters as he saw it and had no time to fool around with the understrappers.

As he came through, every one naturally turned to see what was coming, all except Morton. He had been standing close to Putney; and as Red came through, the circle of rifles spread a little as some of the men ran toward where their comrades had fallen.

Morton's hand flashed to Putney's holster and came back with Putt's .45, which had been holstered while the Wa-Kerewe was orating. With the quickness of a cornered rat, Morton ran to the break in the circle, firing twice at the nearest men, who pitched forward on their faces.

Red had stopped with an expression of ludicrous surprise on his face; and it was so fast that Jimmie Cordie did not turn until Morton had reached the opening in the line. Jimmie's Colt jumped into his hand—but Morton's back was turned to him. He did not fire, but shouted "Go get him!" He started after Morton himself, still holding his Colt.

As Jimmie started running, the Nine Red Gods of Luck took the matter over. Morton swung out to clear a tree, and as he got to a clump of grass squarely ahead of him there rose from behind it the head of a great hamadryad, the most viciously poisonous snake of the Orient—a snake more feared than the king cobra.

Morton was running full-tilt, his head down a little. The snake struck him on the side of the neck, the force of the blow throwing Morton off balance. As he went down, the hamadryad released its fangs, coiled, and struck again. This time the fangs went deep in Morton's side. Again the snake released and coiled to strike once more. As it did, Jimmie Cordie halted and blew its head off from where he stood.

THE MALAYS were bunched together. Most of the riflemen who were of the Beaneater's crew were around the two that Red had upset. The Wa-Kerewe were still in the wedge formation. Red was still walking toward the Yid and the others. Carter was standing as if paralyzed.

Jimmie, his Colt ready in case there was another snake, walked to where Morton lay face down. He knew there was no hurry. No man struck twice by a hamadryad where Morton had been lives more than a minute, if he does that long.

Jimmie had not taken two steps before the snake's mate rose from behind the clump of grass and came toward him with the swiftness of attack that makes the hamadryad snake so feared.

As Jimmie fired, there was another *"pow!"* so blended together that it sounded like one detonation. Four other Colts had joined in with his; and the head and a foot's length of the body of the snake disappeared.

The Wa-Kerewe and the Malays grunted approval of the fast, accurate shooting. To hit a hamadryad in action took just that.

"All right," Jimmie called. "Give me a hand with him, one of you birds."

Red came over. "What the hell is it all about, Jimmie?" he asked as he helped pick Morton up.

"I don't know much about your last part myself," answered Jimmie, as they carried Morton's body into the clearing. "I know my ball game went south when you busted in. Put him down, Red."

"But what are ye doin' with the—"

"Hold it, old kid. I'll tell you later. Right now I've got other fish to fry."

The Boston Bean came up and looked down at what had at one time been Colonel Morton of His Majesty's Tenth Hussars.

"It looks to me, Jimmie, as if the goose that was going to lay the golden egg is dead."

"Take another look and be sure of it," answered Jimmie curtly. He turned and looked at Carter, then walked up to him and put the muzzle of his Colt not any too gently in Carter's ear.

"Come clean, you louse, and come fast, or I'll blow the top of your head off. Where is the tree that the image of Nong Chik is pinned to?"

"I don't know," gasped Carter. "He never told me. He—the medicine man gave him a map because Morton thought he couldn't find it again without one."

"What did he do with it? Come on, you must know. I'll give you until I count three. One—two—"

Jimmie's tone was death itself, and Carter knew that as the word three was spoken he would be dead.

"In his money belt," he said.

"Yid, go over and see if he has a money belt on him." Jimmie holstered the Colt. "If you run, as he did," he went on, "I'll send the Wa-Kerewe after you and let them have you after they catch you."

"I don't intend to run," Carter answered firmly.

"Jimmie!" yelled the Yid. "I got it." And he held up an oiled silk money belt. He brought it over, and Jimmie searched through the compartments. In the third he brought out a roughly drawn map. It showed two streams coming together with a little hill in the angle, and a larger stream off to the right.

For the first time since Red arrived, Jimmie grinned. "Go get one of your army, Red. Maybe-so your bamming in here at the wrong minute was the right one. Figure that out on the way, Mr. Dolan."

The Malay looked at the map, called to two or three of his fellows, and they went in conference. After considerable talk, they came to an agreement, and announced that they knew where the place was.

"Red and I will go with them," Jimmie announced. "You gents wait for us right here. Take good care of Mr. Carter. The British consul wants to see him. Come on, General Dolan."

"Vait," said the Yid. "I go mit. I vant to see dot squeegee dot has made me leave de shade und everything."

"Come on, then; but one thing, Yid—no foolin'. No funny cracks or smirks, you hear me?"

"Oi, Jimmie! For vy should I?"

"Darned if I know—but don't do it. This may be funny as hell and high water to you, but it's life and death to them. Get the army strung out, Red."

CHAPTER VI

THE IMAGE OF DEATH

"NOW, YE SHRIMP av the world," Red said sternly as he and Jimmie walked along, "tell me all. First, why the divil didn't ye tip me off that ye had a frame-up? I was sleepin', and all at once in busts me little brown men wid the news that the two English scuts had disappeared. Out I gets and runs all night wid Nong Chik's 'army,' as ye call it. In I comes, havin' looked through the trees and seein' only them monkeys wid shields and spears; in I busts, and there is ye and the rest!

"Tell me, but how ye got in Nong Chik's stockade to get them widout bein'— Oh, I'm shut!"

"Well, I got back to the Bean's yacht and told them about things," Jimmie began, then told Red about going to get the Africans in Hongkong. One of them, they found, was a half-breed Wa-Kerewe.

"Who were the lads in khaki, Jimmie darlin'?"

"The Bean's crew, nitwit."

"I thought I recognized the monkey faces av them. Go on, 'tis plain. Did ye plan this torturing by the phony Wa-Kerewe?"

"They are born actors, Red, and we didn't have any trouble teaching them what to say or do. Dog-goned if we didn't have to curb 'em instead. When I saw that smoke from the brush on Carter's chest I thought that they were living their parts too fully, no foolin', You see, the game was that we were to arrive just in time to save Morton and Carter when the Wa-Kerewe were making things hot for them. Then in payment for stopping the massacre or what not, I was going to lead gently up to the subject of pay. If they didn't think of the jewels they were going to get, I was going to lead up to the fact that a little bird in Pahang had whispered in my ear that they had some, or had gone to get some. They would know that they had talked in front of their native girls and would think that one of them had tipped me."

"How the hell was ye to know their native girls?"

"Sweet daddy! Do you suppose they would stop and figure that out, with the Wa-Kerewe still there? Every one in Pahang knew that they were living with native girls, you red-headed ape. Listen, while I—That reminds me. What became of their escort back at Nong Chik's?"

"I had them decoyed over to wan side," answered Red, with a grin, "wan by wan—and see-questrated."

"Good work. What did you do that for, Red?"

"Well, I thinks that ye must be framin' something—knowin' ye full well, ye scut av the world. I says to meself, maybe-so now Jimmie will be wantin' a clear path, and 'tis meself that will give it to him."

"Darn good work, Mr. Terrence Aloysius Dolan."

"Sure, 'tis all too deep for me. Anyway, we have the map and are on our way. Why didn't ye just grab them off and stick a gun under their noses?"

"Morton was hard-boiled, Red. He would know that white men wouldn't kill him in cold blood, but the Wa-Kerewe had him fooled. I think he would have come through if we had pretended to march on and leave them. Of course, if I had guessed he was fool enough to carry a map on him, it would have been easy enough. You see, if we had waited to take the jewel ransom away from them, they would have notified Nong Chik and tried to make him come through with more—framing a new spell with some other medicine man."

"What did ye intend to do wid them, after ye went through wid the frame?"

"I was just going to tell you. Turn 'em over to the British. Their man Friday, a Eurasian, is already in the *cartel,* giving up all he knows, which is plenty. The thing to do now is to get to the tree, then back to Nong Chik, and call it a day."

"'Tis a nice little trip to see a shrine we do be havin', ye uneasy-footed omadhaun," Red grinned.

LATE THAT afternoon a Malay who was in the lead called and pointed. The stream shown on the map was ahead, and farther off they could see the two smaller streams and the hill. An hour more of hard going and close hunting, and they stood before a tree. About four feet up the trunk there was a crudely made wooden figure. Driven through the navel and into the tree was a sharp splinter of wood. Along the splinter sap was dripping.

The Yid, scouting ahead with the Malays who had recognized a kindred fighting spirit, looked at the figure and stepped forward to look at it closer. As he did, one of the Malays yelled.

"I vasn't going to touch it, Mistaire," protested the Yid.

"There you go, you fat ape," Jimmie said bitterly. "Go and sit down and don't move—not even your jaw!"

The Fighting Yid grinned unabashed and obeyed. As he did, two of the Malays, with their swords for a pry, and neither man touching the figure, drew it away from the tree as gently as they could, splinter and all. It came away easily enough as the sap had greased the way. Once away from the tree, they eased the figure to the ground by their swords and held it down while two more, using their swords as pliers, drew the splinter out. All this was done without touching the figure with their hands.

Red had walked over and was sitting by the Yid; and now Jimmie came and sat down with them.

"What now, Jimmie?" Red asked.

"Darned if I know. Just sit and watch, Mr. Dolan. They are going to build a fire."

The Malays built a fire and lifted the figure and the splinter by their swords, and placed them in it. Then they began singing a chant, squatting around the fire. As soon as there was nothing left but a pile of ashes, they scraped them up very carefully and took them to the little stream. Still chanting, they threw the ashes out in the current.

Then one of them came back to the tree and with his razor-sharp *creese* cut a long splinter from it.

The leader came up to Red and said, "It is over, *tuan*. Now we must hurry back."

"Go ahead wid the rest av it," Red said royally. "Sing another verse."

"He says it's over, Red." Jimmie rose. "Come on."

AS NONG Chik's hand closed over the splinter brought to him from the tree, and listened to the story of the destruction of the image, he became well before their eyes, such is the power of utter faith even in superstition.

He felt his stomach and patted it. Drawing Jimmie's Foreign Legion clasp out from where he had it under his *sarong*, he handed it to Jimmie, got up, walked around.

The hut was packed as full as it could be with his sub-chiefs and fighting men. He began an oration that lasted fully a half hour. Everything he had or his tribe had was theirs. He and his tribe to the last baby were their slaves. Once he had seen the always smiling black-eyed one and the one with the hair that flamed like the sun, whose child he no doubt was, he had known that no medicine was powerful enough to withstand them; and so on for a long time.

The escort that had come with Morton and Carter were brought out and headed down the hills with the simple statement that if they were caught in that neck of the woods again their heads would adorn Nong Chik's stockade posts. The escort did not linger.

On the way down to where their camp had been made, Red said, "Jimmie, 'tis all as plain as day to me save for wan thing. How did the scuts ye brought up get in the stockade widout the Malays hearin' them? I didn't think it could be done."

"I don't think it can either, Red. The Bean and I were along, and we came up on the side where guest huts are. The two guards on that side were on us before we had come ten feet out of the timber. I flashed my light so that they could see my face just in time. Man howdy, maybe you don't think their swords were up! Then the Bean was introduced as a topside medicine man come to help. Then in a minute or so, while the Bean was showing them the radium dial of his wrist watch, they both went to sleep—and in we went. Simple, isn't it, Mr. Dolan?"

"It is. What did ye hit them with?"

"I didn't hit them with anything. Maybe-so the butt of a spear hit them, I don't know—anyway, they went to sleep. I hunted them up before we left just now and told them that the enemy medicine man must have sneaked up on 'em."

"Did they believe it?" asked Red, with a grin.

"Wouldn't you—if you believed in medicine men? Anyway, I gave each of them a button off my coat, and told them that would stop any such doings in the future; and they acted tickled to death."

Red walked along for a few minutes, then as the Yid came up asked, "What about the wan that is left—the wan they was building a fire on?"

"I'm going to introduce him to the British official in Pahang," Jimmie answered shortly. "I don't care much about this killing of little girls, myself."

"Me either," Red answered promptly. "Whatever the scut gets will be too little for the likes av him."

"That being the case, let's step on it a little, Mr. Dolan. I feel in need for some of the quiet and peace on board the palatial yacht of the Duke of Massachusetts."

"Und also mit it," put in the Yid, wiping his face with a gaudy colored handkerchief, "a few high vons—mit four of the fingairs in dem, ain't it, Jimmie?"

"For once, Mr. Cohen," Jimmie Cordie answered gravely, "I do not seem able to say 'it ain't.' Especially now that we have cured Nong Chik's tummy-ache."

THE NINE RED GODS DECIDE

Straight toward a fiendish trap set by Chinese treachery and revengeful hatred go Jimmie Cordie and his five fellow soldiers of fortune, gay adventurers in the far places of the Orient

CHAPTER I

A WAR LORD'S ATTACK

IT WAS A murderous thing to face, the machine gun fire that sprayed from the walled city of Meng Wu, in Chinese Turkestan. The troops of the War Lord K'ung skulked in the timber across the little valley until they were literally driven to the attack by swordsmen in their rear.

But human life is the cheapest thing for sale in China, and wave after wave was sent across the valley and up against the gates. K'ung knew that once the attack had started it was up to him to press it home, otherwise his stay in that part of China would be limited to the time it took him to flee out of it.

He also knew that in such case he would be more than lucky if he got out. If he were captured by the Manchu prince Chieh-yu, who held the city, his body would remain indefinitely while his spirit went on high. K'ung was under no illusions as to what a Manchu prince would do by way of repaying treachery.

So from his headquarters on a little knoll, far enough back as he thought to be out of range, K'ung ordered regiment after regiment forward, hoping that eventually Chieh-yu would run out of ammunition. He held back his swordsmen and a regiment composed of his own bodyguard for the final push.

The six machine guns on the wall of Meng Wu, two at each corner that faced the valley and two just above the gates, picked up the running men on each flank and then sent a merciless cross-fire into the center.

"The dogs waver," K'ung snarled to an officer standing beside him. "They stop—and run back! May the curse of the Nine Thousand and Eight Devils of the innermost blackness be on the foreign devils who are manning the machine guns! Order the regiment of Wen forward."

As the charge broke and those of K'ung's men who survived it ran back toward the timber, the Fighting Yid rose from his machine gun.

"Don't touch it," he ordered the two young Chinese who were helping him. They were both very apt scholars and were more than anxious to operate the gun instead of merely holding belts ready for the Yid.

"Maybe-so ven it comes de next attack, I lets you do de shootin'," the Yid added with a grin as he saw the pleading look on their faces.

He walked over to the next gun. "Hey, Beaneater," he said, as he squatted sociably down beside a tall, lanky man who had grinned up at him. "How much ammunition have you got it?"

"Four, eight, ten—a little more than ten belts, my distinguished friend from Hester Street," answered that gentleman gravely. He was John Cabot Winthrop, according to the Massachusetts Blue Book, but all over the Orient he was much better known as the Boston Bean, or Beaneater, or the Codfish. He answered to any or all of those titles readily.

The Bean was a millionaire several times over, with town and country houses, apartments in more than one Continental city, yachts and all the rest that goes with unlimited money—and his one idea of a perfect time was to be in a place where bullets or swords were singing the death song. His grave, thin, aristocratic face and melancholy look hid a gayly reckless heart.

"OI!" THE Yid exclaimed. "Dot is just three more than I have. Maybe-so Jimmie and Red vill have some to spare, ain't it?"

The Yid, whose name was Abraham Cohen, was about as broad as he was tall, and looked fat and roly-poly. His eyes of china blue seemed always popping out of his head with surprise at such naughty things happening in a bad old world.

"I am Plincess Chi Huan of the Nine Clans!"

That look and the seeming fat had fooled more than one man. The Yid's fat was all steel-like muscles; he was never surprised at anything, and he thought and moved as quickly as a grizzly bear—and he was just about as strong when aroused. According to Jimmie Cordie—with whom the Yid and the Bean stayed as much as possible—the Yid was "a soldier of fortune, neither pure nor simple."

The Yid had fought as a machine gunner in the A.E.F. and afterward in the Orient for War Lord or potentate; and when he couldn't find one who had some fighting he wanted done, he would go off on some expedition of his own, getting the Beaneater to come along if possible. But both he and the Bean would promptly drop whatever they were doing if there were a chance of getting with Jimmie Cordie and big, Irish, brick-topped Red Dolan.

"I don't think they have," the Bean answered. "In fact, Mr. Cohen, I know that Jimmie hasn't. I saw him go over and get some from Red. Wait till this bird's swordsmen come over the wall, you'll be cut up into—hop to it, Yid!"

The Yid looked at what was coming from the timber, and rose.

"Oi, such a business! Here comes it all. Beaneater, vait! Look—over there on de little hill. All de higher-ups und everyt'ing. Maybe-so you und me mit de right elevation could knock 'em off und vin de var, ain't it?"

The Bean looked. "Too far, Yid, get to your—by gosh, we might at that! No sighting shots. Raise her as high as she'll go and then right on the target. Make it snappy!"

Jimmie Cordie, at one of the guns over the gates, already at work, shouted to Red Dolan, who was operating the other beside him: "The Yid and the Bean must be out of ammunition. Well, for Pete's sake! What do they think they're doing? Red! To the left! The left! I can't hold it all—hold 'er."

There was no more need of machine guns. The Yid and the Bean had landed on the target—full on it—and the little knoll had become a shambles.

Most of the higher officers had assembled there to get further orders from K'ung, and the two machine guns had wiped them out. As the men in the charge saw what had happened to their leaders, they turned and ran, and this time they kept right on. The swordsmen and troops in reserve, scattered through the timber, started also, from where they stood.

In China, where War Lord fights War Lord, and deserting units from any one of three or four armies will fight any that they think they can whip, it is a wise thing to start away from a battlefield as fast as possible, once it is seen that the men responsible for the fight have gone down.

K'ung rolled off the top of the knoll, a bulletin his chest. His War Brother, Hsai, who had been coming up the side and was unwounded, caught him in his arms.

"I—go—on high, O War Brother," K'ung gasped. "These foreign devils have killed me. I—would have—revenge. No, do not interrupt, Swear—that I may—sit—on high with my venerable ancestors and—see you torture them."

"On my house of Hsai Wu, I swear it. Rest quietly, War

Brother. It may be that your wound is not—" He stopped talking. The spirit of K'ung had already started on its journey.

CHAPTER II

DEBTS OF HONOR

THE MANCHU PRINCE CHIEH-YU sat in his gardens with the men who had helped him save his city of Meng Wu and his people from the burning and slaying that K'ung would have inflicted on them. With him sat his little daughter, the princess Chi Huan.

They were both old and tried friends of the Americans who had arrived just in time to beat the attack back. Chieh-yu had been first secretary of the Chinese Embassy in Washington for several years and the little princess had gone to school in Chevy Chase. A year before she had been seized and taken to Hongkong by some English adventurers, but had been rescued from them and returned to her father by these soldiers of fortune.

The Manchus do not bind the feet of the girl babies, neither do the eyes of the pure-blooded Manchu slant up, as do those of the Chinese. The Princess Chi Huan was as lovely as some exotic Oriental flower, with black eyes, blue-black hair, straight little nose and daintily curved lips. The silken robes of a princess of the blood could not hide her perfect little form as she sat as straight as possible beside her father.

As far as she was concerned the men sitting there were her "honolable big blothels" and she didn't care who knew it. Her English was not as perfect as Chieh-yu's, but very good, except for the fact that the fatal letter "r" tripped her when in the beginning or middle of a word. When it was at the end, she could almost always handle it.

"You gentlemen arrived at a very busy moment," Chieh-yu

said with a smile, "and I did not have time to explain why I sent for you."

This brought a wide smile from Jimmie Cordie, at various times Foreign Legion sergeant, captain of an A.E.F. machine gun company and fighter in the far places ever since. Slim, black-eyed, deeply tanned, he moved with the ease and grace of a snow leopard.

"We found out the reason twenty minutes after we arrived, Chieh-yu," he said. "We are darned glad we got here in time to give you a hand."

"You gave me more than a hand, captain," answered Chieh-yu gravely. "If you had not come, I am afraid that I could not have held my city against the inexhaustible force that this dog K'ung seemed able to throw against my walls."

"He did not dale to meet my honolable father with a swold in his hand, the cowald!" announced the Princess Chi Huan, who had inherited her full share of Manchu fighting blood. "I am only solly that he did not come close enough to die on my swold."

"Quit being so bloodthirsty, Missee Iron Hat," teased Jimmie.

"I am not Missee Ilon Hat!" she retorted promptly. "I am the Plincess Chi Huan of the Nine Clans, Mr. Jimmie Coldie." This was an old and tried joke between them.

"And well the scut knows it, darlin'," soothed Red Dolan, who had carried the little princess in his brawny arms over many miles of rough going. "Pay no attention to him, alanna. Come and sit by me."

"I will, Led. Then you and I will—will—oh, yes, we will flame something on him."

They all laughed. They had done some framing in their time, too, but it had been with Jimmie's connivance.

Chieh-yu explained, as he patted his daughter's hand: "Once this cur, K'ung, whose spirit is no doubt wailing in the outer coldness, dared to look with longing eyes on the Princess Chi Huan. That is why the princess feels as if she would have liked to attend to the matter of his death herself. When I sent word to you in Hongkong that I was hard pressed out here, and asked you to come and help me, I had no idea that K'ung would attack so soon. He was my lieutenant while I was in the Army of the North, and he came here with me. I gave him a city to rule over and he repaid me with treachery. Finally he became, as he thought, strong enough to drive me from the province of Yunnan. He tried," Chieh-yu added grimly, "with the result you gentlemen know."

"WELL," JIMMIE answered, "if you can arrange to have a junk for us at the river, we better be starting back. We promised the Mandarin Liu-kan that we would—"

"What?" the princess interrupted, something the Manchu seldom does. "Jimmie! Led! You are not going to stay and lest in my galdens? You must not go away!"

The tears came into her velvet, midnight eyes, although she tried hard to wink them back. "You are my—please, Gligsby and Putney"—she held out her slim rounded arms that blazed with bracelets of priceless jewels—"and you, Yid and Codfish: Please stay here and lest."

"We cannot in honor, O Princess of the Nine Clans," answered George Grigsby, a tall, lean, quiet man from the Hills of Breathitt County, Kentucky. He had served in the Foreign Legion with Jimmie Cordie, Red Dolan, and Arthur Putney; he had won a major's commission in the A.E.F. Since the war he had been always in the Orient.

Like Putney, the Vermonter, who sat beside him, Grigsby was more or less silent most of the time; and like Putney also, he fought with a frozen little smile on his lips and in his eyes. He was a Kentucky mountaineer and he looked and thought and acted as one in spite of his long absence from the hills.

He smiled at the very distressed little princess and went on, "It is a debt we owe, Chi Huan. Shall a Manchu princess tell us to rest in gardens when there is a debt of honor to be paid?"

"No, Geolge," she answered bravely. "I did not know that it

was a debt of honor. Of coulse you must go and pay it. But I wish—I wish that you did not have it to pay."

"Come and show old Red the pretty swans," Red Dolan coaxed, seeing that the little princess was having a hard time holding the tears. "Sure 'tis something you and I will frame that will bring us all back quicker than ye can say scat to a jaybird."

"Pelhaps we can, Led," Chi Huan answered, rising with a brave smile.

Chieh-yu watched his little daughter and the big brawny Irishman go hand in hand toward the lake of the swans. "The Princess Chi Huan has given to all of you the place of the brothers she has not," he said gently. "The junk will be ready for you at the river to-morrow morning. I will send an escort. And there is the matter of payment to be taken up."

Jimmie Cordie laughed. "We don't need any escort, Chieh-yu. We'll take two of the Brownings and part of the ammunition that is left. We've all got our 30-30s and Colts. As far as payment goes, does one friend speak of payment to another? It has been payment enough to see the Princess Chi Huan again."

THE WAR BROTHER of K'ung stood in front of a little shrine in his city of Shun, about fifty miles south and east of that blood-washed knoll where he had sworn the oath of vengeance. Hsai had been in the shrine, praying that the gods would lead him on the path of his revenge. And now, as he turned to the spy he had sent to stay as close as possible to the city of Chieh-yu, Hsai smiled.

"You have my permission to speak," he said curtly to the bowing man.

"This I have to tell, O Lord of the world and mighty leader of fighting men. The foreign devils have left the city of the Lord Chieh-yu and have embarked on a junk which headed east down the great river."

"How many men have they got with them?"

"Their bearers only, Lord. With them went two of the little guns that speak of death so fast."

"When did they sail?"

"This morning at dawn. I have run all day, Lord, and—"

"Silence, jackal. Your tongue is always in motion. It shall be torn out by the roots unless you learn to control it. Was it a war junk?"

"I could not see, Lord. It is a small one, carrying, it may be, five or six as a crew."

"Was there a favoring wind?"

"No, mighty one. They floated slowly with the current."

"You have my permission to go. This time I will spare your tongue—but guard it."

Hsai walked slowly toward his palace, his bodyguard of swordsmen behind him. He knew that there was no hurry. The river Yarkand wound around through the valleys, and even with favorable winds it would take the junk at least two days to get near his city. He would think of some strategical plan that would result in the capture, unwounded, of the men he wanted.

He knew that he could take the junk by force, but he also knew that the men who had manned the deadly machine guns would all be dead or wounded by the time the fight was over.

He went to one of the balconies that overlooked the gardens and sat down in a high-backed chair near the railing. All Chinese, when able, have beautiful flower gardens, with little artificial lakes in them on which swans and rare waterfowl swim. No matter how cruel or merciless they may be, they love their scented gardens and spend as much time there as they possibly can.

Hsai looked at the flowers with unseeing eyes. His clever brain was forming and rejecting plan after plan.

His face and eyes were impassive as he sat absolutely motionless. An hour went by, then another. Finally he clapped his hands, once. The heavy silken drape at the door was almost instantly pulled aside and a palace officer stood in the entrance and bowed low.

"I desire the presence of Captain Yao Wu," Hsai said without looking around.

The officer bowed again, and a few moments later a young Chinese army officer halted ten feet away from the motionless figure in the chair and saluted Hsai.

"There is a matter in which I will use your services," Hsai said. "I know that you speak English. How well?"

"I was educated at the English University of Oxford, and for three years before joining your forces, resplendent one, I acted as interpreter in the army of General Hu-Ta-Hai of the South."

"Listen, then, O Captain Yao Wu. It may be that the time has come for you to win your regiment."

CHAPTER III

THE WOUNDED MAN

"I COULD WALK as fast as this thing they call a junk can sail," Red Dolan announced in disgust as he sat up from where he had been sprawled out on the deck, using the Fighting Yid's leg for a pillow.

Red Dolan, two hundred odd pounds of bone and muscle, topped with a flaming mop of brick-red hair, had frosty blue eyes and a heart that went out to anything in pain or trouble unless he was engaged in his one and only love, fighting. That is not quite correct, as Red had another love and that was for the slighter built, black-eyed, smiling, Jimmie Cordie.

Red had served with Jimmie in the Foreign Legion and in Jimmie's company in the American Expeditionary Force. Mr. Dolan had one or two rules of life. He would, under any circumstances, ask Jimmie Cordie: "How about that, Jimmie?" or "What now, ye scut av the world?" and the answer always satisfied Red. He was also a firm believer in the policy, "Aw, slap 'em out of the way." It made no difference how many there were to be slapped or where it was.

"Vell," suggested the Yid sleepily, "vy don't it you get out und walk den, Mistare Dolan? Dare is only forty-nine million und six little yellow brothers dot vould gif de shirt off de back to get it a chance at puttin' de hot eggs on you."

"Put on a jaw tackle, you red-headed ape, I want to sleep," Jimmie said from where he sat propped up against the mast of the junk.

"Me keep quiet?" protested Red. " 'Tis not me that's doin' the talkin', ye black-muzzled shrimp. 'Tis this gibbon here from Jerusalem."

"Und proud of it," smirked the Yid. "Do it vot Jimmie says or ve vill kick de slats loose from you, Irisher."

"Who will?" demanded Red. "Not you two—or any six more like you. Wan Dolan could lick a million—"

Putney looked up from cleaning his Colt. "You've told us before about what one Dolan could do, Red. Why not start now and begin telling what two of them could do?"

"Sure now, Putt," Red answered with a grin, " 'tis enough I have to do wid these two scuts on me back widout ye helpin' them."

"I'll help you if they jump you, Mr. Dolan. They both need a good tanning."

All of the reckless, carefree soldiers of fortune laughed. The fact that they were slowly drifting down a hostile river in China, penetrating into a more hostile country teeming with men who would cheerfully put them to the torture, did not make the slightest difference. They believed that when their number went up they'd go, and not before.

Arthur Putney was almost as big as Red and fully as strong, with stern, rough-hewn features that were exactly like those of his ancestors in Vermont who had fought the Indians for their right to live. In the Legion, in the American Expeditionary

Force as a captain, and all around the Orient afterward, he lived always up to his almost Puritan code in every way.

"That saves you from a beating up, Red," Jimmie said lazily. "We better keep our fingers crossed that this warship arrives in port without having to fight many battles. There is darned little ammunition, gents."

"What do you care?" demanded Red. "Who can stop us?"

"Besides, James," Grigsby said from where he sat with the Boston Bean, "don't ever forget that Red can always find 'me good sword'."

They all laughed again, Red as well as the rest. The fact that he would drop a gun any time to pick up a sword and get to close quarters was a standing joke.

"If I do," the red-head answered, "I'll clear the path for ye lily-livered old ladies. Wid Jimmie beside me wid his Colt, 'tis a broad path we will make for ye—won't we, Jimmie?"

"Yeah, boy," Jimmie answered with a smile. "We sure will, Red."

THE YID got up and stood by the rail, looking out over the yellow river.

"Oh, look!" he said suddenly. "Dare goes it a raft mit a man on it! Vounded man."

"Tell that bird at the steering oar to ease over that way, Jimmie," Grigsby said as he rose. "You seem to be able to make them understand better than the rest of us."

Five minutes later Captain Yao Wu stood on the deck of the junk. He looked very different from the trim, nattily uniformed young officer who had reported to Hsai. Now his uniform was torn and dirty and there was a bloody bandage around his right arm, high up, and another was also wound around his head. There were real knife cuts beneath the bandages. Hsai left nothing to chance.

"I—I wish to thank you, gentlemen," said Yao Wu in faultless English, swaying a little from genuine weakness and loss of blood. "Another day on that raft and my spirit would have ascended on high to join my venerable ancestors." He took hold of the rail to help hold himself up.

"Break out that bottle of brandy I know you've got, Yid," commanded Jimmie Cordie. "Make it snappy."

"My unworthy, miserable name is Yao Wu, honorable one. I—I have had no food for three days and—"

He would have fallen if Red had not caught him. "Take him below and lay him on one of the bunks," Jimmie ordered. "I'll make him some rice broth."

An hour later Yao Wu, looking and feeling much better, sat on deck facing the six men, who smiled at him in friendly fashion.

"Don't tell it if it takes too much effort," Grigsby said. "You are all right now and whatever you have to tell can wait!"

"I am much better now, Major Grigsby," answered Yao Wu. "And if I am—there is not much time. I will tell you from the beginning. I am, or rather I was, Captain Yao Wu, attached to the staff of General Hu-Ta-Hai of the Army of the South. At the battle of Yo-fei I was severely wounded and would have passed on high if it had not been for an American doctor named Harris. It may be that you gentlemen, being Americans, have heard of him? Dr. Charles Seton Harris."

"We were at the battle of Yo-fei," answered Jimmie Cordie with a grin, "although not with the Army of the South. We have all heard of Dr. Harris, but I don't think any of us have ever met him."

"You were there—and with the Army of the North? It may be then that I have to thank one of you gentlemen for the machine gun bullet in my leg," Yao Wu said with a smile equal to Jimmie Cordie's. "But such are the fortunes of war, gentlemen."

"You speak surprisingly good English, captain," Grigsby said.

"I should, considering the fact that I spent some eight years at English schools. First at Harrow and then at Oxford. I—but I am afraid that while we talk, Miss Harris may be in great danger or even—"

"Who?" demanded Red. "What the hell now? Are ye sittin' here wid the ready wah-wah and a woman in danger?"

"Pipe down, Red," ordered Jimmie sharply. "Captain, tell us as quickly as possible."

"Dr. Harris saved my life and a possible amputation of my leg. I owed him a debt, and still owe it. After the Army of the South disbanded, he went north with the Mandarin Chang Kwang and with him he took his little daughter, a girl of twelve."

"And what the livin' hell did he mean by it?" Red demanded. "The scut had no sense at all to take a girl up in that corner of—"

"Red, for Pete's sake, keep still," Jimmie pleaded. "Don't you see you are throwing him off the main line?"

"I'm shut. Go on wid it."

"DR. HARRIS stayed up there until the Mandarin Chang Kwang was defeated by a War Lord from the Thian Shan. Then he, with his daughter and few faithful servants, started for the river in an attempt to escape. What happened during the trip I do not know. The two bearers that were with the girl when I arrived with my men were not in condition to tell much about what had passed. Dr. Harris had died or been killed *en route,* and as I say, when I got there, most of the bearers had been killed by the bandits' attack."

"So," said Red, forgetting his promise to keep still, "ye got there in time to rescue her, did ye?"

Yao Wu smiled at the big Irishman. "I do not know about the rescue part, Mr. Dolan. I was on my way to join a War Lord with whom I have been before. I had only a few men with me. At any rate we took Miss Harris from the bandits, killing most of them in doing it. I lost what men I had and also received one or two superficial wounds. After the fight I found that I was in possession of Miss Harris, the two bearers, one of whom had been the doctor's topside boy, and my own worthless body."

"Did ye know it was her when ye started in wid them scuts?"

"No, Mr. Dolan. I had no way of knowing that. I could tell from where I was in the timber that she was a European and I am more than friendly with any of the Anglo-Saxon race for favors I have received; so I went in. After the fight was over she told me who she was. My debt to her father called for payment, so I hid her and the two bearers in an old temple, and started for the city of Tzu-lu which lies below here some forty miles."

"Why did ye not take herself wid ye?"

"My gosh, Red," Jimmie Cordie said in deep disgust. "That is one hell of a brainless question. One man wounded, with two bearers, to take a girl through country swarming with bandits and what-nots?"

"That is the reason, Mr. Dolan," Yao Wu went on. "Once at Tzu-lu, whose War Lord I know, I could return with a strong enough force to take her in safety down the river. I made the raft and in doing it I must have bled freely, because when you gentlemen lifted me over the side I was about to go on high."

"You say that you hid Miss Harris in an old temple?" the Boston Bean asked.

"Yes. It is a very old temple that once was very large. Now it is in ruins. It is the temple of Lun Yu. I do not think any man of your race has ever seen it. But it may be that some of the bandits who did not join in the attack, or some of my men who ran, came back and are searching for her. I do not care to think of what would happen to her if she fell into their hands.... If you gentlemen will assist me in getting to Tzu-lu as soon as possible, I can—"

"Assist hell!" Red snorted. "We'll assist you back to the temple right now. The six of us will slap outta the way all the damn bandits and War Lords in China, won't we, Jimmie?"

"We will, old kid Dolan, and half of Persia added. How far had you come down the river, captain, when we picked you up?"

"The sun was high in the heavens, Captain Cordie. About noon, I think."

Jimmie looked at his wrist watch. "Three o'clock now; and this current is about four miles an hour. All right, we'll go back with you and get Miss Harris."

Yao Wu smiled. "I was hoping that you would suggest it." His story was air-tight and he knew it.

CHAPTER IV

AMONG THE TEMPLE RUINS

IT WAS A self-sufficient little column that went at a ground-covering dogtrot through the timber that lined the river. The junk had been left in a sheltered cove, and with it remained the four or five members of the crew.

Leading the column were two bearers who had come from Hongkong with the party, both swordsmen of the T'aip'ing, the most dreaded and merciless secret society in the Orient.

At M.I.T. Jimmie Cordie had saved the life of a fellow-student, the only son of Yen Yuan, the head of the T'aip'ing; and when Jimmie arrived in China, his classmate, now a member of the organization's all-powerful Board of Foreign Affairs, had met him and taken him to Yen Yuan.

That fat, bland old Chinaman whose word was law and whose orders were obeyed without question by more than four million Chinese, had bowed low before the slim, smiling American:

"You are my honorable elder brother, O peerless one who saved the life of my only son," he had said. "Deign to mention anything you may wish."

Word had gone out through the T'aip'ing, through all its countless branches and ramifications, throughout the Orient, and to all part's of the world where there were T'aip'ing members, that the slim, black-eyed, smiling one named Cordie was the honorable elder brother of Yen Yuan, to be treated, obeyed, and protected as such by all who wished to live and enjoy good health.

And afterward Mr. James Cordie seldom, if ever, went

anywhere but what there were at least one, or two T'aip'ing in the offing.

After these two T'aip'ing—one of whom was Shih-kai, a war captain who had been with Jimmie and Red several times before—there came a party of ten of the bearers who now had nothing to carry but their swords. Then came Jimmie and Red and the Boston Bean and bearers carrying the two Brownings, more carrying the tripods, and three or four more with the remaining boxes of belt ammunition and cans of water. Following them were ten more swordsmen, then Putney, Grigsby, the Fighting Yid, and Captain Yao Wu; then five more sword-armed bearers as rear guard. They went through the timber as they would advance across No Man's Land.

Yao Wu's face and eyes were impassive, but inwardly he smiled at the precautions taken. He knew that the country between the river and the temple held no men. It had been a game drive by Hsai; his men had cleared the timber and villages of all human beings.

Jimmie Cordie suddenly loosened his Colt in the holster, then laughed softly at his action. The Boston Bean, walking on his right, saw him do it and automatically his hand flashed to his own gun butt. As Jimmie relaxed, the Bean grinned. "Seeing things, James?" he asked.

"Darned if I know," Jimmie answered. "I had a hunch or something. It's too quiet. Did we ever come this far without flushing up at least some of the population? I have a feeling, Codfish, that we are making some kind of a sacrificial procession, with us as the ultimate sacrifice. I've been fussing around in this neck of the woods for a long time and this is the first time that I ever felt it."

"Felt what, Jimmie darlin'?" demanded Red, hearing the last part.

"As if there ought to be a Band ahead playing the Dead March from Saul. I had a sudden feeling, Mr. Dolan, that all is not well in the State of Denmark."

"Yeah?" demanded Red. "And what the hell do ye care, Jimmie Cordie? Out av the way we will slap any that gets in it, do they be playin' that Dead March thing or not."

"To say nothing of the fact that you can probably find a sword if worse comes to worst," grinned Jimmie. "It's passed from me, whatever it was. *Allons, mes enfants.*"

AN HOUR later Yao Wu came up to Jimmie. "The temple is close, Captain Cordie. It may be better if I go ahead. If Miss Harris sees strangers, it may frighten her."

"How far is it from here?" Jimmie asked.

"About a quarter of a mile. See, where the timber thins out on the right."

"I'll call the bearers in. It may be possible that some of the bandits have returned, Captain Yao Wu. If they have they would be very apt to send you on high before we could get in. We'll tag along right behind you."

The temple, which looked from the timber to be a vast heap of ruins, covered with vegetation, must have been a very large and ornate one in the days of old.

There were also the ruins of a good many smaller buildings around it and what looked as if they had formerly been the foundations of several palaces or a city.

" 'Tis a fine place to hide," Red announced. "A regiment could hole up widout any wan knowin' they was there at all."

Jimmie noticed one of the bearers that had come up with the rear guard and was standing just behind Red. He looked more intently, then beckoned the boy in closer.

"Who invited you to the party?" he demanded.

The boy grinned broadly and answered; "The Plincess Chi Huan sent me with vely honolable Mistel Led. I go Hongkong to lealn English and evel-thing."

"Oh, so that's it. I knew darned well you weren't among those present when we started."

"I was goin' to tell ye, Jimmie darlin'," Red said, "but the little spridhogue clear slipped me mind wance we was on the junk."

"Glad to have you along," Jimmie said with a smile that won the Chinese boy's heart. "You better stick a little closer to us—what is your name?"

"My name is Chung, honolable captain. I stick vely close, maybe-so I lealn shootee little gun go *lat-tat-lat-tat?*"

"You'll learn lots of things if you stick around with us, young feller," Jimmie answered as they started toward the ruins of the temple. There were the bodies of several men lying in a group, then, a little beyond, more bodies.

"Some are mine," explained Yao Wu. "And some are the curs who tried to take Miss Harris."

They all were prisoners that Hsai had brought there and shot or cut down in cold blood. The War Lord Hsai was very thorough and left nothing to chance. Yao Wu was to tell of a battle, so here was evidence of it.

The Fighting Yid walked with the Boston Bean, his keen eyes searching for some sign of life. "You know something, Beaneater?"

"One or two things, my distinguished friend," answered the Bean gravely. "Not more, I will admit, but I will stand on the statement that I know at least two things. One of them is that you need some good fast running like we got up in the Kyzyl-kun desert, you are fifty pounds over—"

"Oi, Codfisher, vy remind it me of dot—look, here comes somebody."

TWO CHINESE were running toward the party from the left side of the ruins. As they came up they began calling to Yao Wu, very excitedly. On arrival they both talked at once.

One of them, seeing that white men were with Yao Wu, switched to English, "Missee lun hide—lun hide! No can find! Vely much aflaid! Lun hide in luins. Me topside boy, Doctol Hallis."

"Miss Harris has become frightened and hidden herself away in the temple," Yao Wu announced, a little frown on his face. "I am afraid that we will have a hard time finding her."

"I don't see why," Jimmie answered curtly. "George, supposing we make camp over there where the walls offer some chance to stand off attack, then start a search. She will come out if she hears an English voice."

"An attack? But from whom, Captain Cordie?" asked Yao Wu, looking very puzzled. "There is none within twenty miles that is strong enough to—"

"I don't know from whom," interrupted Jimmie, "and care less. We always make ready to receive it, Captain Yao Wu."

"What caused the hair to rise along your back, Jeems?" asked Grigsby with a smile.

"Darned if I know," answered Jimmie, "but it is sure up for some reason."

"What the hell is all the wah-wah about?" Red put in. "Sure, herself is in some dark corner shiverin' wid fear and here we stand like an old ladies' sewing circle."

"Who always sat down, Mr. Dolan," Putney said. "Let's go, Jimmie."

A camp was made between standing walls of one of the buildings. The two Brownings were set up and the ammunition boxes opened.

"Red and I will go first," Jimmie announced. "We'll take these two birds with us. They can show us where she was last."

"Better take some of your highbinders, Jimmie," the Bean said. "If you are jumped, they will come in handy."

"She might see them first," Jimmie grinned, "We won't go so far but what you can hear us hollering—will we, Red?"

"You and me, Jimmie, we can handle all that comes widout any hollerin'—ye black-muzzled shrimp av the world."

"Yid," Jimmie said as he and Red started, "you and the Boston Bean start over at the right and work toward the middle as much as you can. Yid, you sing one of those songs of yours as loud as you can. She'll know you are no Chinaman. George, you and Putt be the garrison until we get back, then you can go take a look-see if we can't raise her."

"Get going, Jimmie," drawled Grigsby. "It isn't going to be light much longer."

Shih-kai stepped up to Jimmie and bowed. "Lord, my insignificant head depends upon your safety. Grant that I also may go with you."

"You see, Shih-kai," Jimmie answered gently, "I am afraid that if by chance she saw you first she would not know that you are a Manchu. She might run, or burrow deeper and get hurt. If I do not come back in a half hour, you may come for me, little brother."

Jimmie really liked the grim-faced, sword-scarred young Manchu, who was one of Yen Yuan's most trusted captains.

"Red and I can hold anything off that long. If you hear shots, come sooner."

"We all will," said Putney. "Get going. The Yid and the Bean are already starting in."

JIMMIE AND Red, with the two bearers who had supposedly been with Miss Harris, walked to the ruins and began to climb slowly over them. Those in the camp who could hear the Yid's reedy tenor singing "On the Sidewalks of New York," which he thought would be the best tune to tell the girl that Americans had arrived.

They could also see Jimmie and Red for quite a little while as they climbed up and down, and before the two got very far in they could hear Red shouting, "Where are ye, alanna? Answer, darlin'. We've come to get ye." Jimmie Cordie claimed that anything in skirts from nine to ninety-nine could take one look at Red and know at once that she could twist the big Irishman around her little finger. He was quite right, only he did not have to put any age limits on it.

A quarter of an hour went by, then another, and Shih-kai, who saw Putney look at his wrist watch, stood up and snarled an order to the T'aip'ing swords, who by now had thrown off any attempt to pose as bearers.

None of them had liked to see the "Black-eyed Smiling One" go toward the ruins practically alone, even if the "Lord of the Flaming Hair" had gone along with him. They all knew just how far any excuse's would go with Yen Yuan, and they liked Jimmie for his own sake; he was always courteous to them, and was in truth, as far as they went, their "honorable elder brother."

As Shih-kai started with half his men the two bearers came running out of the ruins.

"Hold it, Shih-kai," said Grigsby softly. "Something has happened."

As he spoke, the Yid and the Bean could be seen coming out of the middle of the ruins.

"Whatever it is, they don't know it," Putney said.

" 'Melicans hide flom us!" the topside boy shouted. "Go ahead and hide, like Missee! Me plenty 'flaid! Maybe-so devils in temple no likee, see—"

Yao Wu said something in Chinese. The man shivered and answered.

Yao Wu turned to Grigsby and Putney as the Yid and the Bean came up. "I told him to calm himself or I would give him the death of the thousand cuts. He says that the two white men were a little ahead of him going down a passageway under some of the fallen pillars and suddenly they disappeared."

"Yeah?" drawled Grigsby. "Ask him—"

"There is no use in asking him anything, Major Grigsby," interrupted Yao Wu. "He is so afraid of devils that what little sense he possessed has fled. I suggest that we go to the temple and, two by two, cover it all. If we scatter out and act quickly we may—"

"Well, suh," answered Grigsby, "I reckon we don't do that, just now. I want to ask you some questions. The first—"

Shih-kai suddenly stepped forward into full sight of the two Chinese bearers who had run from the ruins.

"You I know, dog who answers to the degraded name of Lei. Is there anything you wish to say before I take you before the Mighty Head? It may be that if you speak—and quickly—that in his supreme conception of generosity he will make the death you and all your repulsive relations are to die one that will not last over five days."

The Chinaman looked at the fierce, scarred face of the young war captain of the T'aip'ing, whom he had not noticed before, as Shih-kai and the T'aip'ings had been a little in the rear. If he had counterfeited the shiver before, it was real now. He was a T'aip'ing himself, although a branch far outside the inner one near Yen Yuan. Once in Hongkong, before he had fled to the north, he had been used in a small matter, and he knew the War Captain Shih-kai.

CAPTAIN YAO WU'S eyes widened as Shih-kai spoke, and he gave an order for the Chinaman to keep still. But the bearer Lei was past hearing anything except the soft purring tones of the T'aip'ing swordsman. He knew what was coming for his family and all relations to the uttermost degree if he could not in some way get mercy granted.

"I do not know, Mighty One!" he wailed. He sank on his knees.

As he did, Yao Wu made a movement as if to draw the gun which Jimmie Cordie had given him along with a belt and holster. His hand had hardly got more than tense before he was looking straight into the muzzles of four Colts, steady muzzles behind which were cold eyes.

"Don't move," said Putney softly.

"Go ahead, Shih-kai," Grigsby ordered. "Jimmie and Red may be getting further and further away every minute."

The bearer Lei gasped out the story—as much as he knew of it, which was plenty. While not one of Hsai's lieutenants, he was high enough up to have been taken partly into the confidence of Yao Wu in the planning. Long before he was through the face of Captain Yao Wu was gray in color.

"And so, O Lord of all the Swords of the Mighty Head," the bearer said at last, "the foreign devils were to be separated and decoyed to the traps that I arranged. There was to be no fighting."

"Where were they to be taken?"

"To the Lord Hsai in his city of Shun."

"Who directed the arrangements?" asked Shih-kai suavely.

"He who stands there, Captain Yao Wu."

As the young Chinese captain saw the terrified Lei point to him, he took the one remaining chance he had for life, knowing fully how slim it was. The white men had seemingly relaxed their tenseness. Their guns were still in their hands, but not pointed directly at him. He crouched with the quickness of a cat and his right hand went to his gun butt. He was fast enough to get his hand there and close it around the butt. As he did, four heavy .45 soft-nosed bullets tore into him from four different angles and Captain Yao Wu died before his body started toward the ground.

The Fighting Yid had been standing a little in the Boston Bean's line of fire and as he holstered his gun he remonstrated, feeling his right ear. "Oi, Beaneater, for vy take it my ear for a gun rest?"

"Keep your big ears out of the way. I only had a half inch clearance," the Bean answered gravely. "We better get going, George."

Shih-kai drew his sword and stepped in closer to the decoy bearer.

"I will take the responsibility of pardoning your family and relations," he said softly. "And because of the fact that you have told all, make your death an easy one." The blade flashed in with a slicing upward stroke.

The other bearer, also on his knees, wailed in terror and fell forward on his face, groveling on the ground. He fully expected to get the same dose, but as Shih-kai stepped forward, Putney said: "Hold it, Shih-kai, he can guide us to the city."

The T'aip'ing bowed and sheathed his sword, giving a curt order to two of his men, who raised the bearer none too gently.

"Vait," the Yid said as they started for their packs and the machine guns. "If dey vos framed to do all dot, dare are more of dem holed up vaiting for us, like dey did Jimmie und Red. Ve get dem first und—"

"Not so good, Yid," Putney interrupted. "Let 'em stay where they are. If we make it snappy we may be able to cut off the party that has got Red and Jimmie. Red is some load to pack, to say nothing of Jimmie, and it's a cinch that both of them are knocked out in some way or we would have heard them."

"Shih-kai," Grigsby commanded, "get the nearest way to the city out of that bird, and see if you can find out which route the prisoners were going to be taken. Then throw out a line of your men behind us. If any one tries to get through, stop 'em. Ready? All right, let's go."

This time it was a war party that went through the timber with drawn guns and swords. Darkness came with the suddenness that only the Orient knows, but the little column, as ready to strike as a coiled rattlesnake, went steadily on toward Shun, the city of Hsai.

CHAPTER V

A HANDFUL AGAINST A CITY

IT WAS GRAY dawn when Lei's fellow-decoy whose life had been spared held up his hand, then pointed up the side of the old canal bed that the party had been advancing in for the last hour.

"The city of the Lord Hsai," he whispered to Shih-kai, who was beside him, within easy sword reach. Shih-kai nodded, and his sword flashed. The decoy's head nodded too—and fell to the ground.

The four grim-faced soldiers of fortune climbed the steep

sides of the canal and cautiously parted the tangle of weeds and second growth, looking at the city of the man who had tricked them.

It was not a walled city, but lay in a position of natural strength as far as resistance to attack went. It lay in the Y of a turbulent little river that roared down from the hills. Both branches of the river were spanned by bridges that could be almost instantly dropped, being held by ropes against the sides. Any machine gun or rifle fire would be expended vainly against the blank walls of stone houses across the river.

The road leading into the city, up the shank of the Y, ran up a steep slope for about a quarter of a mile and was absolutely barren of any cover. The houses that lined it as it entered the city were also of stone and built so that, in case of attack, they would have to be taken one after the other.

The Fighting Yid took one look and grinned. "Vot we need right now, Beaneater, is dot de navy comes it up de creek und lands de marines."

"That's a good suggestion, Mr. Cohen—I mean General Cohen. Then why not have the 31st Division walk up the road while the bombers are—"

"You kidders keep your voices down," warned Grigsby. "Some of the populace may be out for an early morning stroll."

Putney had been studying the approaches and now settled back, letting go the weeds he had parted.

"She's going to be a hard nut to crack, George. If we take the road and this bird has any guns be can mop up on us before we get to the first row of houses."

"One of the bridges would land us closer—given that we could get across before they dropped her," the Bean announced.

"It will be up to us to do that little thing, Codfish," answered Grigsby, "or take a thousand-foot drop. You and the Yid take the Brownings. Putt and I will cover you. Shih-kai, get your men on either side of us, not in front. We'll go—"

"Vait!" the Fighting Yid protested. "Maybe-so ve have got it here first. If dey is carryin' Jimmie und Red ve beat 'em here, I bet you. If ve go in und don't find dem—"

"Listen, Yid," Grigsby interrupted. "I don't dare to take the chance of their not being here. This bird is all set to do a little high-class torturing, and he'll start it off as soon as he gets the chance. Jimmie and Red may have been brought through some shortcut. The thing for us to do is to shoot our way right in to him and find out. We probably can pick up some one *en route* who will be able to tell us. If they are in there, we'll get them. If they're not, we'll come back out. Maybe we can find something in there that this gent thinks a lot of that we can swap for Jimmie and Red."

"Jake mit me," agreed the Yid with a grin. "If some von tells us de way to de palace ve can bring it him out to trade."

Putney and the Boston Bean laughed. "That suggestion, General Cohen," the Bean said gravely as he tightened his cartridge belt another hole, "is worthy of your brilliant strategical mind. Let's go."

"The bridge ahead," Grigsby ordered. "As soon as we get in, Shih-kai, get hold of some one that can show us the palace. Straight shooting now, Yid. No fancy shots or betting."

"Oi, George! For vy you varn it me und not de Codfisher? He is de von dat is always up to dat."

FOUR MEN, with some fifteen or twenty swordsmen and two machine guns, aside from their rifles and Colts, were going to attack a city of five thousand people; and they laughed as they calmly stood up and began to walk toward the narrow little bridge. The machine guns were set up and ready to go, each carried by three of the T'aip'ing who strutted proudly under the burden. Grigsby and Putney carried their 30-30 Winchesters across their left arms, as if walking through a hunting field.

Shih-kai's T'aip'ings had taken off their loose outer robes and marched on either flank, their lithe bodies in the sleeveless silk undergarments eager for the swordplay to come. They were all young men, picked swords, and fully confident of their ability to cut their way through any odds.

As they reached the little bridge, the Yid stopped. "Oi, vait! I got it a thought. Vonce ve are over de bridge und on de vay, vot stops dem from lowerin' it, I esk you? Den if ve vant to come back, not so good, ain't it?"

"Since when have you been hunting ways to come back, Mr. Cohen?" demanded the Bean gravely. "Generally your slogan is, 'On with the dance and—'"

"Heads up!" Grigsby shouted. "Here they come! Get over, Yid. You too, Bean! Take your men across, Shih-kai. Keep them back of the machine guns. We have walked right smack into it."

WORD HAD been brought to Hsai of the advance of this party by a man who had won through from the old temple. He had been one stationed at a trap in one of the outbuildings and had seen what had happened. He didn't know what had become of the other two foreign devils, but on witnessing the death of Captain Yao-Wu he had slipped away to warn his War Lord.

Hsai could not figure out what had happened. At the moment all he knew was that he was shy one captain, and that his plan had failed partly, if not altogether. Now he was going to get a fight from men whose ability along those lines he had full reason to respect.

All thought of capturing them unwounded, for torture, was promptly banished. He knew what machine guns could do, and he had brought up all he had to overwhelm by one sweeping charge this audacious attempt to attack him in his city. It had taken him until morning to get his force together, some fifteen hundred men, which was the reason that the attacking party had come unmolested up the canal bed.

Hsai knew better than to try a fight unless in greatly superior numbers. The War Lord was under no delusions as to his men, who were mostly mercenaries from South China. If there were enough of them to make the charge a foregone conclusion they would go into it; but not otherwise.

From out of the row of houses that fronted the bridge, about an eighth of a mile away from it, there poured the swordsmen of Hsai. With them came a company armed with bayoneted rifles. Down the road from the city there came another body of men, and from the canal bed, up from where the party had gone over the top, came a third. The men on the road turned sharply to the left and completed the triangle with the bridge in the middle.

The Yid and the Bean, with the men carrying the machine guns, did not hesitate an instant, but ran lightly across the swinging bridge, followed by the T'aip'ings.

Putney laughed. "Is it your idea, George, that you and I will hold this side?" he asked, calmly watching the rapidly moving Chinese troops.

"No, I was trying to figure the best out. We'll shoot our way straight into that stone house that stands out a little and take it. He's got most of his men on the sides and coming up from the road. Red and Jimmie will have to take pot-luck for a while."

They ran across the bridge, and as Grigsby got to the other side he turned and held out his hand for one of the T'aip'ing swords. With it he cut through the four ropes that held the bridge and they all watched it crash against the other side and fall part way into the chasm below.

"Vot de hell is George doing that for, Codfisher?" asked the Yid.

"Damfino," answered the Boston Bean cheerfully. "He's got a hen on of some kind. He better tell us which way to start the ball rolling or they'll be on top of—oh, I see. Look, coming up the canal bank!"

"Straight ahead, you birds!" shouted Grigsby. "To that stone house that sticks out! Shoot the way! Back 'em up, Shih-kai. Putt and I will take care of the rear. Let's go!"

THERE WAS absolutely no show of even nervousness on the part of the soldiers of fortune, and none at all on the faces of the T'aip'ing. The latter were smiling happily at the thought of such gorgeous swordplay as was rapidly rolling toward them. Besides, they all thought that they were going to get the "Black-eyed Smiling One" who was their honorable elder brother.

"Take it from de left, Beany, und I take it from de right, ain't it? My, how could it I miss it mit dis set-up?" and the Yid's gun began to hammer out a harsh staccato of death.

"You better not do much missing, old kid Cohen," the Bean answered.

Two expert machine gunners, a level space, and a massed body charging in!

The faces of the T'aip'ing swordsmen grew long as they saw the men they had hoped would give them sword-exercise go down like pins in a bowling alley. One or two, over-eager, took a step forward on the right side, but stopped at a snarled order from Shih-kai, who stood and watched the machine gun work.

The Chinese who had come up the old canal bed were put out of action by the dropping of the bridge, at least until they could get back to the one higher up or the one below.

The party coming up from the road was the most dangerous, as far as guns went. Hsai had only three hundred men, mostly swordsmen, to face the first shock of the machine guns and the two 30-30 rifles that were handled by men who could empty the magazines in less seconds than they had shells and place their bullets with cold, merciless accuracy while doing it. The fire of two machine guns had often slowed and stopped that number of men with rifles, men of other and better-trained races. Before the Chinese got much closer they stopped, wavered, and fled under the pitiless hail of steel-jacketed bullets that tore through two or three of their ill-nourished, thin bodies at a time.

The Yid and the Bean stood up, and, with the gun bearers, ran forward, followed by the T'aip'ing like a lot of fox terriers. When they covered about a hundred yards they halted and knelt behind their guns.

Putney ran up. "To the right! Get on the bunch coming from the road, you dam' idiots! Do you think George and I can—"

The prompt response of both Brownings drowned out the

rest. The troops from the road were better men or more disciplined than the ones who had come from the city, and in spite of the fire they came on—some of them. The survivors were mostly on the extreme left and right.

SOME OF the fleeing swordsmen halted on seeing the machine guns pointed away from them, and, as their brothers were coming up fast, they tried once more for much honor and glory, and charged in.

The T'aip'ing swords, led now by Shih-kai, ran to meet them in a compact little wedge that was, at close quarters, as deadly a thing to face as the machine guns. Shih-kai was a Manchu and had learned the wedge formation in the north. The wedge cleared in front of all resistance, but lost five men doing it. Shih-kai led the remainder back, pointing out errors in swordplay like a schoolmaster.

Just as he arrived, Grigsby ordered another advance. The party that had come up the canal had finally reached the upper bridge and were over.

"Right up and into the house this time," Grigsby shouted. "Drive 'em back! That's the boy, Yid! Now—let's go! Shih-kai, send your men in to mop up! Bean—go in right after him and hold the door facing the city!"

They made the house, which had a low window without glass that looked out at the canal and the T'aip'ing disappeared. The Bean threw one long leg over the sill, turned and lifted in the Browning with the help of his T'aip'ing assistants. A moment later Grigsby and the rest heard the gun begin, from the other side of the house.

"Codfish is tryin' some fancy shootin', George," said the Yid as Grigsby reached his side. "Speak to him about it mit severity." In spite of the oncoming Chinese, the Yid smirked.

"Get in there," answered Grigsby with a smile. "Shove the muzzle of that gun back out this way and get busy. You'll get all the fancy—snap into it, Yid! They are pretty close."

They were, very close. Quite a few bullets were coming close also, spattering against the walls of the house on all sides.

The Yid crawled in, booted by Putney, and after him came the T'aip'ing bearers, then Putney and Grigsby went through the window. There was a wild yell of hate and exultation from the Chinese attackers, who were now sure that they had the foreign devils trapped.

CHAPTER VI

INTO THE DRAGON'S LAIR

THE HOUSE ON the outskirts of Shun had been used for a sort of officers' club, and as the T'aip'ing came in through the windows, four of Hsai's officers stood by the door which was open. Hsai by chance had selected that very house to see the battle and had been there with his staff.

He was brave enough, as brave as most Chinese, but he saw no reason why he should stay, being commander-in-chief, and meet shock troops personally. As it was, he barely had time to get out of the building, leaving the four officers to hold the door long enough for him to order up men. So close were the T'aip'ing to him that as his officers bowed and stepped two to each side of the door, Shih-kai and three of his swordsmen were on them.

Hsai's officers were swordsmen of ability, but they faced some of the best swords in China, wielded by men who thought that their opponents stood between them and the "black-eyed, smiling one" on whose rescue they were quite sure their heads depended.

Shih-kai, his war-scarred young face now like that of a cold, merciless devil, engaged the young officer nearest the door on the right. The swords met and the officer parried the lightning-like cut. But he had no parry for the blade that started from where the parry ended in a slash driven by a moulinet of steel-

There was no sign of an opening in the stone cell

like wrist, coming in a half circle from the right, neck high. The young officer went down, his head almost severed from his body.

As he fell, the officer on his left went down as did the one nearest the door on the other side. The one farther away on the left side killed the T'aip'ing that faced him. But his number was up and the respite was short—a matter of seconds. The T'aip'ing who stepped up was the War Brother of Shih-kai. There was a cut, a parry, a thrust, a parry, a feint that drew the blade of Hsai's man out of line, then a fierce point that went home.

"Get away from the door, Shih-kai!" shouted the Bean who had arrived as the last officer went down. "That's the boy! Let me speak to the gentlemen outside."

The machine gun was in action in the doorway before the words were out of the Bean's mouth—and, like Hsai's escape from the house, just in time. A company of swordsmen were coming up on the double. But the street was a narrow cañon between two- and three-story stone houses, mostly without windows fronting the street or having at the best one small cell-like opening above the door.

The oncoming Chinese filled it from side to side, and as the Bean opened up he swept the street from house to house on either side. The attackers did not even try to face it. The instant that first burst came, they started back to wherever they came from. Most of those who had been in the front ranks could not go back but lay still or writhing in the street.

As the Bean quit firing, the Yid and Grigsby and Putney arrived via the window. As soon as the Yid had clearance, the muzzle of his Browning slid out of the window at the rear and like the Bean he began to "speak to the gentlemen."

THE NECESSITY of continued firing did not last much longer out there than it had in the street. The Chinese coming up from the canal bed and the road had absolutely no cover at all. They either threw themselves flat on the ground or turned and ran for the canal. The Yid might have stopped a second or so sooner than he did, but he was trying for a small bunch way out on the left by the road who were not running fast enough to suit him. He stood up with a pleased grin to find Grigsby looking at him.

"Oi, George," the Yid hastened to explain. "I thought maybe dot if I knocked it some of the staff officers off de tree, dare vould be less for—"

"What are you explaining to me for?" Grigsby asked curtly. "You know how much ammunition we have left as well as I do. It seems as if you always have a certain amount of—" He stopped as he saw the expression on the Yid's face, then went on, "It's all right, Abie, old kid. I'm a little fussed up about Jimmie and Red, I reckon."

"Here come some more callers," the Bean put in hastily. "They've got an old brass cannon."

Grigsby ran to the window. "We can't stay here. Right out and to the palace. We'll catch this trap-setting bird right where he lives. Get out with that gun, Bean. Go with him, Shih-kai. Putt, you and the Yid take the rear guard. Let's go! There's the palace on that hill. We'll sock this charge home."

The Boston Bean laughed, as his helpers picked up the Browning. "That's the boy, George."

The Chinese in the street wavered as they saw the lean brown muzzle of the machine gun appear in the doorway. Their old brass cannon was loaded and one of the gunners was blowing on a brand before applying it to the touch-hole.

He promptly dropped it and dived behind the gun-carriage. The Bean fired two bursts, then his helpers picked up the gun.

Out of that house into the street came an outfit that was as deadly and hard to stop as a wounded grizzly bear. First the Bean and a machine gun, then the T'aip'ing, then Grigsby, and close behind him, the Fighting Yid and Putney.

The company that had come in with the cannon turned and fled. They did not like the machine guns at all and when they saw the T'aip'ing swordsmen at close range, they liked them even less. All of the heads that had been peeking out of windows and over roof tops disappeared as if by magic.

"Now you see 'em und now you don't," said the Yid, with a grin.

"You'll see plenty, Mr. Cohen," Putney answered laconically, "if you will look back and up."

The Yid looked and swiftly knelt behind his gun, saying, "Oi, de houses und de roofs is leaking Chinks, ain't it? Watch poppa use de mop."

The Chinese from the canal bed and the side of the city facing the road, seeing that the defense had been withdrawn from the stone house at the rear, had closed in and were now coming through every opening. But they faced one of the most expert machine gunners in the Orient, and an equally expert rifleman who fired with true New England economy, getting the most for his outlay.

Putney and the Yid, ignoring the bullets that were beginning to hum and spatter on the walls around them, literally did what the Yid said, the mops being steel-jacketed bullets.

Grigsby ran back to them. "All right! Close up—we're going around the corner and across the square."

THERE WAS no resistance offered along the rest of the street. But when they got to the middle of the little square that was at the bottom of the hill on which the palace stood, there was a fast charge from all four sides.

Hsai had been notified of the break from the house while he was feasting with some of his officers in his gardens. He had thought that he had the situation well in hand. The foreign devils were holed up in a stone house, he had plenty of men to send in, and he was confident that sooner or later the white men's ammunition would be exhausted. Then it would be a case of overwhelming them in a rush of swordsmen. His plans for torture had again seemed feasible and he was smiling when the messenger arrived. In that moment he heard the machine guns in action and sprang to his feet, the gloating smile gone from his lips.

These men had dared to approach his city and now, instead of fighting for their lives behind a stone barricade, they had further dared to try and shoot their way into its very heart.

Hsai snarled an order to an officer beside him to have his crack fighting troops brought up, withdrawing the ones he cared nothing about; then, being no coward personally, he ran to command them.

The charge was met and stopped by the guns of the Bean and the Yid before it had got halfway across the square. It was stopped—but at the cost of all ammunition but some twenty belts for the machine guns and what 30-30 shells were left in the cartridge belts—not many. All four had almost full belts of .45 cartridges left for their Colts.

"Up the hill!" Grigsby shouted. "We couldn't hold the palace. To that shrine on the left! Go through the palace with your men, Shih-kai. We'll cover you outside. Bring some official back with you. Get goin'. You shoot the way through, Codfish. No more from your gun, Yid; use your Colt."

Two belts more were used by the Boston Bean and all foes between them and the little shrine fell back—or down. As they made it, they could see Shih-kai lead the T'aip'ing through the door of the two-story palace of Hsai.

The shrine was built of wood and while it offered some little protection against rifle fire, it gave none at all against anything heavier. What it did do was to command absolutely any approach to the palace on three sides, being on a higher hill.

"Dig in," Grigsby commanded. "There's water here and—"

"Vat mit?" the Yid asked. "Ve got it no digging tools. I vish it dot ve vould find a sandwich or some—"

"Use your nose," the Bean suggested, grinning at his sidekick and starting his own trench with the heel of his boot. "Don't worry about any sandwiches, Mr. Cohen. You won't need any climbing the golden stairs, which you will be doing in a few minutes."

"I should vorry about dot, also. I vish I—vait, I see it some loose boards dot vill make svell spades. See, George, over by de—"

"Here they come trying to make the palace," Putney announced. "Show us later, Yid. Get on that gun."

"Just stop them," warned Grigsby, raising his rifle. "Let 'em know they can't make it—but save your ammunition."

After the first try, Hsai made no further attempt to enter the palace from that side or from any side that the shrine commanded. He drew completely out of sight all the troops he had, and a sudden unnatural-seeming stillness came over the city.

SHIH-KAI CAME out of the palace with eight men; the rest had died inside. With them ran an old man, dressed in the uniform of a high official.

"This dog," Shih-kai said, after they arrived, "tells that none have been brought into the city as prisoners. He would know of it, had it been done."

"Ask him if he knew of Hsai's plans," Grigsby ordered.

Shih-kai spoke in Chinese and the old man answered, then Shih-kai said: "He did, yes. He is the ranking officer of the palace and of the prison. He tells of Hsai's actions when we arrived and is sure that something went wrong. He asks that his life be spared, being old and not a fighting man. He is sure that none have entered, as they would have been brought to him."

The Yid whispered to the Bean. "In again, out again, gone again—ain't it, Codfisher?"

"The 'in again' is correct," the Bean answered, "except for the fact that we have never been here before. But as far as the 'out again' goes, not so good."

Grigsby was talking and the Bean stopped to listen. "—his life will be spared. Tell him that he may live if he will go to Hsai and say that we will leave the city quietly, if we are unmolested."

The old man agreed to that eagerly and went down the hill in a dog-trot, so anxious was he to get away from the gleaming swords of the T'aip'ing that he had seen at work in the palace. In the hunt for the "Black-eyed Smiling One," the T'aip'ing had cut down all that stood in the way.

A half an hour later, an officer walked calmly up the hill under a flag of truce.

"The War Lord Hsai states that you will never leave his city alive. But if you surrender, he will make the torture short."

Shih-kai translated that curt statement and Grigsby smiled as he answered, "We will not surrender; and we will leave the city as we choose, after we have rested as long as we wished. When we do we will hunt for the War Lord Hsai and send him to join his ancestors in the cold darkness before we go."

The officer turned on his heel and walked down the hill and as he did, the Yid said, "And dot is dot. Vait till I dig it de trench a little deeper, Beaneater, und den you and me go und hunt for something to eat, ain't it?"

"That's a good idea," the Bean agreed gravely. "We can probably find a restaurant open at this time somewhere down town."

"Bring me back a ham sandwich," Putney said. "While you are waiting for the Yid to get his trench deep enough, count your cartridges, Mr. Winthrop."

"Here it is," Grigsby said. "Jimmie and Red have disappeared into the blue, as far as we are concerned. In trying for them, we've got ourselves into a trap that is going to take some—"

"Vot kind of a trap?" the Yid demanded, straightening up from his trench. "Ve valked in—vy can't ve valk out de same vay?"

"We can, if you and the Bean will stop and get some more machine gun ammunition on the way back from that restaurant. How far do you think we would get on that walk with what we have, Mr. Ammunition-user?"

"Oi, George! For vy pick it on me? Beany shoot two to my von, all de vay."

"Which is past history," drawled Putney. "George, the best thing to do is to wait until night and then go over that wall at the rear of the palace. These birds that have us jammed don't like night fighting if they are like most Chinese, and we stand a pretty good chance of getting in the clear. If we get out there are plenty of places in the hills we can make a better stand than here. Hsai can knock us off the Christmas tree at any time, here, if he's got any heavy stuff. Jimmie and Red aren't here and a running fight in the hills will make a lot of noise that they might hear, if they are loose and looking for us." It was a long speech for the taciturn Vermonter, and as sound as his suggestions always were.

"That's right," Grigsby agreed. "We'll pull just before dawn. These birds will be holed up against the cold more or less and those that are on watch will be full of hop. In the meantime I'm going to get some sleep. Shih-kai, stand guard with your men. Don't stay too long at that restaurant, Yid, you might miss the train."

"Dot being de case," the Yid said, as he curled up in his trench, "I don't think it I'll go mit, Codfisher. Vake me early, modder dear, for I'm to be kveen of de May."

Shih-kai's grim face smiled as the four men promptly went to sleep in the very heart of a hostile Chinese city, knowing that torture or death awaited them if they could not win out of it.

"Truly," he murmured to his War Brother, "the friends of the Black-eyed Smiling One are men unafraid."

CHAPTER VII

THE UNDERGROUND TRAP

JIMMIE CORDIE AND Red had climbed over or worked their way around the ruins for some little while before Jimmie halted and beckoned the Chinaman up who had claimed to have been Dr. Harris's topside boy.

"Show us the exact place she was standing when she became frightened and ran," he commanded.

The man pointed down a narrow stone-paved walk and Jimmie and Red started down it. The two Chinese walked behind, about ten or twelve feet in the rear. About a hundred feet further on, there was a big pile of fallen stone in the way, forcing Jimmie and Red over to the left unless they wanted to climb up and over. The two or three steps they had to take to clear the obstruction brought them close to a standing wall.

"Ye would think now, wouldn't ye, Jimmie," Red said, taking off his hat to fan himself. "That herself would answer a call in American. Maybe-so she ran all the way—look out!"

The stone beneath their feet had dropped away. It had not moved because overbalanced; they had both feet on it and were about in the middle when it went down—not slowly, but as if it were falling through the air.

Red, with his hat in his hand, had absolutely no chance to draw a weapon. Jimmie Cordie, as fast always as a northern wolverine, had his gun half out before his head disappeared. Another stone slid swiftly from the wall across the hole and in a split second after the stone dropped, everything on top was as before except for the fact that there was no Jimmie Cordie or Red Dolan in sight.

They dropped about eight feet and lit on a pile of brush that had been put there to break the fall. Both of them got to their feet like big cats and as Red lit, his Colt also was out. It was absolute black darkness, but as Red drew, Jimmie Cordie's flash light went on and a moment later, Red's.

"Stand still, Red," Jimmie said calmly as he played his light along the smooth stone walls directly in front of him. "Throw your light over to the right."

Without moving, or speaking another word they threw their lights around the four walls, the ceiling and the floor. Except for the pile of brush in which they stood, they were in an absolutely bare stone room, the walls within ten feet on all sides. There was nothing to show an entrance or any kind of an opening.

They could not see, in the beams of the flash lights, even where the slab of stone that had slid over to form the roof joined the walls.

Jimmie laughed. "Back over to the corner on the left, Red. Something will slide back in a minute. It won't be a corner. Snap your light out."

Red obeyed instantly and it was not until their backs were against the wall in the corner that he spoke.

"What the heck now, Jimmie?"

"Darned if I know, Mr. Dolan," answered Jimmie cheerfully. "All I know is that I stepped on a stone and fell through right after. You take a guess."

"I did the same. This damn place is so dark I could cut it wid me knife. Why did ye order out the lights, Jimmie, ye scut?"

"They lit up the whole works to a certain extent, you big ape. Enough to enable any one to take a pot shot at us through a loophole. Now, if you keep still we can hear anything that comes and maybe-so get a shot or two ourselves before we go 'on high.' They'll have to have some light and I'd a darn sight rather they held it than us. *Sabe,* Mr. Dolan?"

Red was silent for a moment then whispered: "I wonder now did the Bean and the Yid get dumped like we did."

"Maybe-so," answered Jimmie softly. "If they did, and as quick, there isn't much chance of George and the rest hearing anything. Shih-kai will come bustin' in, but it looks as if whoever framed this was hooked up to take care of—"

"What are ye stopping for, Jimmie?"

"Do you smell anything, Red?"

RED SNIFFED audibly. "I do not—beyant the damp, grave-like smell." He sniffed again. "I do, now. 'Tis like—like—now what the heck do be the name of that flower that stinks to—"

Jimmie made no attempt now to keep his voice down. "Cease searching for the name, old kid Dolan, and also put your gat up. What you smell is not a flower by a damn' sight. It's gas."

"What kind of gas?"

"Darned if I know. It's some kind of a narcotic gas. If you stay in it long enough, it's curtains. But if you are in an atmosphere that's composed partially of it and not left in it very long, you'll go to sleep. First you breathe hard and your face gets flushed and your pulse gets feeble and your tongue swollen and—"

"Enough," Red interrupted. "I see ye know the symptoms, ye shrimp."

Both of them laughed. In a pitch-dark, cell-like stone room under a part of a ruined temple in China, with gas seeping in, both laughed as if sitting in Grigsby's apartment in Hongkong.

"While there is time," Jimmie said, "I want to say that all in all, from the time I saw your red topknot in the Legion, I've had a good time at your party, Mr. Terrence Aloysius Dolan of Dublin."

"The same to ye," Red answered promptly, "and many happy returns av the day. Will it be all right, Jimmie, to put the flash on? If we are to go West, 'tis wan more look I'd like to have at the homely mug av ye."

"Go as far as you like," Jimmie answered, a little thickly. "It doesn't seem to be getting you, Red, as fast as it is me."

"It is," Red answered. "I feel as if I had the weight av the world on me chest. Jimmie, alanna, 'tis ye who have been always to me, like a—like a—there now, I do not know the words I want. Ye know how I feel, Jimmie."

"It's always been you and me, Red, in the last analysis," Jimmie answered gently. "Take it easy—old kid. We will—go—"

"Maybe-so ye think now that I'm afraid to go, ye half-sized portion av a shrimp?"

Jimmie laughed. "I know you are—you red-headed ape. I can hear your teeth chatter and—and—no, Red, you're not—"

"The wall! The wall!" shouted Red, his flash light steady on the wall to the left of them. "Jimmie! Come to! Heads up, Jimmie!" he pleaded. "Here they come! Are ye wid me, Jimmie?" His Colt was out and ready.

Jimmie Cordie, already relaxing against the wall, raised his head and with a terrible effort that took all he had of gameness, shook off the feeling of suffocation. He pulled himself straight, a smile on his lips, his Colt .45 in his hand.

"I'm right beside you, Red," he said clearly and distinctly.

Almost half of the stone wall on the left had slipped noiselessly back and now the light was like the gray of dawn.

Hsai's man who was in charge of the gas tank had made a mistake. He had figured the gas that had gone in had made the men in the room unconscious. It would have done so with the ordinary man, but both Red Dolan and Jimmie Cordie were in the pink of condition, as they were always from clean hard living in the open.

This man was a European chemist who after the war had taken service with Hsai's War Brother, the late un-lamented K'ung. There is no question but that he knew gases and how to produce them, but what he didn't know—and it cost him his life—was the physical stamina of Red Dolan and Jimmie Cordie.

He had instructed the men that now massed in the opening to hold their breaths while they ran in and got the two men who by all laws of chemistry should be fully unconscious. As they waited for the side wall to slide back the chemist began calmly disengaging the tubes from the tank of gas in the corridor outside of the room.

Quite a little of the temple had fallen in, here and there, heaping loose stone and timbers. The part that Jimmie and Red were in was like a series of big and small caves.

THE CHINESE started in, four of them, the rest standing in the opening or just back of it. Before their eyes could get adjusted to the darkness enough for them to be sure they saw the two standing figures, the room seemed to rock with the detonations of the heavy Colt .45s.

Red fired three times and Jimmie once, and the four Chinese pitched forward on their faces. The powder-smoke mingled with the remains of the gas, which luckily for Red and Jimmie was not of an explosive nature. The men still in the doorway let out a yell of terror and ran back along the corridor on either side.

"Outside, Red!" Jimmie panted, staggering forward.

As they reached the opening there was a swift rush of men from both left and right. Hsai had announced that the foreign devils must be taken uninjured and that if hurt, the men responsible for it would be tortured to death; he had added that if the foreign devils were caught and then escaped, the same thing would happen.

It was lighter outside the door and the Chinese in the party assigned to aid the chemist could see that Jimmie was very weak and that the bigger man with the red hair was also swaying. Knowing Hsai and knowing also that the foreigner in charge of them would report any hanging back, they rushed in from both sides, bare-handed, relying on their wrestling skill once they got to close quarters.

That the deadly guns in the hands of the two men would no doubt wound or kill three or four of them, they knew, but that death was much preferable to the one that Hsai would hand out.

Red had reloaded as he started for the door and now, as the rush came he felt Jimmie Cordie's back come against his, as it always did in a tight place and he yelled a wild Irish yell of the love of battle. "Give 'em heck, Jimmie!"

With Jimmie Cordie in full possession of his mental and

physical powers, the fight would not have lasted nearly as long. Slighter than Red and not nearly as heavy, he was like a black panther of the jungles of Brazil in quickness and strength.

Red emptied his Colt, holstered it, unslung his thirty-thirty rifle and began using it as a club. As he reached for it, he felt Jimmie's back slowly slip from his, but at the same time he heard the *pow-pow-pow* of Jimmie's Colt. Slower by far than his but still going.

Red turned and straddled Jimmie, who was holding his body off the stone floor with his left hand, firing up at the sea of faces and bodies that to his fading senses seemed like phantoms. If Red was fighting before from sheer love of fighting, now he began to fight like a buffalo cow in defense of its calf.

He charged the Chinese coming in at Jimmie, and the lighter Chinese went down under the crashing blows from the rifle stock like pins in a bowling alley. Red cleared Jimmie's front in that one charge, started after two or three that ran, stopped, turned and charged back on those that were left in his own territory.

They did not wait to receive him. The torture Hsai had promised was farther away, in that moment, than this red-headed devil who was bigger than any two of them and who had plainly gone mad. He was very close and coming closer, so they ran.

As they did, Red whirled around again and started back toward Jimmie who was trying to get up using the wall for support.

"Wait," Red commanded, "I'll carry ye."

FROM AROUND the corner on Jimmie's side swiftly stepped the chemist. In his hand he held a Luger pistol and as Red spoke, he calmly raised it and fired point-blank at Red's right shoulder. Both Red and Jimmie, in the split second it took to see the action, knew that he was deliberately trying to cripple Red, not kill him.

As the man shot, Jimmie Cordie stopped trying to get up, slipping back to the floor, raised his Colt and put a .45 caliber bullet squarely between the eyes of the man who had sneered as he shot at Red. Hsai's chemist had paid in full for his mistake.

As he fell, Jimmie said, "That's my last shell, Red. Load this gat for me."

"Wait till I load me own," Red answered, dropping the rifle, the stock of which was shattered. "I'll do the family fightin' fer the both av us until ye come out of it."

"He got you in the shoulder, you big ape. Load this gat, then help me up. Bleeding much, Red?"

"Naw, 'tis nothin'. Gimme the Colt. Now, can ye walk, Jimmie darlin'?"

"I don't know. Give me a hand up. Holy cats, that gas sure made me—yeah, I can walk. Put your hand under my left arm. I'm getting better every minute. We'll go around the corner where that bird came from."

Red transferred his Colt to his left hand and slipped one brawny hand under Jimmie's left arm.

"What the heck is it all about. Jimmie?"

"Damned if I know. Some gent had it in for us and played spider and fly."

"Has he got the rest, do ye think?"

"I don't know that, either. If he has, you and I will—I can't talk much, Red. Wait till we get outside. My gosh, the air feels good."

Jimmie drew one or two deep breaths, then straightened up. "All right, Red. Let's go. I'm much better."

As he said it they came to what at one time had been a room beside the one they had been in, backing up to it from the rear. On the floor close to the wall was a steel tank, a little pump at the base and a tube running from the top of the tank into the wall.

"That's what he was sending the gas in from," Jimmie said as he leaned against the wall for a minute. "Why the hell and high water he didn't put us clear under is—well, for Pete's sake!"

Red had seen a row of swords against the wall, left there by the Chinese that had started in after them.

As Jimmie spoke Red was over to the swords. "Come and get ye wan, Jimmie."

JIMMIE LAUGHED, not a very strong or full-chested laugh, but a laugh just the same. Red heard it and looked up. "So, 'tis back ye are. That time I felt the back av ye go away from mine—Mary Mother! I thought ye was gone!"

"Never mind what you thought. Pick out the one that appeals to you and let's go. There's a good-looking one over in the corner, Red. That one with the jade hilt."

"Tis too light," objected Red. The fact that they were in some kind of a series of rooms underground in an old Chinese temple and without question surrounded by enemies, and the added fact that he had a bullet in the shoulder, made no difference to Red. Jimmie was up on his feet and able to laugh, and Red had some swords to choose from; and that was all that Terrence Aloysius Dolan needed at any time.

"Listen, you big red-headed—"

"The same to ye"—Red interrupted absently with a sword in each hand, weighing them and considering the beauty of the hilts—"ye shrimp av the world."

"Oh, my sainted Aunt Maria!" Jimmie said, sitting down on a fallen stone. "You and your darned swords! Well, make it snappy, Mr. Dolan. The Yid and the Bean are probably trapped and the good Lord knows what has happened to the rest by this time. Pick your sword out and let's go."

"If ye had the choice av 'em, now," Red said, "which wan av these two would ye take, Jimmie, alanna?"

Jimmie laughed, a real laugh this time. "You can't be beat. Red, do you realize for John's sake that we are liable to get an attack any minute, or that this darn roof might fall in on us or what-not? And here you are picking out swords."

"And why not, ye pink-gilled shrimp? What attack could them scuts bring that we could not slap outta the way now that ye are all right. The bullet in me shoulder is in the muscles only.

'Tis sore I feel up there and some stiff, and that's all. Why should I not pick me a sword?"

"Go ahead and pick it, old kid," Jimmie answered cheerfully. "I'll wait. The sight of you jumping over me on that last charge of yours amply repays me for a little wasted time now, Mr. Dolan. Tell you what—cut the Gordian knot, take 'em both. I'll pack one for you."

" 'Tis a fine idea," Red answered promptly, "and well worthy av ye, Jimmie darlin'. Are ye fit to travel?"

"I am."

Red handed Jimmie one of the swords. "You take this wan. Wait, give me your 30-30 to carry."

Jimmie took the sword in his left hand after Red had slung the rifle over the unwounded left shoulder.

They walked slowly through the mass of corridors, now more like tunnels, and through many rooms, some big, some small; but nowhere did they find any opening to the sunlight.

"What the hell kind av dump is this?" Red complained finally. "In and out and in and out, then round about and up and down."

"It's a cinch there is some way out," Jimmie answered. "The Chinese came in and they brought the gas tank in. Also, Mr. Dolan, there is a certain amount of light; but of course that may seep in through the cracks. If we can find a pick and shovel, you can start straight up, Red, and dig us out."

"And if I had a bucket av water in hell I could get a million dollars a cup for it," grunted Red who didn't care much about being underground or in any way penned up.

Jimmie laughed. "Has Ah lived to see de day dat Misto' Dolan's goat am jumpin' 'round and 'round?"

"Ye have not," Red grinned, "and well ye know it, Jimmie Cordie. Only 'tis outside I'd rather be, and so would ye and well ye know it also, ye—"

They were in a fairly big room, into which they had crawled over a pile of fallen material that closed the entrance to within two feet of the top.

Before Red uttered whatever blasphemous pet name he had in mind, a voice with an English accent called out, "I say, you chaps, go back through the doorway and turn to the left, then climb the stairs and push up on the rock that covers them. I couldn't budge the thing."

CHAPTER VIII

A KINDRED SPIRIT

THE VOICE SEEMED to come from the ceiling. Before the second word was spoken both Jimmie and Red had their Colts out and ready. Once more Red felt Jimmie's back to his and this time it felt firm.

"Oh, I say!" the voice went on. "It's nothing like that, really. I'm in the same bally position myself and I haven't a weapon of any kind, you know. Please hurry, some of K'ung's men may be along any minute and jolly well scragg the three of us."

"What now, Jimmie?" Red demanded.

"Well, we better accept the gentleman's invitation. We can't do much else, Red," answered Jimmie calmly. "It may be another trick, but for the moment, who are we to be choosey?"

"There is no trick," the voice assured, "word of honor. I say, you fellows better do what you Yanks call 'make it snappy.' The place literally swarms with K'ung's men."

"Which, of course, you are not," answered Jimmie. "All right, Mr. Voice, we shall go and push the rock up for you."

"And if ye are foolin' us," Red answered grimly, "and I get the two hands av me on the neck av ye, I'll twist it like a—"

"Don't threaten, Red," Jimmie chided, "unless you are in a position to do something."

"I said 'if,' didn't I? Do ye want me to boost ye up, Jimmie?"

"No, I can make it. I'm all right now. This double-damned sword of yours is in my way, that's all."

They climbed back over the pile in the doorway and after three or four paces found a flight of stone steps. They ran up about ten or eleven feet and seemed to end at a stone floor.

"All right," Jimmie called, as he and Red got as high as they could, "Here we come! Get that big back of yours against it, Red, and shove."

Red obeyed, in spite of the bullet in his shoulder that was making it sore and stiffer than he would admit. Jimmie, in the small crowded space, managed to get his shoulder under the stone also and together they shoved up. It gave slowly and Red grunted as he put all his strength into the push up. As it tilted, a pair of hands appeared over the edge and in a moment more, the stone went up and back like a trapdoor.

"Righto," the voice said cheerfully. "Here, give me your hand."

"Get out av the way," Red answered, still breathing deep from the exertion. "Jimmie and me have got up outta worse holes than this widout help."

Red came up like a big grizzly bear coming out of his den and turning, even before looking to see who had helped them, took Jimmie Cordie's outstretched hand. Out came Jimmie's one hundred and seventy-five-pounds like a jack-in-the-box.

THE SLIM, boyish-looking man dressed in soiled flying clothes chuckled as Jimmie's feet hit the floor.

"I say," he remarked to Red, "you are strong, what, what? Coming to grips with you would be like trying to outhug a polar bear, wouldn't it?"

Jimmie Cordie looked at the young man, whose clean-cut face was unmistakably English, and grinned. "Granted that Mr. Dolan is the strongest man in the world, where do we go from here?"

"First we'll put the jolly old stone back, what?"

Without a word they all stooped to the stone and turned it back. As it went into place Red straightened and demanded:

"And now, who the hell are ye, and what are ye doing here?"

"At the minute, the same as you are, old dear," the young man replied with a grin. "Dodging K'ung's men. I say, was it for you that our chemist friend was turning on the gas?"

"K'ung's men?" answered Red. "That scut has no men, me bucko wid the flyin' panties on. 'Tis dead he is, and a lot av his men wid him."

"K'ung dead? Since when? Then who— I say, you chaps are not by any chance trying to spoof the old man, are you? There isn't much time."

Jimmie laughed. "Let's sit down for a moment. There's a cross-fire here."

"Not here; come to my diggin's. We can see in every direction from there. I say, this is news to me. Is Hsai in control now?"

"We don't know the gentleman," answered Jimmie as they started. "K'ung is very, very dead, though. He was killed at Meng Wu by machine gun fire. Who, by the way, is one Captain Yao Wu?"

"He is one of the officers of the staff of Hsai, K'ung's war brother," answered the young Englishman promptly. "You know him?"

"Fairly well," answered Jimmie with a grin. "We met him personally a day or so ago. K'ung we only saw once or twice at a distance, but we heard quite a lot about him, haven't we, Red?"

"We have—and none av it good about the omadhaun, Jimmie darlin'," answered Red. "How long does it take to get out av here?"

"Not long—from where I hole up," answered the young man. He had been looking first at Red, then at Jimmie as they walked along, and then said: "I say! You're Red Dolan and Jimmie Cordie!"

"That's right," agreed Jimmie. "I'm Jimmie Cordie, and that small boy on your left is Red Dolan."

"My word! I thought you were, when you began speaking to each other. I've heard about you chaps ever since I landed in the Orient. I wish that I had—"

"What's the name av ye?" interrupted Red as they climbed some more steps this time that ended at a landing above.

"I'm John Cecil Carewe; and until I resigned to come and fly for this rotter K'ung, I was flight commander of the Essex squadron. I say, I'm glad to have met you chaps, and— Here we are at my chambers—not bad, what?"

"Darned good," answered Jimmie, as he looked around the room they had entered.

IT WAS much higher up in the ruins than the ground floor, and while the roof was caved in on one side, it opened onto the blue sky. In one corner was a stone bench, and in the middle was a larger stone that served as a table. What was obviously more interesting to Red was the fact that the table was covered with things to eat, such as roast chicken and rice cakes, and there were several squat little stones or earthen jugs that evidently held wine.

"Where did you get it?" Red asked as he started for the table.

Carewe smiled. "This is a great place for the ancient and respectable worship of ancestors. They leave all kinds of food. Last week I had roast young suckling pigs and—"

"Give Red the bill of fare after we get out," Jimmie interrupted. "We have friends outside somewhere that are by now getting darned good and fussy about our being away so long."

"Friends! Outside? I say, I thought I heard four shots when I—"

"Ye did?" Red demanded, "Come on!"

"It may have been the Bean and the Yid," Jimmie said. "We better get started, Carewe. You can tell us later."

"I know you chaps know that I'm not afraid, but have you enough men to stand off any attack in force?"

"Have we?" mumbled Red, his mouth being fairly full of roast chicken. "We have, young feller me lad. We have enough, once we are all together, to stand off all the Chinks in China, and then some."

Jimmie grinned. "By that, Mr. Dolan means that we have four other men out there and some swordsmen, also two Brownings. Let's go."

"You have enough if the rest of them are like you chaps," answered Carewe. "I say, are they the other men that you both are usually with? The one called the Yid, and the Bean and—what were the other names?"

"Grigsby and Putney," supplied Jimmie as they started. "Yes, they are all there, or ought to be. The Yid and the Bean started in to do a little searching the same time we did. Red, give Carewe the rifle. You know how to work a Winchester, Carewe?"

"Yes; lever action, isn't it? My word, it feels good to get something in my hand again."

"Here's the belt that goes with it. Give Carewe your belt also, Red. He can take command of the rifle brigade. Got anything here you want to pack?"

"Nothing except what I stand in. I say, could I call you Jimmie and Red?"

"Ye can," answered Red, picking up a whole chicken, much to Jimmie's amusement. "Quit laughin', ye scut. I'm takin' this to Putt. He loves 'em."

"So does the Yid. Take two of them, why don't you?"

"How can I, wid dis sword and me Colt? Well, I might, at that." Both Jimmie and Carewe roared as Red tucked two chickens under his left arm.

"Lead the way—Jonathan," Jimmie said gravely to the Englishman. "The commissary is all hooked up."

AS CAREWE led, Jimmie told him of K'ung's assault on Chieh-yu's city, of their part in it, of the trap that had been set there, and how he and Red at least had fallen into it. When he finished, Carewe started in.

"I came out to fly for K'ung because the blighter offered more pay for a year than I could draw in six at home. One day I ran out of petrol and landed to get some near the city of Shangtow.

I went in and got some, fussed around for an hour or so, and then took off. I got home all right, and told K'ung what caused the delay. About a week after that there was a surprise attack that very nearly captured the city, and who do you think it was made by?"

"Seeing you here," answered Jimmie with a grin, "my first guess is that it was made by the War Lord of Shangtow."

"C'rect," answered young Carewe with a grin. "And what made it worse, old dears, was the fact that it came down through a pass that K'ung thought only he and his War Brother Hsai and a few higher officers knew about."

"Including Mr. John Cecil Carewe, his flyer," supplied Jimmie.

"Double c'rect this time," answered Carewe cheerfully. "Then what happened, Mr. Fortune Teller?"

"The chief of the flying department was placed under grave suspicion, and, hearing about it, took on the well-known lam?"

"C'rect as far as the first part goes. What is this lamb thing? I—there was no lamb connected with it, to my knowledge."

"Lamb thing? Oh, I see. In the language as she is spoke by Yanks, Jonathan, l-a-m—not l-a-m-b—means to run. You take it on the lam—you run, see? A lamster, a man who runs. The same as 'make your elegant.' Is that clear to you?"

" 'Tis way back ye are, ye scut," Red announced through a mouthful of chicken.

"Why, I think it is," Carewe answered. "Quite expressive, what? Lam, run; elegant, run also. But to get back to our muttons—my word, there's a real pun, what? See, lam-lamb—mutton. Not bad, what?"

"Darned good," answered Jimmie gravely. "But to get back, as you say, what happened to you?"

"Why, just as you guessed. The good War Brother Hsai and I never—er—took tea together; and when the attack was repulsed he suggested to K'ung that I had tipped off the path to the War Lord of Shangtow. I pointed out that if I had done so, I would hardly have come back and told them of my visit, but K'ung said that was just what I would do to throw off suspicion. Cagey chaps, these Chinese, what?

"I went back to my quarters, leaving K'ung and Hsai to argue it out, and when I reached there I found one of the palace officers whom I had chanced to do a favor. He told me that Hsai had persuaded K'ung to order my arrest, to be tortured until I confessed. So, from where I stood, I—took it—on the lam. Ha! That's neat, what, what?"

Both Jimmie and Red laughed with the gay, reckless-eyed young flyer, whom they had both promptly accepted after the first look.

"I made it out of the city after trying for my bus and failing. I holed up in the woods all day and at night I traveled toward the river. I got as far as the temple here and was resting up, having found the food and what not. Then I saw what I thought were K'ung's men coming, so I dug in a little deeper. When I smelled gas I knew that the chemist—whom I didn't like either—must be around somewhere, so I started to do a little scouting. I was going to fog up his giddy game if I could. I heard you chaps underfoot and peeked down through a crack. So there you are, old beans."

"Supposin' ye would have run onto some av them Chinks wid swords," demanded Red with a grin as he waved a chicken leg. "What would ye have done, me foine banty, widout a sword or a gun?"

"Tried for one of theirs," Carewe answered promptly, "or—what the deuce was it?—Oh, yes, or taken it on the lam. By George! I'm getting fair at that talk, what?"

"You are," Jimmie answered as they suddenly stepped out into the open air. "This isn't the side we came in on."

"This is the south side. You must have come from the west, the river side. We can swing around."

A SMALL party, ten or twelve Chinese, burst from the timber, not more than a hundred yards away, and charged. They were armed, this party, and dressed in the nondescript uniforms of the Army of the North. Four or five stopped for a moment and blazed away with their army rifles, but, as usual, the muzzles were more or less pointing up in the air.

"The nerve av them scuts," Red growled as he carefully laid his chickens down and drew his Colt. "If the chickens get dirty I'll be as mad as—"

Pow-pow-pow-pow-pow!

Carewe raised the 30-30, a happy smile on his face, and Jimmie, as he saw that expression, smiled also. He had sensed that the young Englishman was as game as the breed he came from, but he had not seen him in action. Carewe calmly unloaded the magazine, then lowered the rifle to reload. An expression of sorrow blended with deep disappointment took the place of the smile as he saw that after he reloaded there would be no more bandits to shoot at.

"I say," he protested. "You chaps shouldn't try for them all with revolvers, you know."

"And what were ye doin' wid that Winchester?" demanded Red sternly. He had also seen the little smile on Carewe's lips. From that minute on, the young Englishman was counted as one of Red's friends. "Playin' ring-around-the-rosy wid them, ye small-sized portion av nothin'?"

"You took a little more than your share, Jonathan," Jimmie added.

Carewe laughed and finished his reloading. "I've heard about what you chaps could do with a gun," he said, "and now I've seen it. My word, what shootin'!"

"Who was them Chinks?" asked Red as they started.

"I don't know. The woods are full of disbanded armies and all that. Probably a bunch that just arrived from somewhere. They saw us and thought they would look us over."

"Well," said Red grimly as he tucked his chickens under his arm once more, "they did it."

The three men walked around the ruins, not slowly, but in no hurry whatever. If hungry eyes watched them from the timber, there was no attack. What had happened to one party was more than enough to make others confine themselves to just watching.

In about ten minutes they came to the place where Captain Yao Wu's body lay almost alongside of Hsai's decoy who had paid for his mistake with his head. Jimmy looked at the body.

"Four holes—that means that the Yid and the Bean got back," he said slowly; "unless George and Putt fired twice—and they wouldn't need to. They found out that this bird knew something he wouldn't tell—or he did tell and then made a break."

"Here's the shells," Red announced as he picked up four empties. "Wan here and wan there and two close together."

"Fair enough, Red. Well, here it is, as I dope it. Something happened that made them suspect Yao Wu. He tried to get away, or at any rate did something that made them all crack down on him at once."

" 'Tis right ye are, ye scut," answered Red. "Here is the Colt ye lent him on the junk."

"He started to draw, and they let him have it. Now turn that bird's head over, Red."

Red carefully put the chickens down and did as ordered. The head of the Chinaman slain by Shih-kai was hanging to the body by a thread of flesh, face down. Red lifted it for a moment, then let it drop.

" 'Tis the wan that went down the path wid us," he announced.

"That's right. Well, that simplifies matters. He made some break, or told, and Yao Wu tried to—"

"Make his elegant," interrupted Carewe, without meaning at all to be flippant in the presence of death.

"That's right, John. He tried to make his elegant," Jimmie concluded gravely, knowing in what spirit the young English flyer meant it. "The fact that the bunch has pulled out means that they have got it in some way that we are supposedly being taken to the city. Only thing to do is to catch up with them as soon as possible. Counting the time we were in the hole and

The Chinese closed in triumphantly

all, they must have three hours start on us. We ought to—we ought—damn this fog! Why, I can hardly see a—"

Jimmie swayed and would have fallen if both Red and Carewe had not caught him.

"What is it?" demanded Red as they eased Jimmie to the ground. "Is he dead? Jimmie, ye damned scut—come to!"

"He's not dead," Carewe answered. "Feel his heart. Overplayed his hand after the gas. He's got to rest, Red, and have absolute quiet. Let's carry him over there where we can make hole up. I've seen that gas work before. By morning he'll be all right, if he lies flat on his back until then."

"He will," promised Red as he lifted Jimmie in his arms. "He will, if I have to sit on the spridhogue all day and all night. You be the army, now, till we get there."

The place Carewe indicated was one of the little outbuildings that had fallen in. It made a perfect little fort, as there was a spring of clear cold water in one corner and more than enough stones lying around to make a roof as well as to fill up the gaping holes in the sides.

Red laid Jimmie gently down on the ground and tucked his coat under him for a pillow, then helped Carewe build the fort.

After it was finished, he sat in the opening facing the north and east, and Carewe sat at a peephole that faced south and west.

"Now let 'em come," Red announced grimly as he lighted a cigarette after passing them to Carewe. "You and me will make 'em keep quiet so that Jimmie can rest, if we have to shoot hell outta all China."

Carewe laughed softly. "Tell me about your outfit, Red," he requested, as he settled back comfortably. Not half as big as Red and bred from a different strain, inside they were as much alike as twin peas in a pod—at least in their reckless daring and contempt for all danger.

CHAPTER IX

PRINCESS OF MANCHU SWORDS

THE PRINCESS CHI HUAN sat beside a little artificial lake in the gardens of the palace at Meng Wu. She should have been at peace with the world in such beautiful surroundings, but she most distinctly was not. As a matter of fact, she was in a very bad temper, this little Manchu princess, and nothing looked at all good to her.

Her maidens and the swordsmen of her bodyguard knew it and were keeping themselves in the background and as inconspicuous as possible. Not that the Princess Chi Huan was feared by them; she was loved by all the city and all of her father's troops, and they all knew that she loved them. But she was a pure-blooded Manchu and was very apt to act like one in the heat of temper.

Her retinue had in mind the old adage, "Out of sight, out of mind," and were acting on it as far as possible. They all knew what the matter was. Two days before, her father, Prince Chieh-yu, had left the city with a regiment or two of crack infantry to demonstrate to two or three lesser War Lords the unwisdom of siding with traitors like K'ung. Chi Huan had wanted to go along, dearly loving anything that even smacked of a fight; but her father had decided that for the moment she had seen enough fighting in the siege of the city. Left at home, she had instantly developed this wrathful attitude.

An old palace officer came up to within ten feet of her and bowed very low. As he approached, he saw the gleam in the midnight black eyes and knew that the little princess's feathers were ruffled. He made the bow extra low.

"O Princess whose smile lights up the world, a youth has come to the palace who craves admission and audience with the Princess Chi Huan."

"A youth who wishes audience with me? Am I to be bothered with the requests of youths? No; refuse him both admission and audience. Furthermore, instruct him sharply as to the proper channels of bringing any matter to my attention; and also— Who is this youth, Ta Ch'ing?"

"His name is Chung, resplendent one. He was in the second class at the school of swordsmen. He is the youth you picked out to go with the Lords with the fast-talking guns."

"Chung! Here in Meng Wu?" The Princess Chi Huan rose swiftly to her little feet. "Bring him to me instantly, Ta Ch'ing. No, I will waive the ceremonious bows. Go quickly."

Five minutes later the boy whom Jimmie Cordie had noticed in his column on the way to the temple stood in front of her. Both he and his clothes looked as if they had been through a hard route. They had indeed, for Chung had started out from where he stood on a bee line for Meng Wu, after the disappearance of Jimmie Cordie. He had come straight to the palace.

"Speak," commanded Chi Huan curtly.

"The Lord with the Flaming Hair and the Black-eyed Smiling One have disappeared," the boy began promptly. "The other Lords killed one who led them into a trap and one other who had helped the traitor. Then the other Lords left for Shun, the city of one named Hsai, to rescue the two Lords who—"

"Start at the beginning and tell me. Speak quickly and do not omit anything. Start from the time the junk sailed."

The boy obeyed, and while of course he had not understood everything, especially the conversation in English, he had a pretty fair version of what had happened. The lovely face of the little princess became set and the black eyes cold as she listened.

At the finish of the boy's story the Princess Chi Huan said: "You will report back to the school of swords. The matter of reward for your services I will take up later. You have my permission to go."

The boy Chung would have given anything he possessed and quite a few years of his life to have asked the Princess Chi Huan to include him in any plans of rescue, but he had better judgment. One does not ask Manchu War Lords or their princesses to change an order; so Chung bowed and retired.

THE PRINCESS CHI HUAN, followed by her maidens and bodyguard, started for the palace. At the entrance she dismissed them with a smile and a friendly wave of her hand. Now that there was something to do, her wrath had fled. Her father's War Brother, Yang, was in full command of the city and the territory it protected, and the princess was going to see him, no matter what he might be doing.

She found him studying some jade that was laid out on an inlaid table. Hearing her light footsteps, he looked up, and his grim, scarred old face became less harsh as he smiled. He rose and bowed.

"You honor me, little flower, by coming to see me. Deign to accept this chair until I may have one brought more suitable for your comfort."

The Princess Chi Huan crossed her hands on her firm young breasts and bowed. "My honorable father would not be pleased to see me sitting down while his War Brother the Lord Yang stands, even if I would so far forget what has been taught me. I ask you to resume your seat, O Lord Yang."

Yang smiled and clapped his hands together once. A piece

of tapestry was drawn back on the side of the room and an officer saluted.

"A chair for the Princess Chi Huan," Yang ordered, and as the tapestry dropped, he continued to Chi Huan: "The jades you see, beautiful one, are of the Kin dynasty. This morning they were brought to me. See," he traced an intricate design with delicate touch. "This always you will see in jade of the Kin.... But you have something to tell me, peerless one?"

A chair was brought and placed beside the princess, but she did not sit down, and Yang also remained standing back of the table.

"Yes, O Lord Yang, who takes the place of my honorable father. It is this. The men who came here and helped him—and you—to defend this city, have been trapped by a cur named Hsai."

"Hsai? He was K'ung's War Brother. May I ask you to be seated, little flower? My insignificant wounds are a trifle painful."

Chi Huan sat down promptly, and as she did, Yang resumed his seat.

"Now, radiant one, tell me," he said.

Chi Huan told him what the boy had told her, and at the finish kept right on with: "We will lead what regiments there are in the city to Shun and take it. If this mongrel called Hsai has even touched them, we will give him Ling-Chi, the death of the thousand cuts."

"No, courageous one. There can be no regiments led from the city."

The Princess Chi Huan stood up. "What?" she demanded hotly. "You do not understand, Lord Yang. I said that the men who had helped us are in danger! The men who took me from the curs that held me prisoner, and brought me back to my honorable father, and to you, my other father, in all safety and honor."

"I understand, little princess whom I love as a daughter. But the order of your mighty father still sound clear in my ears. It was that no troops were to be sent from the city until he returns."

"But this is something that my wise father did not foresee! He would be the first to go.... You held me in your arms when I was a baby. I am the Princess Chi Huan of the Nine Clans—you are the War Brother of the Prince Chieh-yu, my honorable father—I command you to lead his troops to the city of Shun, at once!"

Yang shook his head. "No, gallant little heroine. See, it is war-time, and the hills boil always with enemies. Keen eyes are always on watch. We hold what we have only because those who would take the city and burn and slay know that we are prepared to meet them. That is why your father gave the order. It would require five thousand men to take Shun, and much time. My heart bleeds at the thought of the men who, as you say, helped us defend our city, but until the Prince Chieh-yu returns and orders differently, no men leave the city. In trying to rescue those men, we would expose our own thousands of helpless people to the slaughter."

PRINCESS CHI HUAN had known the grim old Manchu noble from the days when she first began to know anything or anybody, and she knew that any attempt to swerve him from the position he had taken would be like throwing water on a polished steel shield in hopes of breaking it.

She had tried out saying "I am the Princess Chi Huan," and the giving of a direct command more as a forlorn hope than anything else. She didn't think it would succeed, but she was desperate. If he had only gone with her father, she thought bitterly as she bowed.

"I ask your permission to depart," she said softly.

Yang had hard work restraining a smile as he saw the hot flames dancing in her eyes. "You have it, O lovely one in whose veins flows the blood of Aisin Gioro. Do not be wrathful with me. I but obey orders. On the return of your exalted father I will be glad to lead a rescue column. See, little flower, two more days and the Prince Chieh-yu will have returned."

The Princess Chi Huan did not answer, but bowed again and walked out, holding her slim young body as straight as possible, her proud little head well up.

Yang smiled as he sat down and picked up a piece of jade. He thought that the need of rescue was greatly exaggerated, and that if any one needed rescuing it would be Hsai, Yang having seen the white men in action and knowing that the bearers were of the T'aip'ing.

Even if he had thought that the need of rescue was great, he would not have sent troops from the city intrusted to him. He had received definite orders, and come what may, he was going to obey them. He smiled again as he thought of the hot-tempered little princess, then calmly resumed his study of the jade.

Chi Huan walked slowly through the palace, her exquisite lips a tight red line. Jimmie and Red in danger, and she not able to help them? Well, she would help them. That—she began to think in the English she had absorbed at school in Washington—that darned old Yang! She'd show him that she could—

Her cousin, Kwang-si, a first-class man in the school for swordsmen, crossed her line of vision and she at once stopped thinking about Yang. Here was a tried and true confederate. He was a year older than Chi Huan—of the same blood and also general make-up.

Seeing her, he came up to greet her. As he got closer and saw the angry look, he grinned cheerfully. Although in the first-class, his handsome, boyish face was still unscarred, and he looked a good deal like Chi Huan, only in a masculine way.

"What are you laughing at?" demanded Chi Huan.

"Lots of things," he teased, "especially that look on your face. Are you going to slay all in the city, O mighty warrior, or are you going to spare a few? Count me, your cousin, among those you spare, I beg of your—"

"Stop that at once," Chi Huan commanded. "Stop it and take that idiot's grin right off your lips or—or I will not tell you what

I am going to do. I was planning on letting you help me—but now I do not think I will."

"It's off," Kwang-si answered promptly. He was fairly spoiling for something to do, and from past experience he knew that if the Princess Chi Huan had anything on tap there was generally excitement connected with it. Sometimes altogether too much when it came to explaining things afterward to the powers that be.

"Keep it off, then. Come into the gardens. I'll tell you about it there."

"I haven't much time," Kwang-si protested as they walked along. "The class trials start in two hours. I am to fight Ta-hai."

"I do not care with whom you fight. Here is a quiet place to sit down. Now listen, and do not interrupt me, either, as you have a bad habit of doing."

"I won't," promised Kwang-si, as they sat down under a flowering tree.

CHI HUAN told him the news the boy Chung had brought, and indignantly related what happened when she tried to get Yang to send troops to the rescue. Long before she had finished Kwang-si was as much interested as she was.

"I've just decided what to do," Chi Huan announced. "I will go to the War Lord Yo-fei. His city lies close to Shun, and he will do anything I ask."

"You? Go to Yo-fei? But how, Chi Huan? The country between here and there is up, and there are many bands of bandits—"

"Of course," Chi Huan interrupted, which she had told him was a bad habit, "if you are afraid to go you need not." She looked at her cousin calmly, her lovely eyes impassive.

"You mean that you and I—we couldn't make it, Chi Huan. You know I am not afraid, but—"

"There will be much honor and glory to be written in the

scrolls of our house if we are the ones that make payment for a debt owed."

"That is true," he answered, his eyes shining. "I will go. The hills are no place for a—" He was going to say "girl," but the expression in her eyes made him change his speech. "It's best that none go but swordsmen."

"If I do not go," Chi Huan said very firmly, "then no one goes. I know that you were going to say 'girl,' Kwang-si. I can climb the hills as well as you can and am as good at swordplay also—that is, I would be if my wrist were a little stronger," she confessed. "No, it is my expedition. Is the first class at liberty after the trials?"

"Yes. Not all, but most of them. Those that win, at any rate. See, Chi Huan, we could whisper quietly to those of our House and—"

"And to those of the House of Wang who owe us allegiance. Do it, Kwang-si. We will leave the city at the first darkness, one by one, and meet at the shrine on the hill."

"Splendid," her cousin agreed. "That will give us twenty swords anyway. We can cut our way through any who try to stop us from reaching Yo-fei."

"We will go; and the Lord Yo-fei will lead his troops to rescue Jimmie and Red and the rest. My honorable father did not order me not to leave the city." The princess was jubilant.

CHAPTER X

A RESCUE THAT MISFIRED

IT WAS DARK, about ten o'clock at night, when the little party started away from the shrine. The princess Chi Huan was dressed exactly the same as the Manchu youths; her hair was tightly coiled and tucked under a cap.

Twenty swords in all, counting the princess as one. None

of them over seventeen and all, with the exception of herself, members of the first class in the school of swordsmen. Each boy had the keen sword presented by the Master of Swords after the trials that afternoon. Chi Huan also carried a sword in her silken sash—a smaller, ceremonial sword, but a real weapon just the same.

There were guns in Meng Wu, plenty of them, but they were heavy army rifles, and guns and cartridges alike were closely guarded. Every Manchu prefers swords, having practically been born with one in his hand. The use of the sword was formerly the better part of Manchu education, and is to a great extent to-day, in the North. Guns and shells are scarce in the hills, and swords are many.

They went like shadows down the hill on the side away from the city. This was an old game to them all, playing countrymen and bandits in the hills in the evenings. When they reached the level, they entered the timber, fading into the thick second growth like lean young panthers. From then until dawn, they went steadily toward the city of Yo-fei without any stopping, Chi Huan demonstrating the fact that she was not boasting when she had said, "I can climb the hills as well as you can."

She could—and slide down the next one, also. Twice they skirted flickering campfires in the distance and once almost ran on to a big party of Chinese bandits, marching without patrols or scouting parties ahead or on the flanks. The Manchus lay hidden in the timber on the side of the pass and watched them go by, with scornful eyes.

Just as it was getting fairly light, they stopped for a drink at a little spring where two of the paths from the hills joined the one that led into a valley.

"We cross the valley," the Princess Chi Huan announced, "then up the hill on the other side and follow the stream that goes down. That is the way my honorable father and I came when we visited Yo-fei."

"I do not like it," a slim young Manchu said. "This valley is all in the open and the ruined temple of Lun Yu where Hsai set his trap is just across on the right side. There are many masterless men who use the ruins as headquarters. My father has told me tales about them. If we cross now in the light we will be seen and attacked. It is better to—"

"You question our safety, Liu?" the princess asked silkily.

It was the same as asking if he were afraid. She knew that he wasn't and so did the rest, but she flung the taunt to spur him forward.

The Manchu youth reacted as a thoroughbred horse would at the touch. His head went up as he answered haughtily, "I am Liu of the House of Yin, O Princess of the Nine Clans. I question your safety, not mine. I was going to suggest that we skirt the valley, thus avoiding delay which would come if we were attacked."

"What! You question my safety? Because I am a girl! I am not to be considered as a girl while on a—"

"Swords!" shouted Kwang-si. "A circle, two deep! Around the Princess Chi Huan! Quickly, brothers!"

HIS KEEN eyes had picked up the glint of steel among the trees on his right. As he shouted, from right, left, and rear ran groups of Chinese swordsmen, each group outnumbering the Manchus that instantly formed the circle and faced them courageously. The Chinese, outnumbering their foes more than three to one, formed a larger circle inclosing the Manchu ring, and with a yell started in.

"Stay inside," Kwang-si commanded as the Princess Chi Huan drew her sword and tried to get past the youth who stood in front of her and into the first line.

"I won't!" she answered hotly. "Step to one side, Yi-yan."

The boy addressed made no effort to obey. He did not intend to do so, nor did any of the rest. To go gayly in the woods or on an expedition with the Princess Chi Huan was one thing, and to let her expose herself to swordplay in deadly earnest was another.

In spite of her efforts the princess could not get by the second line before the Chinese closed. The first-class men took their stand as they had been taught in the school and awaited the attack, their young faces calm.

Some of the Chinese outdistanced their comrades and hit the line first. Those who made that mistake went down under the lightning-fast cut that followed the easy, graceful-looking parry.

The Chinese leader had seen Manchu swordplay before and recognized it now. He knew if they were going to capture the youths to sell as slaves, be had better use caution in attack. The bandits were older men and much heavier, and the leader figured that once he broke the circle, by using two or three men to each Manchu, he could come out with at least a few of them still alive.

His men stopped running in, formed, and came in a compact charge. The Manchus met it without a single backward step being taken, and the first eight or ten men in the charge went down, but the sheer weight of it broke the circle.

There was a mad swirl of lighting and the Chinese drew off. The leader was finding it not an easy matter to take alive a Manchu who had a sword in his hand. It was like trying to pick up a rattlesnake in August with the bare hands and not get bitten.

Now the odds were much more even than before. Of the Manchus fifteen were left as they formed another circle around the Princess Chi Huan, who, when the first one had broken, had charged eagerly into the mêlée.

A Chinaman had cut at her, to have the blow warded off by Kwang-si who was beside her. As his sword darted in to reach the man's throat, the Princess Chi Huan had sputtered like an angry little wild cat. "T-take your own! He was mine!"

Kwang-si was too busy with the next man to pay any attention to her words, and she ran over to where Liu of the House of Yin, not quite sixteen, was engaged with two Chinese, showing that deftness with sword and footwork to keep them apart which was afterward to make him a master swordsman.

Whatever the leader had originally planned, there was no

attempt now to disarm the Manchus. His followers fought to kill, knowing it was a case of kill or get killed.

One of the Chinese drew off and crossed blades with the Princess Chi Huan. He had no idea that she was a girl and it would not have made any difference if he had. He cut at her, about knee-height, intending to let his sword be carried by the parry up to where he could slash down.

Chi Huan seemed to float over the sweeping sword and as she cleared it, she cut with a back-hand stroke that almost severed her opponent's head. Without stopping at all to see the effect of the blow she ran to the next man, who was trying to get in on a little circle that had three of the Manchu youths surrounded.

Some one saw her and yelled a warning. The Chinese turned and his heavy sword came forward to meet her lighter blade. He was tall and gaunt, with a reach of arm almost twice as long as the princess, and his sword also was much longer than hers. Kwang-si saw it and with a desperate effort killed the Chinaman he was fighting and ran in.

The cap of the princess had fallen off and her hair had loosened from the tight coils. Now it hung far below her knees in two braids. The Chinese leader, who was still on his feet, recognized her and shouted, "Back, Kao! Back! Do not strike! It is the Manchu Princess Chi Huan! Kill the rest, but she is worth many thousands of *taels* to us! Disarm her."

That was much easier said than done and the man Kao had no time even to try it. Kwang-si was on him, inside of his reach, and Kao had all he could do to protect his own life by raising his sword hilt as guard until he could jump back.

LIU AND one other Manchu broke through the little circle at Chi Huan's side. "Out!" Liu ordered. "Out! This way, princess. To the hills! I am in command and—"

"You are not! I am in command. I will not go—O brave sword, Kwang-si! See, Kwang-si has killed the cur who led!"

Four of the Chinese ran up, their swords bloody, evil smiles of triumph on their distorted faces. The three young Manchus, their eyes flaming with joy of battle, actually took a step toward to meet them.

The odds had been too great to start with; of the twenty who had started from Meng Wu, fourteen lay dead on the ground, their young faces as impassive in death as they had been while watching the Chinese charge in. Around them lay the bodies of twice, and in some places three times as many Chinese. The members of the first class of the school of swords had died like Manchu swordsmen, in defense of their princess.

Of the sixty-odd Chinese, eighteen were left, the rest were dead or badly wounded. The Chinese were fresh and the six Manchus were tired, very tired. They had traveled all night and had then fought men much larger and stronger, though less skillful. Kwang-si was back to back with another youth, a little space away from the princess and her two companions. The other Manchu, Tseng, wounded in the right arm, had transferred his sword to his left hand and was fighting from a rock.

"Give me sword-room," commanded the Princess Chi Huan calmly. "We will lesson these curs and then go to Tseng's assistance."

"Get back of us!" Liu ordered.

There came the sharp crack of a rifle from the timber near the spring and the Chinaman nearest the princess fell back, his face curtained in blood.

With it there came the heavier detonations of Colt .45s, so fast that they sounded like a drum roll.

The other three Chinese pitched to the ground, the ones milling around Kwang-si and the other youth fell away, and the ones at the rock striking up from all sides at the young Manchu, Tseng turned to flee.

"Jimmie and Led!" the Princess Chi Huan announced in English. "They have come and lescued us."

From the timber came Jimmie Cordie, Red Dolan and John Carewe, Red in the lead. He ran to the little princess and swept her up in his brawny arms, sword and all.

"Are ye hurted, darlin'? Tell old Red. We saw the fight from the hill and got here as soon as we could. Have the dirty scuts touched ye, alanna? Mary Mother! Is that blood on the arm av ye? Show me the divil that done it and I'll take him apart with me hands. Speak to Red, acushla!"

"I'm all light, Led," Chi Huan answered. "That is not my blood. It is the blood of a cur that I killed. I am vely glad you came. Put me down."

Before he did it, the slim young arms of the Manchu princess tightened around the neck of Red Dolan and her velvet cheek pressed against his tanned rough one.

"We came to lescue you, Jimmie," she announced, "but you have lescued us instead."

"We thank you just the same," Jimmie answered gravely, "taking the will for the deed. From the looks of things, if you had had about ten or twelve more swords, you wouldn't have needed rescuing."

"How did you escape, Jimmie? Wold came that you had fallen into a tlap."

"We did, a bearcat of a trap. Wait until we see if we can do anything for the wounded, then I'll tell you all about it, Chi Huan."

THERE WAS not much that could be done. None of the fallen Manchus was alive. Those of the Chinese who were wounded were made as comfortable as possible and left beside the spring.

Kwang-si, with the help of Red Dolan, Carewe and the remaining five Manchus, laid the bodies out in a shallow cut up on the hillside, covering them with rocks to remain there until they could be removed to Meng Wu for proper burial.

"I am aflaid that my honolable father will be vely angly with me," Chi Huan said as she sat with Jimmie Cordie near the spring. "But when I heald that you and Led were in tlouble I had to come, Jimmie."

"Of course you did," Jimmie reassured her firmly. "Your father will understand. He will be so glad to see you that there will be no room for anger in his heart."

Chi Huan wasn't so sure about that, but she brightened up a little. "I—my healt glieves for the men of my House that have died for me. That is it, Jimmie, more than the anger of my honolable father."

"What better death than to go sword in hand fighting for their princess?" Jimmie asked gently. "They were Manchus, O Princess of the Nine Clans, and they fought and died as their ancestors have done, with a smile of joy on their lips and in their eyes. Their first fight was their last, but what difference does it make when death comes? Their spirits have gone on high to be welcomed with the smiles of the heroes who led the Hordes. It may be that from where they sit looking down on you, their princess, they had much rather see you smile, also, and hear you say, 'You fought and died in all honor for me.'"

Chi Huan nodded her proud little head. "That is light, Jimmie. See, I smile and say it." She looked up. " 'You fought and died for me in all honor'.... Now I feel better. Tell me all about what happened."

Jimmie told her, finishing with, "And when I passed out of the picture, Red and Carewe carried me to one of the outbuildings. I came to, in the morning, and we started for Shun. Red caught the first glimpse of the fight going on down here from the top of that hill and insisted on coming down to take a closer look-see."

"It was vely lucky for us that he did," Chi Huan said. "Now what will we do, Jimmie?"

"Well, it's a cinch we can't take the time to escort you back to Meng Wu. The good Lord only knows what is happening at Shun. George and the rest probably think we are hidden away somewhere, and are raising hell and high—I beg your pardon, Miss Iron Hat."

"I am not Missee Ilon Hat," Chi Huan reproved him. "Jimmie, we will go with you to Shun and make a—a sulvey?

No, that is not the wold. Make an obselvation, that is it. Then we can go to Yo-fei and get help flom him."

"Do you think one of the boys could make it back to Meng Wu?"

"Why, yes, Jimmie. Any one of them could, I think."

"Well, you send one of them back to say that you have made contact with us and are all right. That we are headed for Shun, and after that for Yo-fei. I don't care very much about packing you along, but darned if I want to take the chance of your getting back to Meng Wu with five men."

"What?" demanded the princess, now fully recovered, glaring at him. "You don't care about me being—having me—well, I am here, Mr. Jimmie Coldie! And what is more, I am going to—"

Red, Carewe, and Kwang-si came up. "The Princess Chi Huan has just started to tell me that she is going to Shun with us," Jimmie explained gravely.

"Where else would herself go but wid us?" demanded Red in surprise. "Sure the gas has made ye goofy, Jimmie Cordie."

"I will go with you, Led," Chi Huan announced loftily, "and not with Jimmie Coldie."

" 'Tis together we'll all go, acushla. Jimmie is teasin' ye, darlin'. 'Tis ye that he loves like—"

"He has a vely stlange way of showing it," retorted Chi Huan, still angry.

"You misunderstood me, O Princess of the Nine Clans," Jimmie interrupted with a smile. "I said that I did not care to have you along, meaning that we were going into danger and were not hooked up very well to protect you. As far as you personally go, I am very glad to have you along, because, as Red says, I love you like the dickens, no foolin'."

Few people were proof against the smile of Jimmie Cordie, and Chi Huan was not one of them. She smiled promptly back at him. "I love you, too, Jimmie. I was vely silly not to undelstand how you meant it."

"Now that peace reigns once more," Jimmie said, "let's hold

a council of war. First, O Princess of the Manchu, allow me the honor of presenting to you John Carewe, an Englishman."

CHAPTER XI

ON THE KNEES OF THE GODS

THERE WAS NO further attack on the hilltop shrine in the city of Shun during the day. Hsai had watched the digging of trenches from a roof top, and as he started down had ordered, "Let there be no further attack. The foreign devils lack food. Sooner or later they must come down or starve. Place troops around the hill far back and hold men in reserve."

His officers were glad enough to hear that order, because they knew that to get their men to go up the hill they would have to go with them.

Darkness came, and then, while the T'aip'ing were on watch, it began to get light. Shih-kai was stooping to arouse Grigsby when one of the T'aip'ing warned softly, "One crawls up the hill. Shall I slay?"

"No," answered Shih-kai, touching Grigsby's shoulder. "Let him come in, then disarm him."

Two minutes later a boy stood in front of Grigsby and the others, who had wakened like so many cats at a slight touch. It was Kwang-si, the Manchu cousin of the Princess Chi Huan.

"Do you speak English?" Grigsby asked.

Kwang-si nodded and smiled proudly, "Vely well, honolable captain. Led Dolan and Jimmie Coldie and the Plincess Chi Huan say quit visiting and come out and join them and make it vely snappy, they want to go home."

"Thanks for the invitation," Putney said with a dry grin.

"For de love of Mike," the Yid sputtered. "Den dey vas out all de time, ain't it?"

"Where are they?" Grigsby asked.

"On other side of the liver. Catchee man know fold, make him tell."

"I don't get that. Are we to catch a man that knows a ford?"

"No, we alleady catchee one. He tell us light away. Jimmie Coldie say come before molning—no can see us get back in hills."

"Mr. Cordie," said the Boston Bean gravely, "having got us in this jam, is kindly explaining how we are to get out."

Grigsby laughed. Now that he and the rest knew that Jimmie and Red were safe, the world became once more a happy hunting ground.

"We'll thank Mr. Cordie when we get there. No use of waiting to say good-by to Hsai. Let's go—same formation as before. Out and over the wall. You stay with Shih-kai, young feller. What is your name?"

"Kwang-si of the Nine Clans. Can I have one of the little guns?"

"Take my Colt and belt," the Bean said smilingly. "Don't shut your eyes any more than you have to while shooting it."

"No shuttee eye at all," answered Kwang-si proudly. "I am a vely good shot."

The troops stationed on the side where a wall inclosed the palace were all doing what Grigsby had said they would be doing. Most of them were asleep, and those that were awake were huddled together trying to keep warm. The gray dawn is cold in that part of China, and their ill-conditioned bodies were not able to withstand it. There was some little pretense of keeping a guard line, but not much.

Grigsby, seeing this, changed his order and put the T'aip'ing in front. They, snarling T'aip'ing threats, went through the Chinese like a knife through paper, slashing right and left with their keen swords. The Chinese rolled and tumbled and ran out of the way or threw themselves flat on their faces.

Right after the T'aip'ing came the four white men and the bearers of the Brownings. With them went Kwang-si, his Colt going *pow-pow-pow!* first on one side then on the other, as fast as he could pull trigger. Through, over the palace wall, down a wide street and then into the open they went without losing a man.

But the yells and the Colt reports had roused the city, and they had not got halfway to the river before Hsai's men were in pursuit.

"This way! This way!" shouted Kwang-si, running to the right. They reached the river bank, slid down it and went through the water that came shoulder high and fast enough almost to sweep them off their feet. As they scrambled up the other side, a rifle and two Colts began to fire at the first of Hsai's men who had reached the other bank.

THE BEAN was the first up, with his bearers who had clung desperately to the Browning. He saw Jimmie Cordie and Red, with the Princess Chi Huan and a man he did not know, and two or three youths behind them.

He did not wait to say anything, only grinned, waved his hand, and turned to his work. As the gun was set down he began clearing the top of the other bank with it.

The Yid arrived with full equipment, and his gun joined in. Hsai's men, who had lined the high bank, promptly disappeared, and not even a head showed after the first two or three bursts.

"Never mind any wah-wah!" shouted Grigsby. "Get going! They can cross in two or three places above and below. Start from where you are, Jimmie. We've got a half an hour before they can make contact on this side. Not much ammunition left, Jimmie."

They didn't have a half an hour by at least ten minutes. Hsai had more crossings than Grigsby knew about. As the little band reached the top of one of the hills where the path narrowed and turned an abrupt corner, the Yid, who was looking back every so often, yelled, "Oi, dey short-cutted on us! Assistance for de rear guard!"

Up the path and along the sides of two of the near hills that converged into the one they were on, a little lower than the path, came Hsai's troops.

It was a hard place to charge up, and the Chinese did not try it very long. They sought cover on all sides of the path and on the hills. But they stayed right where they were and did not attempt to run back down.

Putney laughed. "The friends we were visiting are coming right along with us, Jeems. What would you suggest now?"

Jimmie looked at the hills, at the path, down at the other side, then grinned. "I can hold 'em from this time on," he announced. "This is the only path leading through, anywhere near. By the time they have climbed eight or ten of those mountains and crossed that valley, you can be well in the hills. Hop along, you gents. Leave me all the belts and—"

"What?" yelled Red. "Leave ye? I'll stay meself, ye scut."

"Hold it a minute," Grigsby said quietly. "We've got plenty of time at the moment, Jimmie. They don't want any of our entertainment up here until they can attack from both front and rear. Let's sit down."

He also had been looking at the hills and the path and knew what Jimmie meant. One man with a machine gun could delay pursuit from those in front until he was dead. To circle and come up in the rear meant that any of Hsai's men doing it would be forced to swing way out, even if they did find other passes in the hills. It would give the party on the hill at least three hours' start, and in the hills that meant everything. But it meant death for the man who acted as rear guard.

Carewe was introduced, the Princess Chi Huan's presence was explained, and then the Yid and the Bean slipped away to the rear on a reconnoitering trip. They came back in a few minutes, and the Yid announced:

"De hills around de valley go straight up and down, mit no paths except at de end of de valley. If ve can make it across ve are in de clear."

Jimmie Cordie laughed. "Go down and explain to our boy-friends that we want time out while we cross. Right here is where we play Custer's Last Stand, with Jimmie playing Custer."

"You're mixed in your history, Jeems," the Boston Bean said. "You mean Horatius at the Bridge. You know, 'Will not the villain drown? But for this stay, ere close of day, we would have sacked the town.' Inasmuch as you have shown your ignorance, I'll play Horatius. Get going, you—"

"We haven't much time, Jimmie," Grigsby interrupted quietly. "Let's dispense with the kidding. If we did not have the Princess Chi Huan along I'd say to start down and give them all we've got until the finish, but we can't take a chance with her. There are only three belts left for the machine guns, and once in the open down there they'd use rifles. But one man here can hold 'em back until the rest get in the clear."

"BUT, GEOLGE," Chi Huan broke in, "I am not aflaid to die. We can lun acloss or—why not stay light here? I sent back a messenger to tell my honolable father or his War Blother that I was going to Shun with Led and Jimmie. They will come and—"

"They could not make it in time, Chi Huan," Grigsby answered. "Probably right now this Hsai is swinging his troops around. Once they get into the valley, we could not hold this place for twenty minutes without plenty of ammunition."

"Then I will go acloss with my swordsmen and wait for you and—"

"Run right smack into some more bandits or what-not. Nothing doing, Missee Iron Hat," Jimmie Cordie said with a grin. "At that, if Shih-kai went with you, we—"

"What?" demanded Red Dolan. "Herself in the hills again wid only a few swordsmen?"

"Pipe down, Red," Grigsby said. "Let's get down to cases. More of Hsai's men are arriving every minute. Here it is, cold turkey. If we send the Princess Chi Huan across first, even if the T'aip'ing go with her, the chance that she could win through to Meng Wu is one in a hundred. Given that she did, we cannot hold this point for more than a couple of hours at the most, and

Hsai would wipe us out once we were in the valley. If we start for the hills now, they will be right behind us.

"Jimmie is right. One man with a machine gun can hold them back until all of the rest get across. Once on the other side, if six men with rifles and Colts, to say nothing of the T'aip'ing and Manchu swords, can't take the Princess Chi Huan home through the hills where no large force can be thrown against them at once, they better call it a day."

"My swolds can hold this path," declared the princess. "They will stay and—"

"Be a good girl, darlin'," Red answered, "and let us men settle it. 'Tis—"

"If we stay here much longer talking about it," Putney said, "it will settle itself. I'll stay and do what Jimmie calls 'play with the neighbors' children.' They are going to try it out in a minute or so. Get going. I'll take the—"

"Ye will?" demanded Red. "And who the hell do ye think ye are, Arthur Putney? 'Tis me that will stay."

"Vait!" The Fighting Yid bowed and smirked at them all. "I have held it an election, und vish to announce de result. I am elected to stay by a majority of von. I ain't got it no von dot vill miss me, und—"

The Boston Bean laughed. "You were elected by fraud, Mr. Cohen, and the result is thrown out. I'll do the—"

"Heads up!" shouted Putney. "Here they come!"

Hsai had started one company up the narrow path, more to see if the foreign devils could still bite than in the hopes of wiping them out. He was doing what Grigsby thought he would—sending a regiment around to get into the valley at the rear.

"Don't use those Brownings," Grigsby ordered, as he raised his rifle.

The sleet of steel-jacketed bullets that swept down the path proved conclusively that the quarry was still very much alive and could fight. What was left of the company ran back down the hill.

"He's started it off," Grigsby said. "You've got to move out promptly, Jimmie. I'll take this over. Bean, I'll take your gun. All right—never mind any sob-sister stuff. You birds all know how much I think of you. Start off, Jimmie, and make it with the well-known snap."

"Not by a damn sight. I got you into this jam and—"

Carewe stepped up, very casually indeed. "I say, you chaps. You are all together, you know, and I'm quite at a loose end. I can handle the Browning like what-for. So I will—"

"Thanks, old man," Jimmie answered, "but it's our hunt. Pull out a little and let us settle it."

"There isn't anything to settle," Grigsby said. "I am the ranking officer here, and I'll take it over, as I have said. Move out, Jimmie."

"We're not in the army now. I am going to—"

"Me right wid ye, Jimmie, ye scut."

"For vy is de argument? Could it be dot I would let it some von else—"

"I've explained once that I am the proper one to—"

"NO USE, George," Putney said, with a quiet smile. "It's a case of 'After you, my dear Alphonse,' all the way around. Better put it on the knees of the Nine Red Gods and—"

"On the knees of the gods," Jimmie said slowly. "On the knees of the— Listen, you birds. We all know that any one of us would stay and all of us think we ought to be the one. Putt just called the turn. We'll put it on the knees of the gods. We'll draw for it, and the man that wins stays. How's that?"

"Jake mit me," said the Fighting Yid.

"All right here," the Boston Bean agreed.

"That solves it, Jimmie," Grigsby drawled.

" 'Tis a brilliant idea ye have once in a while," Red said, "but how are ye—"

"Let Jimmie tell us, Red," Putney interrupted. "It's the only way out, Jimmie. I'm satisfied."

"All right. Here are six cartridges." Jimmie drew six of the 30-30 cartridges from his belt. "I'll scratch one and put 'em in my hat. Each man reaches for one with his eyes shut—and no damn' feeling around for the scratch, either. Reach in, take the first one touched, and out with it. Never mind rubbing your finger-tips, Yid."

"Oi, Jimmie, look at the Codfisher. He is doing it on de pants vare it is—"

"Shuffle them up and then lay them with the scratch down, Jimmie," Grigsby said. "Each man will turn his back while you are doing it; when you call his name he will turn and pick one up. You will take the last one, old kid. I know you birds full well. None of your sleight-of-hand stuff will work that way. The man that stays does so at command of the gods."

"Let me take your knife, Red," Jimmie said.

Red handed him a knife, and Jimmie made a little scratch on one of the shells. While he was doing it, Shih-kai, who was watching the troops below, said softly to the T'aip'ing next to him: "If the Black-eyed Smiling One draws the cartridge that tells him to stay, he will order us forward with the rest. We will go, but only far enough to turn and come back to die with him."

Carewe came up to George Grigsby. "I say, you chaps, I want to be included. It isn't cricket to push me out, I am a man the same as you are, and I can—"

"Well, suh," drawled the Kentuckian, "it's this way, Mr. Carewe. We all know that you are a man; but, like Jimmie said, this is our hunt. We've been together, the six of us, for a right long time, and don't you see that we couldn't let a stranger do what one of us—"

"I see that, but—but—"

"All set," Jimmie called from the little rock on which he had laid out the shells. "Line up, you gents."

Grigsby looked at the slim young Englishman and smiled.

"I'm sorry, old man. It may be that some day you will not be a—stranger to us."

The little Princess Chi Huan sat on a rock, surrounded by her young Manchus, watching with shining eyes. After the protest that her "swolds" could hold the path, she had been silent, sensing that that was what her honorable big brothers wanted just then.

The five big men, all of them calm-faced, lined up, their backs to Jimmie. He called "Red!" and as Red turned and stooped, Jimmie added, "Don't show until we all have them in our hands."

One by one they turned at their names and picked up their shells. Jimmie, who had stepped away a little, picked up the last one. Each man stood with clenched fist outstretched, a smile on his lips and in his eyes.

"All set? Open up!"

Five of the shells were turned in the opened hands and then dropped. Arthur Stuart Putney, Foreign Legion, A.E.F., fighter in the far places, stood as if at attention, his hand as steady as ever, the smile still on his lips and in his eyes. On the shell in his hand there was the scratch of a knife-point.

"All right," he said, as quietly and calmly as ever. "Move out. I'll take your gun, Yid, I'm more used to it. Let's consider it all said. Good-by and good luck. I'll be waiting for you up behind some star."

THE SHELL was in his right hand, and he transferred it to his left as Jimmie Cordie stepped up to him with outstretched hand. "Good-by, Putt," Jimmie said as they shook hands. "It's all said."

Jimmie's face was as impassive as an officer's on parade, but he could not hide the feeling in his heart from showing in his eyes. As he let go of Putney's hand he ordered: "Shih-kai—start your men down. Chi Huan, send your swords right after and go with them. Carewe, you go with the Princess Chi Huan."

"Filst," said the little Princess of the Nine Clans, as she rose and came up to where Putney stood, "I will say good-by to my vely honolable elder blother, who dies that we may live. Good-by, Althur Putney. Your name shall be englaved in lettels of gold on the tablets of honor of the Nine Clans."

The tears made the velvet black eyes misty, and the proud little Manchu hid her face for a moment against Putney's sleeve. Then, before Putney could answer, she followed her swords around the corner of the path that led to the valley.

Shih-kai snarled an order, and as the T'aip'ing came by Putney their swords flashed up in the salute given superior officers.

Red shook hands. "Good-by, Putt. The light will go out av the world widout the quiet smile av ye."

"Keep that red head of yours up and it will be plenty light. Good-by, Red, old-timer."

The Yid was next. "Oi, Putt! For vy didn't it I got de right shell? Good-by, Mistair Good Player in Everything."

"Good-by, Yid. Don't loot any more than possible and quit trying fancy shots."

The Boston Bean stammered as his hand closed on Putney's. "I c-can't say anything, Putt. Always since I have known you I have—damn it all, it's like Jimmie said—it's all been said many times by actions."

Putney smiled. "Good-by, Codfish. I know what you are trying to say."

Carewe had hung back, but now, as he saw that Grigsby evidently wanted to be the last with Putney, he came up with outstretched hand. "I say, you know, it's awfully sportin' of you. You chaps are—are—oh, I say, you know what I mean and all that sort of rot, what, what?" And without waiting for Putney to answer he hurried away.

Putney laughed and turned to Grigsby. They had, in some ways, been closer together than with the rest. Both big men, both more or less silent men, both fighting men from the ground up, and both with the same code. One from the mountains of Kentucky, the other from the green hills of Vermont, but of the same pure Anglo-Saxon breed.

"There's a chance that we will be met by Chieh-yu's men," Grigsby said. "If we are, you may be able to hold out, Putt."

"You won't if you don't get started, old settler. No need of any wah-wah between you and me. I'll hold 'em."

"That's right, Putt," Grigsby drawled. "No need. We'll all pick you up on the one-way trail sooner or later. Good-by."

The two shook hands, each smiling, his eyes calm and looking deep into the shining white soul of the other. Then Grigsby stepped back a foot, came to attention, saluted, and walked around the corner and down the path.

CHAPTER XII

THE GODS DECIDE

THE ROCKS AT the path were so bunched that Hsai's men could not tell whether there were one or two machine guns waiting for them. Coming straight up in the last fifty yards, they would be able to see the muzzles, if they got that far, which they had not succeeded in doing—yet.

Before the retreating party had got halfway across the valley they heard the *rat-tat-rat-tat!* and stopped to listen.

"Von half a belt," the Yid announced as the firing ceased. "Mit no jamming. I vish dot I—"

"Come on!" commanded Jimmie Cordie. "Make your wish afterward. Do a little running. The sooner we get to Meng Wu, the sooner we can come back for Putt."

Before they reached the hills there was another burst of firing, longer this time, then silence as before. Jimmie Cordie stopped and whirled around. Red saw him do it and instantly turned too.

"Steady, Jimmie," Grigsby drawled. "If you were back there, would you want to see any of us come back? Play the game, old kid."

"That's right, George," Jimmie answered through tight lips. "I won't break again."

As they climbed the first steep hill there came faintly to them another burst of machine gun fire, and then, right afterward, rifle fire almost as fast.

"Oi, Beaneater," said the Yid. "He is down to de rifle, ain't it? Und ve are safe in de hills."

"Two things I know already!" rasped the Bean curtly. So curtly that the Fighting Yid looked at him curiously.

"All men must die," said Abraham Cohen slowly, without a trace of an accent. "Would you want a better death than Putney is meeting—for us?"

"No," answered the Bean, "I wouldn't."

"Vell, den," went on the Yid, with a grin once more, his usual accent strong once more, "Vot is de use of cryin', ain't it?"

"Oh, for the love of the angel chorus!" snorted the Bean in a more normal tone. "Get up there with Jimmie or Red. I should have stayed and—"

"You stay? Und you engaged mit Katherine Neville? Vait until I tell her vot you—"

"Go on away from me, Yid, before I bend a gun over your head. I don't feel like—"

"I am going, Codfisher.... You und me is pudners, ain't it?"

"Yeah, boy, all the time, Abie—only I want to—I'm thinking about Putt and—"

"I am thinking also, but—I am going, Mr. Vinthrop!" The Yid moved up to where Jimmie and Red were with the Princess Chi Huan, who was frankly crying as she ran lightly beside Red who had offered to carry her.

After one look at Jimmie's set face, gray in spite of the deep tan, and Red's scowling one, the Yid decided to run, too, and say nothing. He was not hard-hearted, and he really liked Putney very much, but he had not been with him as much as the rest. To the Fighting Yid, Putney was a good first-class fighting man and a companion to have along anywhere. To the rest he was a brother.

TWO HOURS later, as they came to the comb of one of the hills, the T'aip'ing who were out in front almost ran head first into the advance guard of a Chinese regiment. The T'aip'ing took cover like so many quail and Shih-kai ran back with the news. The Princess Chi Huan climbed up on a spur, took one look and slid down in Red's awaiting arms.

"It is my honolable father! Now we will go back and lescue Putt. Cally me to the top, Led, so I can bully them on!"

The Prince Chieh-yu had returned to his city to be told that the Princess Chi Huan and some of the first class of the school for swords was missing. Right after the messenger from the valley arrived with the word that the princess, with Red Dolan and Jimmie Cordie, were *en route* to Shun.

The Prince Chieh-yu ordered out two of his fresh regiments and left for Shun without a moment's pause.

As he came up the Princess Chi Huan, after seeing his smile, threw herself literally into his arms. "I tried to rescue Jimmie and Red," she sobbed, her cheek close to his. "Yang would not go because you ordered him to keep all troops in the city. I am the one to blame for the acts of the youths of—"

"Quiet, little flower. You are forgiven. They obeyed your orders and died for you, that is all. What else could the princess of the Nine Clans do but go to the rescue of her honorable elder brothers?"

"But Putney is not rescued! He is back there holding the curs of Hsai from our trail."

"What?" demanded Chieh-yu, putting Chi Huan down. "I see that he is not here. Go back with the youths, priceless one."

Jimmie Cordie stepped forward. "Putney is holding a path on the other side of the valley. You spoke once of a matter of payment, Prince Chieh-yu. Order this regiment forward with me."

Chieh-yu turned to the colonel of the regiment: "Captain Cordie takes command. Bring your regiment up on the double."

"Jimmie, ye scut," yelled Red. " 'Tis back after Putt ye are going! I'm wid ye, Jimmie darlin'."

"Fair enough. George, no use for all to go. Red and I will get him if—if—come on, you big ape, show me some running for your size."

When they got to the foot of the hill leading up from the valley and started up, still somewhat in advance of the rest, Jimmie and Red heard the *pow-pow-pow* of a Colt. Mingled in with it were rifle shots, and as they neared the top, now on a dead run, they heard excited yells.

"He's holdin''em, praise be to all the good saints!" Red panted as he and Jimmie with Shih-kai and the T'aip'ing, the Manchu colonel and several of the officers with drawn revolvers, called on all they had for the final spurt. "I heard the— God! The Colt av him is still!"

THEY CAME to the top and around the big rock that made the corner just in time to see Putney, bleeding from countless wounds, go down under a pile of swordsmen who were worrying around him like a pack of dogs around a bear.

Down; then the pile heaved up and Putney came up. As he did, a Chinese rifleman standing over to one side, took aim and fired point-blank at him from not more than six feet. Even as he fired, the rifleman fell dead with a bullet from Jimmie Cordie's Colt in his brain.

Red let out a yell that was like that of a maniac and charged down, followed by the T'aip'ing. The attackers looked up the path, yelled in shrill fear, and ran. The Manchu colonel and the officers with him opened fire on them as Red got to Putney. The rifle bullet had hit him square in the chest and spun him around. He saw Red and knew him through the haze. He tried to stop the turn, but couldn't, and fell across the machine gun. Jimmie reached him almost as Red did and lifted him up.

"Jimmie—and—Red," Putney said thickly through the blood

that was trickling out of his gray lips. "I—knew—that you would come eventu—" His head dropped against Jimmie's arm.

Jimmie turned it so that he could see the still face whose lips held the same little smile as always. He looked, then slipped his hand over Putney's heart and held it there for a moment.

Then he laid Putney gently down and stood up. Red was watching him, his face working in spite of his efforts to hold it.

"God receive the soul of a gallant gentleman," Jimmie Cordie said softly.

ABOUT THE AUTHOR

ANOTHER WRITER WHO makes his bow to readers is W. Wirt—a man whose life has been packed with adventures. We asked Mr. Wirt to stand up and introduce himself so that we can all get some idea of what sort of hombre can spin a salty yarn such as this. Mr. Wirt has the floor:

Born—Boston, Massachusetts, 1876.

People on both sides hard-boiled Maine and Massachusetts Presbyterians of strictly English descent. All but one—but that one was a direct descendant of one of Sir Francis Drake's captains. The King of Spain had a standing offer of one thousand golden crowns to the hombre that would present him with "That pirate devil's head." Every once in a while one of the elect breaks out. The rest of the family at once put it down to the old pirate.

My late pa was one of them, all right. I think he had more than his share of the blood. He was a special agent and one of the very few Americans who served in the Secret Service of foreign countries. He went here and there, all over the world, in the oddest places, from northern China to the South Sea Islands, from there to Alaska and way points. Sometimes for Uncle Sam in the Post Office Department; other times for other people.

My education and experience? They are part and part. If there ever was a scrambled one I had it. When I wasn't much bigger than knee-high to a grasshopper my pa began taking me along with him, whenever he could do so safely. I remem-

ber military, private, public and every other kind of school in a dim way. He'd leave me in one somewhere, go and attend to his knitting, then come back and get me, and away we'd go again. But the constant education I received from him regarding the conduct of "an officer and a gentleman" under any and all circumstance still remains vivid in my mind. One month we'd be in England, evening clothes after six as regular as clockwork, down at one of the big estates for the week-ends, then, in a month or a darn sight less, we'd be in some "flop house" as poor broken-down bums—I acting the part of the devoted son who wouldn't leave his poor old ex-con father, and so forth.

After I reached eighteen I worked with him for a good many years, and when he was called to join his venerable ancestors I carried on alone. No matter where I was, in the Orient or anywhere else, I missed him—with his cool laugh in the face of death and his never failing, slow, amused drawl. His favorite weapon was a sawed-off shotgun carrying buckshot. This, of course, was for use in the places where the little yellow and black brothers congregate mostly. I miss him yet, and always will—and that's that.

I have been behind a badge for Uncle Sam some little time and at present am still special agenting, but on my own, seldom going out of the States and not hunting for any trouble at all, having more than my share already. I've had my gun in the ribs and ears of a few jaspers and used to say "Put 'em up!" so darn often that my longhaired partner—now bobbed haired—every once in a while wakes me up with a demand to know if I have any good reason for poking my fi nger in her side and hollering at her in the middle of the night.

Then there have been many times when the reverse English was in force and I did the reaching for the blue sky, promptly and in haste. All in all, I lived and rambled when things were wide open, no blue laws or anything, just help yourself to the mustard if you wanted any. And I am darn glad I did. Man, howdy, you could go over the mountain, in "them" days and see things—and do 'em likewise, if you wanted to.

I and Schley whipped the Spanish fleet together, I as a volunteer and Schley as a regular. There were a few others present, but we did most of it. In the late argument I did some "hush, hush" stuff.

My present standing? Well, been married seventeen years; have two children, boy and girl. Have an old place in Maryland near Washington, a police dog, three or twenty-six kittens and cats, an old "colored lady" named Medora to make the corn bread, plenty good old corn lick—I mean corn licorice—to drink and am "out of commission."

A lot of my old buddies drift through, hang their hats up behind the door and drink my said good old yellow-with-age corn licorice, eat some fried chicken and curse me in all the living and dead languages because I won't let go all holds and go wild-catting over the hills once more. They don't get a rise out of me at all. I'm like the colored man who, when asked if he wanted to make a quarter, replied: "No, suh, I done got me a quarter." All I want is peace and quiet.

THE
ARGOSY™
LIBRARY

SERIES 5 INCLUDES:
* WORTS * SHEEHAN * SERVISS *
* BRAND * PERRY * ROSCOE *
* BEECHAM *
* WIRT * FORSYTH *
* ROUSSEAU *
THE BEST FICTION FROM THE FRANK A. MUNSEY LINE

1. GENIUS JONES by Lester Dent
2. WHEN TIGERS ARE HUNTING: THE COMPLETE ADVENTURES OF CORDIE, SOLDIER OF FORTUNE, VOLUME 1 by W. Wirt
3. THE SWORDSMAN OF MARS by Otis Adelbert Kline
4. THE SHERLOCK OF SAGELAND: THE COMPLETE TALES OF SHERIFF HENRY, VOLUME 1 by W.C. Tuttle
5. GONE NORTH by Charles Alden Seltzer
6. THE MASKED MASTER MIND by George F. Worts
7. BALATA by Fred MacIsaac
8. BRETWALDA by Philip Ketchum
9. DRAFT OF ETERNITY by Victor Rousseau
10. FOUR CORNERS, VOLUME 1 by Theodore Roscoe
11. CHAMPION OF LOST CAUSES by Max Brand
12. THE SCARLET BLADE: THE RAKEHELLY ADVENTURES OF CLEVE AND D'ENTREVILLE, VOLUME 1 by Murray R. Montgomery
13. DOAN AND CARSTAIRS: THEIR COMPLETE CASES by Norbert Davis
14. THE KING WHO CAME BACK by Fred MacIsaac
15. BLOOD RITUAL: THE ADVENTURES OF SCARLET AND BRADSHAW, VOLUME 1 by Theodore Roscoe
16. THE CITY OF STOLEN LIVES: THE ADVENTURES OF PETER THE BRAZEN, VOLUME 1 by Loring Brent
17. THE RADIO GUN-RUNNERS by Ralph Milne Farley
18. SABOTAGE by Cleve F. Adams
19. THE COMPLETE CABALISTIC CASES OF SEMI DUAL, THE OCCULT DETECTOR, VOLUME 2: 1912–13 by J.U. Giesy and Junius B. Smith
20. SOUTH OF FIFTY-THREE by Jack Bechdolt
21. TARZAN AND THE JEWELS OF OPAR by Edgar Rice Burroughs
22. CLOVELLY by Max Brand
23. WAR LORD OF MANY SWORDSMEN: THE ADVENTURES OF NORCOSS, VOLUME 1 by W. Wirt
24. ALIAS THE NIGHT WIND by Varick Vanardy
25. THE BLUE FIRE PEARL: THE COMPLETE ADVENTURES OF SINGAPORE SAMMY, VOLUME 1 by George F. Worts

26. THE MOON POOL & THE CONQUEST OF THE MOON POOL by Abraham Merritt
27. THE GUN-BRAND by James B. Hendryx
28. JAN OF THE JUNGLE by Otis Adelbert Kline
29. MINIONS OF THE MOON by William Grey Beyer
30. DRINK WE DEEP by Arthur Leo Zagat
31. THE VENGEANCE OF THE WAH FU TONG: THE COMPLETE CASES OF JIGGER MASTERS, VOLUME 1 by Anthony M. Rud
32. THE RUBY OF SURATAN SINGH: THE ADVENTURES OF SCARLET AND BRADSHAW, VOLUME 2 by Theodore Roscoe
33. THE SHERIFF OF TONTO TOWN: THE COMPLETE TALES OF SHERIFF HENRY, VOLUME 2 by W.C. Tuttle
34. THE DARKNESS AT WINDON MANOR by Max Brand
35. THE FLYING LEGION by George Allan England
36. THE GOLDEN CAT: THE ADVENTURES OF PETER THE BRAZEN, VOLUME 3 by Loring Brent
37. THE RADIO MENACE by Ralph Milne Farley
38. THE APES OF DEVIL'S ISLAND by John Cunningham
39. THE OPPOSING VENUS: THE COMPLETE CABALISTIC CASES OF SEMI DUAL, THE OCCULT DETECTOR by J.U. Giesy and Junius B. Smith
40. THE EXPLOITS OF BEAU QUICKSILVER by Florence M. Pettee
41. ERIC OF THE STRONG HEART by Victor Rousseau
42. MURDER ON THE HIGH SEAS AND THE DIAMOND BULLET: THE COMPLETE CASES OF GILLIAN HAZELTINE by George F. Worts
43. THE WOMAN OF THE PYRAMID AND OTHER TALES: THE PERLEY POORE SHEEHAN OMNIBUS, VOLUME 1 by Perley Poore Sheehan
44. A COLUMBUS OF SPACE AND THE MOON METAL: THE GARRETT P. SERVISS OMNIBUS, VOLUME 1 by Garrett P. Serviss
45. THE BLACK TIDE: THE COMPLETE ADVENTURES OF BELLOW BILL WILLIAMS, VOLUME 1 by Ralph R. Perry
46. THE NINE RED GODS DECIDE: THE COMPLETE ADVENTURES OF CORDIE, SOLDIER OF FORTUNE, VOLUME 2 by W. Wirt
47. A GRAVE MUST BE DEEP! by Theodore Roscoe
48. THE AMERICAN by Max Brand
49. THE COMPLETE ADVENTURES OF KOYALA, VOLUME 1 by John Charles Beecham
50. THE CULT MURDERS by Alan Forsyth

Made in the USA
Las Vegas, NV
20 November 2022

59893326R00146